THE GHOST
AND THE LEPRECHAUN

HAUNTING DANIELLE

HAUNTING DANIELLE - BOOK 12

THE GHOST
AND THE LEPRECHAUN

BOBBI HOLMES

The Ghost and the Leprechaun
(Haunting Danielle, Book 12)
A Novel
By Bobbi Holmes
Cover Design: Elizabeth Mackey

ISBN 978-1-949977-11-0

To Scott & SeAnne,
whose Oregon inspired me.
I love you both.

ONE

H e sat cross-legged, hovering in midair beside Danielle's bed, watching her sleep. Propped atop his shaggy strawberry blond hair was a green derby hat, it sat cockeyed on his head. The boney fingers of his right hand absently twisted the ends of his long red beard. He wondered who she was—*why was she at Marlow House?*

With a reluctant sigh, he planted his feet on the wood floor and walked the perimeter of the room, looking for clues. The window shades were open, enabling the moonlight to spill into the room and provide ample lighting for his exploration. The contents of a nearby wicker trash can caught his attention—it held a pair of shoes. *Who throws away shoes?*

Reaching into the container, he pulled out one of the discarded shoes and noticed its broken heel. *I can fix this easily*, he thought, giving his leather apron a pat. Just as he sat down with the shoe to begin the repairs, he heard the bedroom door squeak. Looking up, he watched as it slowly opened. And then he saw it, golden eyes peering curiously in his direction. And then he heard it, a loud high-pitched, "Meow!"

"A cat!" he shouted, jumping up and dropping the shoe on the floor. He disappeared just as the cat dashed into the room and pounced on the spot he had been sitting on.

RUDELY JERKED FROM SLUMBER, Danielle bolted upright in bed. Rubbing her eyes with one balled fist, she glanced around the dimly lit room and yawned. Light from the hallway slipped in through the partially opened doorway.

"Darn, I forgot to lock it," she mumbled. There were guests staying in the bed and breakfast, and she felt more comfortable sleeping with her bedroom door closed and locked. With a groan, she climbed out of bed and headed for the door. En route, she tripped over a shoe. Muttering a curse, she paused, reached down, and picked it up. With a frown, she examined it a moment and then tossed it toward the wicker waste can. The shoe missed its objective, landing on the floor next to her small desk.

Ignoring the missed target, she stumbled to the door and heard a meow. Looking down, she found Max staring up at her, his black tail swishing back and forth.

"Aww...so it's you who woke me up?" she whispered. Leaning down, she picked up the cat and then proceeded to close and lock her bedroom door. Max began to purr as he nuzzled his forehead into her chest.

"Cheeky brat." She tittered, returning to her bed. Climbing back under her sheets and blankets, she snuggled her furry pet and promptly fell back to sleep.

WALT WATCHED in fascination as Danielle's slender fingers adeptly wove her brunette tresses into a tidy fishtail braid. It never ceased to amaze him how quickly and efficiently she performed the task each morning. Just weeks earlier she had discussed cutting her hair and leaving behind her trademark braid, to which Walt had expressed a hearty objection. It wasn't that Walt was particularly fond of the braid—but he did appreciate what it did to her long hair when she released it from its restraints. He wasn't sure if she had abandoned the notion of cutting her hair—or if her life had recently been so chaotic that she simply had no time to consider a new hairstyle.

Danielle sat at her dressing table, her attention fixed on its mirror and her reflection as she wove together her braid.

"Did your mother teach you to braid your hair like that?" Walt asked.

Startled, Danielle turned to Walt. "How long have you been standing there lurking?" She then turned back to the mirror.

Walt chuckled and stepped closer to the dressing table, standing behind Danielle. He stared at her reflection in the mirror—Walt didn't have one. "I don't lurk."

"You do seem to have a habit of sneaking into a lady's room uninvited," Danielle said primly, quickly finishing her braid.

"Only yours." Walt grinned.

Danielle smiled and then explained, "As for your question. No, my mother did not teach me to braid my hair like this. I learned it from YouTube."

"Why am I not surprised?" he muttered under his breath.

Now finished with her hair, she turned around on the bench and faced Walt. Behind him was her bed, and on the bed was Max, who was just waking up. He let out a loud meow.

Walt turned to the cat and studied him for a moment. "Really? Are you sure?"

"Is he sure about what?" Danielle asked, reaching down and grabbing a pair of shoes she had set by the dressing table earlier.

"According to Max, you had some sort of visitor last night. He scared him away."

"Visitor?" Danielle frowned. She slipped on her right shoe. "What kind of visitor?"

Walt shrugged. "Not really sure. He's not making a lot of sense."

"Well, he is a cat." Danielle slipped on her second shoe. "I suspect he's just trying to cover for himself. He woke me up last night. Crazy animal. I think he was playing in my trash."

Walt arched his brow. "Your trash?"

"You know that shoe I broke yesterday? Well, I threw the pair in my trash can last night, and when Max woke me up, one of the shoes was on the floor in the middle of the room. I tripped over it." Danielle stood up.

Walt glanced to the trash can and noticed one of the shoes resting on the floor next to the desk.

"That one?" The shoe floated up in the air and then dropped into the wicker basket.

"It was in the trash last night when I went to bed. Naughty cat."

"Your guests are already at breakfast. Are you going down?" Walt now sat on the edge of the bed with Max, who had closed his eyes and gone back to sleep.

Danielle glanced at the clock sitting on her nightstand. "Remember, I'm going to the bank this morning."

"Aww, that's right. The gold coins. So, you really found a buyer for them?"

"Chris did. He's meeting me at the bank before it closes—and it closes early today so I need to get going."

"Chris is meeting you at the bank?"

"No, the buyer. One less thing to worry about."

"Are you sure you don't want to just keep them?" Walt asked. "It's not like you need the money, and gold can be a good investment."

"You're right. I don't need the money. But the money I can make from selling those coins can do a lot of good."

Walt let out a sigh. "You can't keep giving all your money away, Danielle. I'm beginning to think Chris is a bad influence."

Danielle chortled. "Yeah…right."

"I DIDN'T THINK you worked on Saturdays anymore," Danielle Boatman asked Susan Mitchell as she followed her down the dimly lit hallway leading to the vault room housing the safe deposit boxes. In her right hand Danielle held her key ring—the key to a safe deposit box—poised and ready to open its lock.

Susan opened the door to the vault room, stepping aside for Danielle to enter first. "Ever since Steve's death, I had to take on more hours. I was hoping I'd get my Saturdays back after the new bank manager settled in."

Danielle stepped around Susan and entered the windowless room. She turned to the left, walking toward her two safe deposit boxes. Glancing over her right shoulder at Susan, she asked, "How do you like your new boss? I haven't met him yet."

Susan whispered, "I guess he's no worse than Steve."

Danielle sniggered. "Well, *that* doesn't sound promising."

Susan looked sheepishly to Danielle and cringed. "I suppose I shouldn't have said that."

Danielle grinned. "I didn't hear a thing."

Coming to a stop in front of the safe deposit box they intended to open, Susan put out her hand for Danielle's key.

"I hope you get your Saturdays back," Danielle said as she

handed the key to Susan, its ring and ring mates dangling from its end.

"Thanks. So does my husband." Susan turned her attention to the safe deposit box, kneeling slightly so that she could reach it.

Danielle watched as Susan used the key she had given her, along with the bank's key, to open the lock. Before removing the metal box, Susan handed Danielle back her key ring. She then knelt down and slid the metal box from its vault.

As soon as Susan removed the storage box entirely from the wall unit, she turned to Danielle and said with surprise, "I thought this held the gold coins? Is this the one with the Missing Thorndike?"

"You know better than that." Danielle reached for the metal box, anticipating the weight of its priceless contents. Remembering how heavy the box had been after filling it with the gold coins, she was prepared to use both hands to maneuver the hefty container. Exerting more energy than was necessary in handling the box, it practically flew out of her hands.

Danielle managed to regain hold of the metal container before it landed on the concrete floor. Hunched over, hugging the large safe deposit box to her bosom, she looked up at Susan, her eyes now wide. Slowly standing up straight, still clutching the surprisingly light metal box in her arms, Danielle now understood what Susan was talking about a moment earlier when questioning if they had opened the correct safe deposit box.

Without saying another word, Danielle—standing in the middle of the vault room—hastily flipped open the lid of the large metal container and looked inside.

"It's empty!" Danielle gasped, turning the opened end to Susan so she could see inside.

Confused, Susan gazed into the box. "What's that?" she asked with a whisper before reaching into the open container and picking up the only item it held. Removing her hand from the box, she stared at the green foil object now between her fingers.

Wrinkling her nose, Danielle studied the object. "What's that?"

"It looks like a shamrock—like the kind in the storage room," Susan muttered, turning the shamrock from side to side as she examined it closer.

"Storage room?"

"Yeah, near the bathrooms," Susan explained. "That's where we keep the holiday decorations. This looks like one of the shamrocks from last Saint Patrick's Day."

Danielle handed the box back to Susan. "This isn't mine. There must be some mistake."

Before shutting the box's lid, Susan dropped the foil shamrock back inside. "I don't understand. It has to be yours. Your key fit."

"Then where are my gold coins?" Danielle demanded, sounding harsher than she intended.

"This doesn't make any sense," Susan muttered.

Danielle hastily located another key on her key ring and shoved it at Susan. "Open the other box. I want to see if the Missing Thorndike is there."

It was another five or ten minutes before Danielle's second safe deposit box could be opened. First, she needed to sign the ledger—again. When the box was opened, she was relieved to find it was not empty. It held a velvet pouch—and inside that, the Missing Thorndike, an antique necklace of diamonds and emeralds, valued in excess of a million dollars. Without hesitation, Danielle slipped the pouch with the necklace into her purse and told Susan they needed to talk to the bank manager. Susan agreed.

TWO

They sat in the bank manager's office with the door closed. The only sound was that of Alan Kissinger turning the pages of the safe deposit ledger—flipping back and forth between two of its pages. He sat behind his desk, examining the book, while Danielle and Susan sat silently in the two chairs facing him.

On Danielle's lap sat her purse, which she protectively clung to with both arms. There was no way she was returning the Missing Thorndike to the safe deposit box—at least not until they discovered what had happened to her gold coins. She waited anxiously for him to say something.

Danielle guessed the new bank manager, Alan Kissinger, was a few years younger than Steve Klein had been at the time of his death, maybe in his mid-forties. Conservatively dressed in a blue suit, its jacket hanging on the nearby coatrack, Kissinger was clean shaven with shortly buzzed hair reminding her of a marine—or of those two FBI agents, Wilson and Thomas.

Kissinger might be attractive if he smiled, she thought, yet he had been scowling since Susan had introduced him to her, which Danielle understood, considering the introduction had been made after Susan had informed her boss of the missing gold coins—gold coins that might actually be worth more than the Missing Thorndike.

Glancing around the small room, Danielle noticed the changes to what had once been Steve Klein's office. Its walls had been repainted—now in shades of mauve and beige instead of browns and beige. There were no longer any pictures or paintings hanging on the walls—nor were there any personal photographs sitting on the desk or nearby bookshelf. If Kissinger was married, one couldn't tell by what he had on display in the office.

Danielle was fairly certain the office furniture was the same Steve had used, yet it looked as if it had been recently polished. Although spotlessly clean, the office felt impersonal, as if it were vacant, waiting for someone to move in.

Still clutching her purse, Danielle recalled the first time she had been in this office—not long after moving to Frederickport and finding the Missing Thorndike. That had been a year ago. It was also her first meeting with Police Chief MacDonald. The two had been brought into the bank manager's office to decide what should be done with the Missing Thorndike until its legal ownership could be determined. They had agreed to place it in a safe deposit box—where it had remained after it became clear she was in fact its rightful owner. It had only been removed once—when she had worn it to her open house last July fourth. She prayed removing it a second time wouldn't bring on another disaster.

A moment later, Alan Kissinger closed the ledger and looked up to Danielle. "If anything is missing, you obviously removed it." He pushed the ledger to the side of the desk.

"Excuse me?" Danielle leaned forward, still clutching her purse. "I certainly did not remove it! That box was filled with gold coins the last time I was here!"

Alan let out a weary sigh and opened the ledger. He turned the book around so Danielle could see it.

"Ms. Boatman, is this your signature?"

Danielle glanced at the ledger, noting her signature and the date next to it. "Yes. That's the day I opened that safe deposit box—the day I put the gold coins in it—for safekeeping!" Under her breath she muttered, "*Some safekeeping!*"

He turned the book around so he could see it again. After a quick glance at the page, he closed the book and set it back on his desk. "As you can see, Ms. Boatman, you are the only one who has ever been in that safe deposit box. The day you opened it and today. No one—and I repeat—no one else has been in it. I'm not sure what exactly you're trying to pull—"

"Mr. Kissinger," Susan interrupted, "Ms. Boatman rented the safe deposit box from me. If you will note on that ledger, my signature is next to hers."

"Yes, I saw that," he said, dismissively waving to Susan. "But we aren't responsible for what our customers put into their safe deposit boxes."

"Mr. Kissinger," Susan said emphatically, "I saw Ms. Boatman put the coins in the box. In fact, the first box she rented wasn't big enough, so I had to rent her another one. I saw her fill the box with gold coins."

"And she could have removed them when you weren't looking. As I said, the bank is not responsible for—"

"Mr. Kissinger!" Susan snapped. "When I put the safe deposit box back in its vault the first time, it was heavy. It wasn't empty. I know it wasn't. And I locked it up. Danielle never touched it again until today. Obviously, someone has broken in to our safe deposit boxes!"

"Mrs. Mitchell, would you please keep your voice down!" he scolded.

"Do you seriously think I'm trying to scam the bank?" Danielle asked, her voice calm.

"Ms. Boatman, I don't know you. I have no idea what you're trying to do. Perhaps you put your gold coins somewhere else and just think you put them here. Perhaps you have another safe deposit box?"

"Actually, I have two—both here."

"And your other box? I assume you checked that?" he asked.

"Yes. I keep a valuable necklace in the other box."

Kissinger smiled. "And was it still in the safe deposit box?"

"Yes," Danielle said coolly.

"Ms. Boatman, if someone had broken in to the safe deposit boxes—and mind you, I checked them as soon as Mrs. Mitchell expressed her concern, and nothing has been tampered with—why would they leave behind a valuable necklace?"

"I don't know." Danielle pulled her phone from her purse.

Kissinger frowned. "Who are you calling?"

"Who I should have called the moment I realized the gold coins were missing, the police chief."

"CHIEF MACDONALD, it would be impossible for any of our employees to open Ms. Boatman's safe deposit box without her key." Mr. Kissinger turned to Danielle, who stood between Susan Mitchell and the chief in the safe deposit vault room. "Was the key ever out of your possession?"

"No. But the gold coins are missing," Danielle retorted. "So obviously, someone opened my safe deposit box and took my coins. I'm sure there is a duplicate key out there."

Kissinger let out a weary sigh and shook his head. He looked to the chief. "It doesn't work that way; you know that, Chief MacDonald. And as you can see, these boxes have obviously not been tampered with."

"Then explain the missing coins," MacDonald said.

"As manager of this bank, I have no knowledge of the contents of Ms. Boatman's—or the contents of any of our customers' safe deposit boxes. The contract Ms. Boatman signed when she rented a box from us clearly spells out the limits of our liability."

"Your own employee remembers what I put in the box," Danielle reminded him.

Kissinger looked to Susan. "You saw Ms. Boatman put the gold coins in the box?"

Susan nodded. "Yes."

"And the box never left your sight after that?" Kissinger asked.

Susan started to say something and then paused. She glanced from Danielle back to the bank manager. "I did step out of the room for a minute. I was only gone for a second."

"And when you returned, was the box open or closed?" Kissinger asked.

Susan frowned, considering the question a moment. "It was closed, I think."

Kissinger arched his brows. "You think?"

"Yes…it was closed. But it was really heavy. I remember that," Susan insisted.

Kissinger shook his head and looked from Susan to the chief. "What we have is an employee who *thinks* she remembers the box was heavier when she held it weeks ago." He looked to Danielle, his expression unfriendly. "What are you trying to pull, Ms. Boatman? An insurance claim?"

"Insurance claim? I think that would first require I have insurance on the coins."

MacDonald looked quickly to Danielle. "They weren't insured?"

"No. I didn't see the point." She glared at Kissinger. "I foolishly thought they would be safe here. And since I planned to sell them right away, I didn't see the point of getting insurance."

"You were supposed to see the coin collector today, weren't you?" MacDonald asked.

Danielle pulled her cellphone out of her purse and glanced at the time. "I was supposed to meet him here about ten minutes ago." Danielle shoved the phone back in her purse. "I guess I need to go out front and see if he's waiting for me." Heading for the doorway, she glared back at Kissinger and added, "I'll have to tell him they were stolen from the bank."

"You can't do that!" Kissinger shouted, heading for the door. MacDonald reached out and grabbed his wrist, stopping him.

Angrily jerking his wrist from the chief's hold, he glared up into MacDonald's face. "Are you going to let her just go out there and slander me? The bank?"

"I know Danielle very well, and if she says the gold coins were in that safe deposit box, I believe her. And frankly, I'm surprised how you're treating your bank's largest depositor."

Kissinger frowned. "What are you talking about?"

Susan cleared her throat. "Technically speaking, Ms. Boatman is no longer the bank's largest depositor, not since Mr. Johnson—"

"Mrs. Mitchell, you know better than to discuss our customers' business with anyone—including the police chief. At least not without a warrant."

The chief looked at Susan. "I forgot; Chris mentioned he was transferring a few million here from the Glandon Foundation. If he's a larger depositor than Danielle, he must have transferred more than a few million."

"He was here yesterday," Susan whispered, earning her a harsh glare from her boss.

Kissinger looked from Susan to the chief. "What is this about Ms. Boatman being our largest depositor? I've never heard of her until today."

"I told you about her last week when we were going over the list of major depositors. She's the one who owns Marlow House," Susan reminded him.

Kissinger frowned. "I thought her last name was Marlow?"

MacDonald shook his head. "No. Her name is Boatman. The

last Marlow died almost a century ago. And from what I understand, Danielle deposited a good chunk of her money here—despite the fact it won't all be federally insured due to the amount. But she was trying to be a good neighbor and supportive of the bank. I assume that will probably change now, with the missing gold coins. And considering Chris Johnson is a close friend of Danielle's, I wouldn't be surprised if he'll be transferring his recent deposit out of your bank."

The chief studied the new bank manager and was fairly certain the man's peachy complexion had just turned a sick shade of green.

Shaking his head in denial, Kissinger groaned, "This can't be happening."

"I think we need to all go back to your office—and not touch anything in here," the chief began. "I'll talk to Danielle, convince her not to say anything about the missing coins—until we can investigate."

"Yes…yes…but hurry, before she says something," Kissinger said frantically.

Pulling his cellphone from his pocket, MacDonald dialed Danielle.

"What, you can't walk out here to talk to me?" Danielle said when she answered the phone a moment later.

"Have you talked to the buyer yet?"

Kissinger and Susan silently listened to MacDonald's side of the conversation.

"No. He isn't here yet."

"Have you said anything to anyone about the missing coins?" MacDonald asked.

"Who would I have talked to? I just left you two minutes ago. That new bank manager is a major jackass, by the way."

MacDonald eyed Kissinger before responding to Danielle on the phone. "Yes, yes, he is. But I don't want you to say anything to anyone about the missing coins—not yet."

When MacDonald got off the phone a few minutes later, Kissinger asked, "What did she say?"

"Aside from expressing her opinion that you're a major jackass, she agreed not to say anything just yet."

Susan bit her lip in her effort to keep from laughing over the chief's words. Noticing her attempt to stifle her amusement,

MacDonald flashed her a wink and then proceeded to make another call.

"Who are you calling now?" Kissinger asked.

"I'm having one of my men come over here to stand guard. I don't want anyone to touch anything in here, not until the FBI arrives and takes over the investigation."

THREE

Police Chief Edward MacDonald walked Danielle out to her car in the bank parking lot. Officer Henderson and several other officers had already arrived to secure the crime scene.

"I just wanted to explain why I'm calling the FBI in on this," MacDonald told Danielle as he opened her car door for her.

"You do believe me when I told you I put the coins in the safe deposit box, don't you?"

"Yes, certainly. I just think it's for the best," the chief explained.

"I suppose I understand." Danielle started to get into her car.

"I also need to tell you something else," he said hesitantly.

Instead of getting into her vehicle, Danielle turned to face the chief, the open car door between them.

"What?"

He let out a sigh before continuing. "Samuel Hayman is back in town."

"He's out of jail?" Danielle scowled. "I suppose I shouldn't be surprised he's out. It's been almost a year, and he did make a plea deal. What I'm surprised about, that he came back to Frederickport."

"It's his hometown."

"Sure, but his business is closed. What's he going to do? I didn't even think he owns any property here anymore. Where is he going to live?"

"When he was apprehended with your diamonds and emeralds, he was carrying what was left of his inventory—which had been bought and paid for and was legally his. I imagine had he not entered a plea deal, most of that would have been burned up in legal fees."

"Yeah, and it would have obviously been a waste of money. He didn't even serve a year for drugging my cousin and stealing the Thorndike gems. His actions left her vulnerable and got her killed. He should have spent a lot more time behind bars!"

"I agree with you, Danielle."

"So what is he going to do, open his jewelry store again?"

"I don't think he has the resources to reopen. That's why he did what he did in the first place, out of desperation."

"You don't expect me to feel sorry for him, do you?"

"Certainly not. I'm just saying he can't afford to reopen, or he wouldn't have closed in the first place. From what I was told, one of his friends who owns a restaurant offered him a job. It's menial work, but it is work."

"If he can't open his store again, why doesn't he go somewhere and get a job with another jewelry store and use his skills?"

"Think about that, Danielle; what reputable jewelry store would want to hire him with his record?"

She flashed MacDonald a weak smile. "I suppose you're right. Thanks for warning me. It would have been rather unsettling to run into him around town, not knowing he was out."

———

ALAN KISSINGER STOOD in the open doorway leading to his office and glanced around the bank, observing the activity. He stood there a moment in silence. Finally, he stepped back into his office and closed the door behind him, locking it. Taking a seat behind his desk, he started to pick up the office landline, but quickly changed his mind. Instead, he removed his cellphone from his pocket and placed his call.

A moment later Dave Sterling answer the phone.

"Dave, we need to talk…" Alan began.

FOUR

Danielle had just pulled her red Ford Flex into the side driveway at Marlow House when her cellphone began to ring. After parking the car and turning off the engine, she grabbed her phone out of her purse and looked at it. Chris was calling.

"Hey, Chris," Danielle answered as she removed the key from the ignition and continued to sit in the car.

"What happened to your safe deposit box?"

"That was quick. Who called you?" Danielle snatched her purse from the passenger seat and opened the car door while tucking her cellphone between her left shoulder and chin so she could continue her call.

"I just got off the phone with the buyer. Said the minute he walked into the bank, you told him there was an issue with your safe deposit lock, and you'd have to reschedule. Are you having second thoughts about selling?"

Danielle stepped out of the car, her purse now hung over her right shoulder. Slamming the door shut behind her, she took the phone in her left hand, still holding it by her ear, and started walking toward the back door leading into the kitchen. "This is just between you and me, Chris, I promised the chief I wouldn't say anything just yet. But the box was empty."

"Empty? What are you talking about?"

"Empty as in no coins. Oh, I take that back. It had a shamrock."

"Shamrock?"

"One of those foil shamrocks used for Saint Patrick's Day decorations. Susan said it probably came from the bank's storage room."

"I don't understand."

Now standing on the back porch, Danielle paused. She could see one of her guests sitting at the kitchen table, talking to Joanne.

"Hey, Chris, can we talk about this later? I need to go in the house, and I really don't want to discuss this in front of my guests. Maybe you can come over?"

"I'm at the office right now."

"On a Saturday?"

"I'll speak to my boss about the lousy schedule."

Danielle tittered and then suggested, "Maybe you can stop by on the way home."

"Okay. But first let me know—are we talking bank robbery here? Were all the boxes hit?"

"I don't think so. The Missing Thorndike was still in its box." Danielle glanced at her purse. "At least it was."

"What does that mean?"

"It means I brought it back to Marlow House with me."

WHEN DANIELLE ENTERED THE KITCHEN, she greeted Joanne and her guest and then excused herself, explaining there was something she needed to look for in the attic. On the way there, she ran into Lily, who was just coming downstairs.

"Come with me," Danielle whispered to Lily when they were about to pass each other on the staircase.

Holding onto the handrail, Lily paused. "Where are we going?"

"I want to talk to you…and Walt."

With a shrug, Lily turned around and followed Danielle back up to the second floor and then to the attic, where they found Walt reading a book. At least, Danielle found Walt reading a book. Lily simply saw a book floating in the air over the sofa.

"You do realize we have guests in the house," Lily said as she closed the attic door behind her.

"I can hear if anyone is coming," Walt said, closing the book and setting it on the sofa next to him.

"He says he can hear anyone coming up," Danielle told Lily.

17

She then pulled up a chair for Lily to sit on while she took a seat on the sofa next to Walt.

"So what did you need to talk to us about?" Lily asked.

"Did you close the deal on the coins?" Walt asked.

"They were gone," Danielle blurted out.

Lily frowned. "What do you mean they were gone?"

"The coins—gone. The box was empty." Danielle then proceeded to tell Lily and Walt about her morning at the bank. When she was done, the three sat silently for a few moments.

Finally, Lily spoke. "So what are they going to do?"

"The chief's calling the FBI. Brian arrived at the bank just as I was leaving. The chief wants to make sure nothing is disturbed before they have a chance to check things out. From what I understand, the place is under surveillance cameras, so I imagine that's one of the first things they intend to do—look at the film."

Lily frowned. "They still use film?"

Danielle shrugged. "I don't know. Digital maybe. Whatever."

"But why the FBI? I would think the chief would want to handle this himself. Thought local cops like to do their own investigation?" Lily asked.

"I think this is sort of a gray area. From what I understand, bank robberies are typically under the jurisdiction of the FBI; for one thing, deposits are insured by the feds."

Lily frowned again. "I thought safe deposit boxes weren't insured?"

"They aren't. Which is why this is sort of a gray area. Plus, I think the chief is uncomfortable taking this by himself since we're such good friends."

"Why would that matter?" Walt asked.

"For one thing, the new bank manager insists I never put the coins in the safe deposit box."

"Are you serious?" Lily gasped.

"Pretty much. Although, by the time I left the bank, he was more civil. The chief told me he didn't realize who I was."

Walt arched his brow. "And exactly who are you?"

Primly, Danielle said, "One of the bank's largest depositors."

"You sure as heck don't intend to keep your money there? Do you?" Lily asked angrily. "Dang, I need to find a new bank now too!"

"What about the Missing Thorndike?" Walt asked.

"Oh…that…" Danielle opened her purse and removed the pouch holding the necklace.

Lily eyed the familiar pouch. "You brought it home with you?"

"I couldn't very well leave it at the bank." Danielle opened it and pulled out the necklace. Its diamonds and emeralds glistened.

"Ahh…it is so beautiful…" Lily said with a sigh as she reached out for the necklace. Danielle handed it to her. She sat back on the sofa and watched as Lily slipped on the necklace while admiring it.

"I figure I can keep it in the safe here…and Walt can give it added security," Danielle explained.

"You don't seem overly upset about losing the gold coins," Walt observed, sitting back in the sofa. His gaze shifted from Lily, who sat admiring the necklace she wore, to Danielle, who continued to sit next to him. With a wave of his right hand, a thin cigar appeared. He took a puff.

Danielle propped her feet up on the small coffee table. "I'm more curious about where they went. I wasn't even sure they were legally mine until a few weeks ago. I was going to give the proceeds of the sale away anyway, so personally, it doesn't really hurt me. But I do want to know what happened to them. They didn't just up and walk away on their own."

Walt took a lazy puff of his cigar while considering the recent turn of events. After he exhaled, he asked, "You said the thief left a shamrock in the box?"

Danielle nodded. "We assume whoever took the coins had to have left it. Of course, it wasn't a real shamrock."

"Hmm…shamrock and gold?" Lily snickered as she removed the necklace and handed it back to Danielle, who promptly returned it to its velvet pouch.

"What's so amusing?" Danielle asked as she pulled the ties to the pouch tightly shut.

"What do shamrocks and gold have in common?" Lily asked with an impish grin.

"Leprechauns?" Walt answered.

Danielle glanced at Walt and then back to Lily. "So what, you saying a leprechaun took the gold?"

"Well, maybe." Lily grinned. She leaned forward and said in a low conspiratorial voice, "Did you know there's a leprechaun colony in Portland?"

Rolling her eyes, Danielle said dryly, "Is there now?"

Walt chuckled and said, before taking another puff, "Lily is starting to scare me. I think my haunting of Marlow House is getting to her."

"Oh, I'm serious," Lily said excitedly. "Ian showed me. It's called Mill Ends Park—it's like the smallest park in the world, something like two feet square."

"Hmm, that is pretty darn small," Danielle agreed.

With a nod Lily said seriously, "It has the distinction of being the only leprechaun colony west of Ireland."

Walt frowned. "Please tell me Lily doesn't really believe in leprechauns."

Danielle laughed and looked from Lily to Walt. "Why not, she believes in ghosts."

Lily smiled and looked from Danielle to the seemingly empty spot on the sofa where she assumed Walt was sitting. "What is he saying?"

"He's afraid you really believe in leprechauns."

Lily started to laugh. When she regained her composure, she looked to Walt's space and said, "Sometimes you can be such a goof!"

"Goof?" Walt sounded insulted.

"I don't think he liked being called a goof."

Rolling her eyes, Lily shook her head and said, "No, Walt, I don't believe in leprechauns. I thought you knew me better than that." She looked at Danielle. "But it is true about Mill Ends Park and it's supposed leprechaun colony."

Danielle looked at Lily. "I remember reading something about it. I guess it's one of those things that keeps Portland weird."

Lily nodded. "Isn't that the truth. Anyway, when you said you found a shamrock, and the gold was missing, I couldn't help think leprechaun. After all, aren't they known for stealing gold?"

"I wouldn't be surprised if whoever took the gold left the shamrock in the safe deposit box for that very reason," Danielle said.

"What, to throw the cops off so they'd start looking for a leprechaun?" Walt scoffed.

"Noooo." Danielle rolled her eyes.

"You two need to stop rolling your eyes," Walt scolded. "It really is not very becoming."

"Then you need to stop being so goofy," Danielle retorted.

Walt rolled his eyes, shook his head, and took a puff of his cigar. Danielle began to laugh.

"What's so funny?" Lily asked.

"Just Walt telling us to stop rolling our eyes, and then he goes and does it." Danielle flashed Walt a grin. "Anyway, I figure whoever stole the gold probably has some twisted sense of humor and thought leaving a shamrock in the box would be an amusing touch."

"Could be a clue," Lily suggested. "Look for a thief with a twisted sense of humor."

"I suspect it's got to be an inside job—someone from the bank. Has to be. But if it is someone with a sense of humor, I rule out the new bank manager," Danielle said.

Before anyone could respond, Lily's cellphone began to ring. She pulled it from her purse, which she had tossed on the floor next to her feet when sitting down a few minutes earlier. After looking at it, she said, "It's Ian. Can I tell him about the gold?"

"Sure. But tell him not to say anything to anyone just yet," Danielle told her.

When Lily got off the phone a few moments later, she told Danielle and Walt she needed to get going. She had been on her way to meet Ian when Danielle had caught her on the staircase a few minutes earlier. They planned to drive to Portland, and Ian was wondering what was taking Lily so long.

"When you're in Portland, would you do me a favor?" Danielle asked as Lily stood up and picked up her purse, draping its strap over one shoulder.

"Sure. What?"

"Stop by Mill Ends Park and see if one of those leprechauns has my gold."

Lily grinned. "Sure. No problem."

FIVE

"I once knew a man who insisted leprechauns were real," Walt told Danielle after Lily left.

Leaning back again on the sofa, Danielle looked over at Walt.

Wearing his favorite blue, three-piece pinstripe suit—minus its jacket and tie—with the top two shirt buttons unfastened and its shirt sleeves pushed up slightly, Walt stared off into space, as he recalled that long-ago person, whom he hadn't thought about in literally decades. "Sean Sullivan. That was his name."

"Sean Sullivan? Sounds like a nice Irish name. You think he really believed in them, or was he pulling your leg?"

Walt gave the cigar a gentle flick—it vanished. "No, he really believed it. Peculiar fellow. Was a good friend of Katherine O'Malley."

"My aunt's mother?"

Walt nodded. "Yes, for a time I suspected he might be Brianna's father."

"You never told me that!"

Walt shrugged. "Never saw a reason to. It's not like he was her father."

"But I've always wondered who Brianna's father was. Why did you think it might be Sullivan—and why did you change your mind?"

Shifting slightly on the sofa, he considered the question a

moment before answering. "He was always coming over here when she was working. I know it bothered her; she was afraid he was going to get her fired. She was always apologizing to me about him showing up. Which is why I figured he was probably Brianna's father—and at the time, it explained why they weren't married."

"I don't understand."

"Like I said, he was a peculiar fellow. I assumed she had gotten involved with him before she knew how he really was, and when she finally realized his true nature, she didn't want to marry him, yet couldn't figure out how to get him to stay away."

"So why did you change your mind and decide he wasn't the father?"

"One day I overheard them arguing. They were arguing about Brianna's father. It was obvious to me that Sullivan knew who it was, and he wasn't happy the man refused to take responsibility for his daughter."

"You never asked him who it was?"

Walt frowned. "Ask him? It really was none of my business, Danielle."

With a sigh, Danielle sank back on the sofa. "I guess you're right."

"I usually am."

Danielle rolled her eyes.

"Stop that," Walt scolded.

Danielle smiled. "So tell me about this Sean Sullivan and his leprechauns."

"Nothing much to tell, really. I just remember once he seemed a little agitated when he was leaving, and I asked him what was wrong. He told me, '*He just won't leave me alone.*' I asked him, '*Who won't leave you alone?*' and he said, '*The leprechaun.*' He told me the leprechaun was always playing tricks on him, but that someday he was going to catch him and force him to take him to the pot of gold."

"Pot of gold?"

"According to Sullivan, all leprechauns have a pot of gold hidden somewhere."

"What did you say?"

Walt smiled at the memory. "Not much at the time. I believe I did a lot of nodding. After he left, I had a little talk with Katherine O'Malley. I was concerned for her safety—associating with someone who was so obviously unstable. She assured me that he was an old friend—they had grown up together. Practically a brother, she called him. And she insisted that while he might be peculiar, he was harmless."

"People have thought I was crazy for believing in ghosts."

Walt let out a snort. "Not exactly the same thing."

"How do you figure?"

"For one thing, there are no such things as leprechauns."

"How do you know?" Danielle asked.

"I'm dead."

Danielle laughed. "What does that have to do with anything?"

"I'm dead, so I know things. I would know if there were leprechauns."

"You didn't even know you were murdered until I helped you," Danielle reminded him.

"True. But leprechauns…that's just silly."

"I don't know…" Danielle said in a teasing voice. "Portland is not that far from here, and they do have the only leprechaun colony west of Ireland."

Walt laughed. "Perhaps. The leprechauns must have moved in after I died. I don't remember any colony in Portland."

"Let's see when those tricky rascals arrived…" Danielle pulled her iPhone from her purse and did a quick Internet search. "Yep, you're right."

"How so?" Walt asked.

Danielle looked up from her phone. "Says here the colony was discovered in the forties." Danielle turned off her phone and dropped it back in her purse.

"I've missed so much—now it seems I missed the discovery of Portland leprechauns," Walt said with faux dramatics.

Danielle giggled and then asked, "I wonder what happened to Mr. Sullivan."

"I have no idea." Walt summoned another cigar. "But now that I think about him, I wonder what he thought about Katherine marrying Roger."

"After Katherine and Roger died, Ben Smith's father was Brianna's court-appointed guardian. I wonder why Sean Sullivan never got involved in Brianna's life. You said they grew up together, and he was upset over how Brianna's father wasn't taking responsibility. I wonder why he didn't do something?"

"What makes you think he didn't?" Walt asked.

"I've talked to both Ben and Marie about what happened to Aunt Brianna after her mother's death. According to both of them, Brianna had no one—no family."

"I didn't say Sullivan was related to her."

"True. But if they were childhood friends, and from what you say, they seemed to be close, why would he just drop out of Brianna's life like that?"

"I have no idea. Maybe he didn't."

The two sat in silence for a few minutes. Finally, Danielle said, "I wonder if I could find out what happened to Sean Sullivan."

"What would be the point?"

"Maybe he got married, had kids."

"Lord, I hope not. Nobody home with that one."

"But if he did get married and had kids, maybe he talked about his old friend Katherine. After all, her death was pretty sensational back then. And if he knew who Brianna's father was, then maybe he told someone."

"Danielle, what's the point?"

She considered his question for a few minutes. "I don't know…I guess I like a good mystery."

"And don't you have a more pressing mystery at the moment?"

"What do you mean?"

Walt let out a sigh and shook his head. "The missing gold coins."

"Oh…that…yeah…you have a point." Danielle slumped back on the sofa, once again contemplating the missing gold coins.

"I'M SERIOUSLY CONSIDERING PUTTING in a recommendation to open an FBI office in Frederickport," Special Agent Wilson joked when he greeted Chief MacDonald that afternoon. Standing in the chief's office, the two men shook hands and then sat down, with MacDonald taking a seat behind his desk. They exchanged a few pleasantries before getting to the business at hand.

"I haven't spoken to Ms. Boatman yet, but I did interview Susan Mitchell. She's insistent that box was filled with gold coins when it went into the vault," Wilson explained. "At least, it was heavy enough. Her boss seems skeptical that she'd remember something like that, which doesn't surprise me, considering what this could mean for his bank."

"Those gold coins received a lot of press. The bank was fully aware of what was going into that vault. And from what Danielle told me, the first box she rented wasn't quite large enough, so Susan checked her out a larger one. Under the circumstances, I'd think that's something Susan Mitchell would remember."

"I tend to agree. I have my people over at the bank. I just wanted to stop in, keep you in the loop."

"I appreciate that."

"From what I understand, Ms. Boatman didn't have the gold coins insured?" Wilson asked.

"That's what she told me this morning. She was planning to sell them right away and didn't see any reason to bother with insurance—which I'm sure she regrets now."

"Oh, I don't know about that." Wilson leaned back in the chair. "Without insurance, gets her off the hook for insurance fraud."

"Insurance fraud?"

"Considering her and Ms. Mitchell are friends, we don't have to pursue the angle they are in this together for the insurance money. Of course, their target might be the bank."

"You don't seriously believe that?"

Wilson smiled. "No. But I like to pursue all angles. I suspect we'll know more when we see those surveillance tapes. Now, if nothing shows up on those tapes, then obviously we need to look closer at Boatman and Mitchell. This could be about blackmailing the bank. Danielle Boatman is one of their largest depositors. I imagine with her gold coins suddenly missing, she'd be in a position to destroy that bank's reputation."

"There is no way Danielle is involved in a scheme to defraud the bank. For one thing, she doesn't need the money. Hell, she has already donated a significant portion of her inheritance to charity."

"I understand one reason you called us, you recognize you might not always be objective regarding Ms. Boatman."

"That is not entirely accurate."

Wilson stood up. "Don't worry, Chief. We'll carefully review all the evidence before drawing a conclusion, and I suspect we're going to find something on that surveillance video to help us figure out where those coins went."

CHIEF MACDONALD GLANCED at his clock. It was almost 5 p.m. It was Saturday, and he was supposed to have the day off. His youngest son, Evan, had already called twice in the past hour, asking when he was going to be home. MacDonald had dropped his sons off at his sister's after Danielle had called him that morning. Ever since the plane hijacking in April, his boys—especially his youngest son—grew anxious when they had to stay with his sister. It wasn't that they suddenly disliked their aunt, but when their father was supposed to be home—they wanted him home.

MacDonald was getting ready to leave the station for the day when he received a call from Wilson. Apparently, they had gone through some of the surveillance videos, and Wilson wanted MacDonald to see what they had found.

When Wilson arrived at the office late Saturday afternoon, he handed MacDonald a flash drive.

"What did you find?" MacDonald asked as he sat down behind his desk and inserted the drive into his computer.

"This is from the camera directly aimed at Boatman's safe deposit box."

MacDonald settled into his seat and focused his attention on his monitor, with Wilson by his side, looking over his shoulder.

When the video started, MacDonald watched as it played at high speed. The people captured by the surveillance camera—bank employees and bank customers visiting their safe deposit boxes—appeared to be racing frantically in and out of the camera's view. For a few seconds, when the vault room appeared to be empty, the lens abruptly veered off to the left, no longer aimed at Danielle's safe deposit box, and then it readjusted itself back to its original position. The video then ended.

MacDonald glanced up to Wilson. "I don't get it? What did I just see."

"During this same time frame, the other camera aimed at the only entrance into the vault room did not pick up anyone entering the room. It appears it is empty—no one is there. But inside, something made that camera, the one pointed at Boatman's safe deposit box, suddenly move."

"I assume someone moved it remotely?"

"No. That particular camera can't be moved remotely. It's

stationery. The lens direction was manually moved and then moved back. But according to the other cameras, there was no one in the vault room to have moved it."

"How is that possible?"

Wilson shook his head. "I have no idea. But something moved that lens. And something moved it back."

"You think that's when they emptied the safe deposit box?" MacDonald asked.

Folding his hands together, Wilson rested his elbows on the chair's arms. "What video we've seen so far, no one has touched the box where the coins were supposedly kept. What you just watched is the only time we've found where the camera wasn't on the box in question. There is just one problem—"

"The other cameras didn't capture anyone in the vault room during this time."

"Exactly."

SIX

June's sun would be setting in a couple of hours. Chris turned onto Beach Drive, heading home, but first he would stop at Marlow House. He assumed Joanne had probably taken off for the night and was already home.

In the passenger seat next to him, Hunny stood, looking out the window, her tail wagging and butt wiggling. She began to bark wildly, practically jumping up and down on the seat, her uncropped ears flopping as she did.

Glancing to the sidewalk along the right side of the road, Chris found himself slowing down, curious to get a closer look at what had captured his puppy's attention. There, walking along the road, heading the same direction in which he was driving, was an oddly dressed man wearing a green derby hat, red jacket, leather apron, short green pants, striped socks, and work boots.

"Is there some costume party I don't know about?" Chris mumbled as he pressed his foot on the accelerator, returning to normal speed. A few moments later he slowed down again before pulling in front of Marlow House and parking his car.

He got out of his vehicle and walked to the passenger side to retrieve Hunny. When he glanced back down the street, the peculiarly dressed man was no longer in sight. Shaking his head with a chuckle, he opened the car door and scooped up Hunny, who wiggled energetically in his arms while swiping enthusiastic wet kisses over his face.

Already the size of Max—who was not a small cat, close to twenty pounds—she was a plump little brindle pit bull with a white chest. Max hadn't weighed that much when he had first arrived at Marlow House. Back then, he had been fending for himself and meals were scarce. But after moving in with Danielle, he had plenty to eat—and it showed.

Instead of carrying Hunny to the house, Chris set her on the sidewalk and slipped a harness—its leash already attached—onto her perpetually squirming body. Ignoring the leash, she jumped up on his pants legs, begging to be picked up, her tail wagging.

"Sorry, little girl." Chris gently pushed her off his legs. "I might be able to carry you now, but in a couple months there is no way I'm going to carry you around without destroying my back. You need to get used to the leash."

Hunny sat down briefly and looked up at Chris, her sad little face pitiful as her tail swiped over the sidewalk like a windshield wiper. A moment later she was standing up again, tugging against the leash as Chris practically dragged her toward Marlow House. By the time they reached the front gate, Chris broke down and picked Hunny up, carrying her to the front door.

"OH MY GOD, WHO IS THAT?" Laura whispered to Carmen after Chris entered Marlow House and went into the parlor with Danielle, a pit bull puppy in his arms. They closed the door behind them. Laura and her sister, Michelle, both college students, had checked in the day before and would be staying through the weekend. Carmen had been a guest at the bed and breakfast for almost two weeks and would be checking out the day before Laura and Michelle.

"Danielle just introduced you to him. Chris Johnson," Carmen said with a shrug as she wandered into the living room and plopped down on the sofa, scooping up a magazine as she did.

Laura followed Carmen into the room while repeatedly glancing over her shoulder in the direction of the parlor. "I know *that*. I mean *who* is he. Is that Danielle's boyfriend?" Laura sat on the chair facing the sofa, her eyes darting to the open doorway leading to the hallway.

Carmen opened the magazine and turned the page, skimming its contents. "He lives down the street. They seem to be good friends. But I'm not sure how good. He hasn't slept over since I've been here, and Danielle hasn't slept at his house. Well, not unless she snuck out late at night and returned before I got up." Carmen chortled at the idea and turned the page.

"He is soooo cute," Laura groaned. "So yummy!"

"MAX IS the reason she won't get off your lap," Walt told Chris. In the parlor with Danielle and Chris, Walt sat casually along the edge of the small desk, smoking a thin cigar.

Chris sat on the sofa with Hunny on his lap, her plump body trembling. Danielle sat in a chair facing them, Max on her lap. The cat's golden eyes fixed on the puppy while his black tail swished back and forth, repeatedly brushing over Danielle's face. Each time it did, she shoved it aside and frowned.

"Your cat is scaring little Hunny," Chris grumbled, protectively stroking the puppy's back. She snuggled closer to Chris, never moving her gaze from her tormentor.

"Max, be nice," Danielle scolded. The cat let out a high-pitched meow, sending the puppy burrowing against Chris's chest.

"Enough, Max!" Walt snapped. The cat looked to Walt and blinked. "If I have to put up with Chris, you have to put up with his dog." In response, Max repositioned himself on Danielle's lap, no longer looking at the intruding canine. He closed his eyes.

"Thanks, Walt, I think." Chris chuckled. He stroked Hunny's back and then rubbed her ears. "Maybe she'll seem tougher if I crop her ears?"

"Don't you dare!" Danielle gasped. "That's cruel!"

Chris smiled and rubbed the puppy's ears. "I was just teasing. Anyway, I like the way they flop around."

"I wouldn't worry, when she grows up, just her looks will terrify people—after all, she is a pit bull. The fact she's a lover, we'll keep secret," Danielle suggested.

"A lover and a big scaredy-cat," Walt muttered. Max lifted his head, opened his eyes, and looked at Walt. "Go back to sleep, Max. It's just an expression."

"Hey, is one of our neighbors having a costume party we weren't invited to?" Chris asked after Max closed his eyes again and Hunny closed hers.

Danielle absently stroked Max's back. "Costume party? Why do you ask?"

"There was this guy walking down the street, wearing a green derby hat, red jacket, some sort of an apron—I think it was leather —short pants, and these outrageous striped socks with work boots. Actually, the entire outfit was pretty outrageous."

"Sounds like a leprechaun." Walt flashed Danielle a smile. "Weren't we just talking about leprechauns?"

"From what I recall, leprechauns wear green, not red," Danielle reminded him.

Walt shook his head. "No. In the earlier legends they wore red jackets, I believe."

"Leprechauns? What are you two talking about?" Chris looked from Walt to Danielle. "This guy was a little too big to be a leprechaun. But now that you mention it, he was dressed like one."

"Okay, maybe they did wear red, but I've never seen a leprechaun wearing an apron like Chris described," Danielle said.

Walt arched his brows at Danielle and smiled. "So you've seen a lot of leprechauns?"

"You know what I mean. In pictures and stuff," she said.

Settling back on the sofa, Chris propped one leg over his opposing knee as he absently scratched behind Hunny's ears. "Actually, leprechauns—according to legend—wear cobbler's aprons. They repair shoes, you know."

"No, I did not know." With furrowed brows Danielle added, "Well, if it was around Saint Patrick's Day, I'd understand someone dressing up like a leprechaun, but that was three months ago. And it's a little early for Halloween. Who do you think this guy is?"

"No clue. I didn't recognize him. Of course, I was looking more at what he was wearing than his face."

"Whose house did he go to?" Danielle asked.

"I don't know. When I looked back, he was gone. So why were you two talking about leprechauns?" Chris asked.

"We were talking about the missing coins—one thing led to

another—leprechauns like gold, there was that shamrock…" Danielle shrugged.

"Still no leads?" Chris asked.

Danielle then proceeded to tell Chris everything she knew about the missing gold that she hadn't already told him on the phone.

"So the Missing Thorndike's here?" Chris asked after Danielle told him about emptying her other safe deposit box.

"Yeah, up in the wall safe in my room." Danielle paused a moment and looked at Chris. "You haven't seen it yet, have you?"

Chris shook his head. "No. Just in pictures."

Danielle stood up, gently placing Max on the floor. "Let me get it."

———

WHEN THEY LOOKED HIS WAY, he ducked down out of sight. He didn't want them to find him looking through the parlor window. He recognized Walt Marlow, yet he couldn't remember why he knew who the man was. The woman he also recognized; she was the one who had been sleeping in the bed upstairs. The man on the sofa, he had never seen before.

It wasn't as if he was afraid the people in the room would catch him watching them—they would only see him if he wanted them to, and then, that did not always work. It was the dog and cat that troubled him most—the cat especially. Leprechauns and cats did not get along.

He watched as the woman left the room. Curious as to where she was going, he moved to the second floor and looked in her bedroom window, guessing that was where she was heading. Once he looked into the bedroom, he knew he had been correct. To his surprise, she moved a painting, and there, hidden behind the canvas, was a wall safe. He grinned and leaned closer, his eyes never leaving her. He wanted to see what she was about to retrieve from the safe.

———

HEATHER DONOVAN WAS on her way home and was just about to pass Marlow House when something caught her eye. There, hovering by a window on the second floor, was a man dressed in green and red, wearing a green derby hat. She slammed on her brakes, but not before she ran headlong into the front of Chris's car.

She was still sitting in her car, hands gripping the steering wheel, engine running, while she shakily stared up to the second floor. The man was no longer there, but the front door of Marlow House was now thrown open and the occupants of the bed and breakfast, including the owner of the car she had just slammed into, were all running in her direction.

"Are you alright?" Danielle shouted when she reached Heather's car.

Still trembling, Heather, wide eyed, looked through the windshield at Danielle, her foot still on the brake.

Hurriedly, not saying a word, Chris opened the passenger side of the car and reached in, put the car in park, and turned off the engine. After he did, Danielle opened the driver's side of the car and helped Heather from the vehicle.

Chris slammed the passenger door shut and ran to the driver's side. "Are you okay?"

With a glazed expression, Heather looked from Chris to his car and broke into tears. "Your new car! Oh, I'm so sorry!" She began to sob.

Silently, the guests of Marlow House watched as Danielle gently brought Heather into the house and took her into the parlor while Chris moved her car, parking it behind his.

"Are you sure you don't want to go to the hospital?" Danielle asked as she helped Heather to a chair.

Heather shook her head and broke into tears again. "No, I'm fine…but Chris's car!"

By the time Chris returned to the parlor, Danielle had managed to calm Heather down. Leaving the guests of Marlow House out in the hallway to speculate on what had just happened and why, Chris closed the parlor door. The only people in the room were Chris, Heather, and Danielle—and one ghost—Walt. Hunny remained on the sofa while Max dozed on the floor under the desk.

"I'm so sorry, Chris!" Heather blubbered. "It's your new car!"

Chris knelt by Heather's side. "Hey, it's just a car. I'm more worried about you. What happened?"

Wide eyed, Heather looked up into Chris's face and then glanced to Danielle, and then to Walt, and back to Chris. "There was a man floating by Danielle's bedroom window!"

Walt frowned. "What do you mean floating?"

"Just that. Floating. Just hovering outside her window, looking in." Blinking her eyes, she added, "He was dressed in green with a red jacket."

SEVEN

"That sounds like the guy I saw walking down the street a little while ago. Are you saying he climbed up on the roof and was looking in Danielle's bedroom?" Chris rushed to the parlor window and looked outside.

"I said *floating*," Heather said impatiently, absently combing her fingers through her straight bangs. Strands of her black hair were beginning to escape the confines of her braids.

Chris turned back to face Heather. "So our leprechaun is actually a ghost?"

Heather frowned. "Leprechaun? What are you talking about?" No longer crying, she wiped the tears from her face with the back of her hand.

"Chris saw this guy walking down the street dressed up like a leprechaun," Danielle explained. "But if he's floating around outside, it sounds more like he's a ghost."

"I wonder if leprechauns can fly?" Heather murmured.

"Oh, come on, there are no such things as leprechauns," Walt said impatiently. He waved his hand and a cigar appeared.

Heather looked over to Walt and arched her brow. "Why not? There are ghosts."

"That's what I told him." Danielle flashed Walt a grin and was met with an eye roll.

Chris chuckled and then took a seat on the sofa. "Too tall for a leprechaun."

"Really? I couldn't tell his size. I didn't get that good a look," Heather said, now sounding much calmer. "How tall are leprechauns, anyway?"

Walt flashed Heather a look of annoyance.

"If he was floating by the upstairs window, sounds like a ghost to me," Danielle said. "Unless he was wearing a jetpack, I don't know of any guys who can fly."

"If he's a ghost, who is he?" Heather asked.

Chris shrugged. "I have to admit I didn't get a look at the guy's face. I was too busy checking out his clothes."

"I didn't see his face either," Heather said. "But I don't know of anyone who's recently passed who dresses like that. Heck, I don't know anyone alive who does."

"Why was he looking in my window?" Danielle grumbled.

"Maybe he heard you had a ghost-friendly house?" Heather suggested with a grin.

Max, who had slept through the commotion, opened his eyes and looked around the room. When he spied Heather sitting nearby, he looked over at Walt and let out a loud meow.

Walt's gaze met Max's. He was silent for a moment. Finally, he said, "Really?"

Frowning, Heather looked from Walt to Max, back to Walt. "Are you talking to that cat?"

"It seems Max here saw that man you described. He was standing by Danielle's bed last night."

"What do you mean he was standing by my bed?" Danielle shrieked.

Before Walt could answer, the door to the parlor flew open and Lily walked in, Ian and Sadie trailing behind her.

"What in the world happened to Heather's and Chris's cars? Their hoods are both smashed up."

Heather groaned and slumped down in the chair. "Oh, the car…I almost forgot."

"Heather had a little accident," Danielle explained. She glanced at the clock and then looked back to Lily. "That was a quick trip. What did you do, just drive to Portland and turn around and come back?"

"Car trouble," Ian said. "But it looks like I'm not the only one to have car trouble."

Sadie, who had just come into the parlor with Ian, promptly walked to the sofa, her tail wagging as she nosed Hunny, who immediately attempted to retreat behind Chris, trying her best to wiggle between her human's back and the sofa cushion.

"Sadie," Walt shouted, "leave the puppy alone. You're scaring her."

Sadie glanced over at Walt and made a little grunting sound before flopping down on the floor by Chris's feet. She rested her chin on her front paws while she looked up to the sofa. *They don't let me on the furniture!*

"Is everyone okay?" Ian asked, now standing by the desk.

"Everyone's fine," Chris told them.

"Our cars aren't," Heather groaned.

Ian shook his head in disgust. "This has been a crazy kind of day. First someone steals Danielle's coins and then—"

"Who stole Danielle's coins? What coins?" Heather interrupted.

"The gold coins," Danielle explained.

Heather frowned. "I don't understand. I thought you were keeping them in a safe deposit box?"

"Any word on the theft?" Ian asked.

Danielle shook her head. "No. I haven't talked to the chief since I got home. But actually, the FBI is working on the case."

Sitting up straighter in the chair, Heather looked from Ian to Danielle. "I don't understand? What happened?"

"I went to get the coins out of the safe deposit box this morning because I was meeting the buyer, and when I opened the box, it was empty."

"We are talking about a safe deposit box at the bank, right?" Heather asked.

Danielle looked over to Heather and nodded. "Yes."

"How is that even possible?" Heather asked.

Danielle wrinkled her nose. "I have no clue. From what I understand, they're reviewing the videos from the security cameras."

"Wow." Heather slumped back on the chair. "If you don't get them back, will the bank have to pay you?"

"Typically, a bank is not responsible for the contents of a safe deposit box. For one thing, they don't inventory what their customers put into the boxes," Ian said.

"And I wasn't insured," Danielle added.

"Wow," Heather said again. "And I thought I was having a bad day."

"Exactly what happened out there?" Ian asked.

"A dog darted across the street, and Heather was trying to miss it and hit Chris's car," Danielle told him.

Walt shook his head and chuckled. "It amazes me how easily lies slip off your tongue."

Heather and Chris exchanged glances, yet said nothing.

Lily sniffed the air—she detected a hint of cigar smoke. It wasn't really necessary; she had already guessed Walt was in the room with them. It was obvious to her Walt had told Sadie to leave Hunny alone. And by the way Chris and Heather were acting, she suspected there was more to the car story than they were letting on and wondered if they were discussing something when she and Ian had barged into the room.

Lily grabbed Ian's hand. "Come on, you promised to take me out for pie. Let's walk down to Pier Café." Without asking anyone to join them, she dragged Ian from the room, leaving Sadie sleeping by the sofa.

A few moments later, after Ian and Lily had left the room and closed the door behind them, Chris asked, "So what are we going to do about this new ghost?"

"Not sure what we can do," Heather said.

"He wasn't standing by your bed!" Danielle said with a shiver. She then paused a moment, suddenly remembering something. She dug her hand in her pocket and then pulled out a gold necklace—lavishly bejeweled with glittering emeralds and diamonds. Holding it up for all to see, she said, "I almost forgot! I was coming downstairs with the Missing Thorndike when I heard the car crash. I shoved the necklace in my pocket."

"Oh, that's it?" Heather cooed, standing up to get a closer look. Danielle handed her the necklace. Reverently holding it in her hands, Heather plopped back down in the chair, her gaze locked on the expensive heirloom.

Chris leaned forward to have a closer look, yet he didn't attempt to take the Missing Thorndike from Heather. "It's beautiful."

Turning the necklace in her hands, Heather said softly, "To think my great-grandfather was responsible for removing the original gems from this piece. So much tragedy because of it." She shook her head sadly.

"I used to think it was responsible for Cheryl's death, but it really wasn't. I suspect Renton would have found a way to permanently get her out of the way even if she hadn't taken the necklace. It just made it easier for him."

Taking one last look at the necklace, Heather let out a sigh and stood up, handing the piece to Chris so he could have a closer look.

"I suppose you removed it from the safe deposit box because of the gold coins going missing?" Heather asked.

Danielle nodded. "After I realized the gold coins were gone, I opened my other safe deposit box. The necklace was still there, but it didn't seem smart to leave it at the bank until we find out what happened to the gold coins."

"I'd think if they broke in one box, they'd hit the other ones too. Do you know if any of the others were tampered with?" Heather asked.

"I don't know," Danielle shrugged. "The box holding the Missing Thorndike was above the one holding the coins. All the boxes on the lower level are larger. I suppose it's possible whoever took the gold broke into some of the other boxes along that row. Maybe they figured the larger boxes held more, so they would get more."

TAKING roost on the roof of Marlow House, he watched as the man and woman made their way across the street. The dog was not with them. Ever since the man and dog had moved into the house, he had stayed away. Dogs weren't as bad as cats, but they were still trouble for someone like him. A leprechaun couldn't be too careful.

He jumped down from his perch and landed by the window of the bedroom he had been looking into before a car driving down the street had slammed into a parked car. What he had seen when looking into the window earlier surprised him. He had watched the woman—the same woman whom he had watched sleep just the night before—remove an oil painting from the wall and expose a wall safe.

It wasn't the wall safe that fascinated him as much as what she removed from it. He wasn't sure where—or when—but he had seen that necklace before. Even from his vantage point, he was fairly certain those were real diamonds and emeralds. The fact was, he was old enough and experienced enough to know the difference between expensive fakes and the real things. Leprechauns, after all, were experts in assessing treasures. He just wished he could remember where he had seen that necklace before.

He was about to turn from the window when she reentered her bedroom. With a smile, he continued to watch her through the glass. She pulled the necklace from her pocket and then tucked it into the pouch. After placing the pouch in the safe, she closed the safe's door and gave the lock several spins. Just as she turned to the bed to retrieve the oil painting, she glanced up to the window.

She froze, eyes wide. "Walt!"

HAD WALT still been in the parlor with the rest of them, he would not have heard Danielle's cry. But he had been on his way to her room, wanting to discuss in private what they had been talking about downstairs.

When he appeared in her bedroom, he found her standing a few feet from her bed. She pointed to the window. Walt looked, but whoever had been outside the window was no longer there.

EIGHT

Dropping the sack holding the hamburger and fries onto the side table next to his recliner, Alan Kissinger went to the kitchen to grab a beer out of the refrigerator. None of the interior house lights were on, and he didn't bother flipping the switch. While the sun had not yet set and the pending rain clouds darkened the sky, Alan didn't mind a dimly lit house. Since his divorce, he lived alone and he didn't need every light turned on, as did his ex.

Just as he returned to the recliner, his phone began to ring. Before answering it, he popped open the beer and took a swig. Setting the opened beer on the side table with the sack of food, he pulled the phone from his pocket and looked at it. It was Dave.

"I just got home," Alan said when he answered the phone. He plopped down on the chair and leaned back, propping his feet on the chair's now extended footrest. Reaching over to the side table, he grabbed his beer and took another sip.

"I was wondering about that. I thought you would have called by now."

Putting the cellphone on speaker and turning up the volume, he set it on his armrest and then set his beer in the chair's cup holder. He reached over and grabbed the sack and removed the burger.

"I stopped off to get something to eat and brought it home. I'm starving. Those damn FBI guys and cops were there all day." He unwrapped his burger and took a bite.

"We knew that would happen. So did they find anything?" Dave asked.

After swallowing his first bite, Alan said, "Just that someone moved the camera and then moved it back."

"No surprise."

"Of course, the damn FBI wouldn't be involved if Susan hadn't insisted the box was heavy when it went into the vault. I should have fired her the moment I knew she was going to be nothing but trouble. I thought making her work on Saturdays again would get her to quit."

"You knew that wasn't going to happen. She isn't the first employee who doesn't know when to shut up. But I know you, you'll handle it."

Alan picked up his beer again and took a swig and then set the can back in the cup holder. "I have a question for you, Dave."

"What's that?"

"Are you as good at opening home safes as you are bank safes?"

Dave laughed. "Why do you ask? What are you thinking now?"

"Remember how I told you Boatman emptied her other safe deposit box?"

"Yeah, what about it?"

"It was that necklace I was telling you about. She took it home with her."

"Does that surprise you?" Dave asked. "If I was her, I wouldn't have left it at the bank either."

"That necklace is worth more than a million bucks."

"It will also be a little harder to get rid of than gold coins," Dave pointed out.

"That never stopped you before," Alan reminded him.

"What are you thinking?"

"From what I understand, she had a wall safe installed at Marlow House. That's where she kept the necklace before, when she took it out of the bank. But that was about a year ago. From what I understand, this is the first time she's taken it out of the bank since then. So if she took it home with her, it's a sure bet she's putting it in the wall safe, at least until she decides it isn't the best place to keep something that valuable and moves it to another bank."

"Do you know what kind of safe it is?"

"I suppose Susan is good for something. When I asked her how Boatman thought her necklace was going to be safer at home, she told me about the wall safe. She even knew what kind it was." Alan then told Dave the brand.

Dave began to laugh. "Damn, are you serious? Talk about easy pickings!"

"Easy for you, maybe."

Dave stopped laughing and said, "Well, the opening-the-safe part would be easy, but getting in and out of her house undetected, that's where the risk comes in."

"Her house isn't just a house—it's a bed and breakfast."

"Do you mean like a hotel or something?" Dave asked.

"Yes. All you would need to do is check in and then, when no one is around, slip into the room, take the necklace and leave."

"That's not exactly all that would be involved," Dave reminded him.

"Dave, you still have that credit card I gave you? Come on, isn't Stephanie up to a new adventure? And I bet she'd love to spend a couple nights at a seaside B and B."

Dave laughed again. "I love how you always come up with these ideas, but Stephanie and I are always the ones to take the risk!"

"Come on—the necklace will be a piece of cake, especially compared to cleaning out a safe deposit box in a bank. And no one is as good with disguises as Stephanie is. I bet you two could check in tomorrow and then run into Boatman next week and she would never know you were the same couple who stayed under her roof and then disappeared with her necklace."

Dave didn't answer immediately. Alan knew he was considering his idea. While Dave was silently thinking, Alan grabbed a handful of fries from the sack and continued eating his burger.

Finally, Dave said, "If we do this, I assume we can't wait. I don't know this Boatman, but I can't imagine anyone leaving something that valuable in a wall safe."

"I agree with you. We were asked by the cops not to discuss the robbery while they investigate, but I know the story is already circulating in town."

Dave laughed. "Like something like that won't leak out?"

"From what I understand, Boatman's necklace has something of a reputation in Frederickport. The minute the locals learn about the missing gold, it won't take them long to figure out Boatman removed the necklace from the bank and is keeping it in her safe at home. The safe, by the way, seems to be common knowledge."

"Which is why we need to move fast. Unless Boatman is a fool, she'll be making arrangements to move it to another bank unless her little experience with yours has left her unwilling to trust another bank."

"True, but it doesn't mean she won't decide to keep it somewhere else," Alan said. "There are other options rather than a bank."

"Exactly. So, if we do this, I guess we need to call tonight and make reservations."

"From what I understand, they're full right now, but I heard it should be cleared out by Monday morning. I would assume you'd have a good chance of getting a reservation early in the week."

"Okay. Let me go talk to Steph and I'll get back with you."

After Alan said goodbye, he turned off his cellphone and smiled. Leaning back in the chair, he kicked off his shoes. They dropped to the floor.

SPECIAL AGENTS WILSON and Thomas sat in a corner booth at Lucy's Diner, waiting for their dinner order.

"I really hate going back there," Wilson groaned. "Something's not right about Marlow House."

"I don't know how we can avoid it, not if we want to interview Boatman tonight. I suppose we could ask her to meet us down at the police station tomorrow, talk to her there."

Wilson shook his head. "If we told anyone, they would think we're crazy."

Thomas picked up his cup of coffee. Before taking a sip, he said, "Which is why we agreed not to say anything. We were both there. We both saw it."

"Yes, but what exactly was—*it?*"

Taking a drink of coffee, Thomas shook his head. "I have no idea. I don't know, maybe there really are ghosts."

Wilson leaned back in the booth and let out a sigh. "We need to focus on this case."

"At least we know why the robbers only hit one box."

"That's what we *assume*. They wanted to get in and out of there quick, so they hit the box with the biggest reward. Yet how did they know that box was Boatman's? That it was the one with the gold?" Wilson asked.

Setting his coffee cup down, Thomas leaned forward, resting his elbows on the tabletop. "I think it's pretty obvious it was an inside job. Whoever it was knew where those cameras were. Knew which box was Boatman's. And there is no sign anyone broke in to the bank itself."

Still leaning forward, Thomas absently tapped his fingers on the tabletop while considering the situation. "If it is an inside job, I would tend to rule out Mitchell. Why would she adamantly insist the box was filled with the coins after Boatman put it in the vault? She could have easily claimed she didn't remember. After all, even Boatman agreed Mitchell had left her alone with the safe deposit box before it went into the vault that last time."

"Unless they're in this together," Wilson suggested. "Maybe it's about squeezing the bank? And now that we know someone moved that camera and there are a few minutes when that particular box wasn't under surveillance, it could open the bank up to liability."

Thomas absently fiddled with the handle of his coffee cup. "Sounds pretty farfetched."

"As farfetched as what goes on in Marlow House? Hands that aren't there that grab you? Cigar smoke that comes and goes?"

"There has to be some logical explanation for all that. I've been giving it a lot of thought lately. Maybe that house is rigged like the Magic Castle," Thomas suggested.

"Magic Castle?" Wilson frowned.

"Place down in LA where magicians hang out. I went to it once and sat in on a private magic act. I couldn't believe what I was seeing, especially considering we were all there in this small room together. Nothing like when an act's up on stage or on TV and you assume there are wires or something you aren't seeing."

"So you're saying what happened to us was nothing more than someone playing tricks on us?"

"It's either that or the place really is haunted."

They sat there in silence for a few minutes. Finally, Thomas asked, "Any more thoughts about the significance of the shamrock?"

"We know where it came from. I'm pretty sure when they're finished processing the evidence, they'll say the thief removed it from that box we found in the storage room, since there were other ones like it still there. Of course, anyone could have gone into that room. It doesn't have to be someone from the bank, since it's located next to the public restrooms. And Mitchell admitted they aren't consistent about keeping that room locked."

"But why put the shamrock in the safe deposit box in the first place?" Thomas asked.

"Maybe we have someone out there who wants to make a name for himself. The Shamrock Gang?" Wilson suggested.

Thomas shrugged and then said, "I'm surprised MacDonald called us in on this. It's not like someone hit the bank's cash."

"I suspect since he's close to Boatman, that conflict-of-interest thing was weighing on him."

"I imagine he's questioning his personal judgment these days, considering what his girlfriend did."

"No kidding."

Before Thomas could respond, the server brought their food. After she left the table, Wilson said, "We can talk to Boatman tomorrow. She isn't going anywhere."

"Do you want to have her meet us down at the police station to interview her?"

Silently, Wilson considered Thomas's suggestion for a moment. Finally, he picked up his fork and knife and angrily cut into the rare steak sitting on the plate before him. "No. I'll be damned if I'll let an old house scare me away."

NINE

W hen Lily walked into the kitchen the next morning, she found Danielle standing at the counter, cracking eggs into a stainless steel bowl.

Grabbing a coffee cup from the overhead cabinet, Lily glanced over at Danielle and asked, "Where's Joanne?"

"She won't be in until noon. Carmen is checking out today, so Joanne is coming a little later so she can clean her room." Danielle grabbed another egg from the carton and tapped it against the edge of the bowl. "So I'm making breakfast this morning."

Lily poured herself a cup of coffee. "Can I help?"

"Sure. I'm making breakfast burritos. The sausage and potatoes are already done; they're in the oven, keeping warm, along with the tortillas. Maybe you can grab the grated cheese and salsa from the fridge and put them on the table."

"No problem." Lily took a quick sip of her coffee and then set the cup on the counter. She turned to the refrigerator. "I noticed the dining room table was already set. You must have gotten up early."

Danielle scooped up the broken egg shells and dumped them in the nearby trash can. "I couldn't sleep. Too much on my mind."

"I bet. I still can't believe the coins weren't in the safe deposit box." Lily removed the serving bowl filled with grated cheddar cheese from the refrigerator, along with the salsa. She set them both on the nearby kitchen counter and then closed the refrigerator.

"And then there's that weird ghost leprechaun whatever floating around." Danielle picked up a whisk and started beating the eggs.

Turning to Danielle, Lily leaned against the counter as she watched Danielle finish preparing breakfast. "I suppose I'm getting used to you seeing spirits from time to time."

Danielle sniggered. "The once strange has become normal?"

Lily smiled. "Something like that."

"BREAKFAST WAS GREAT. You should open a restaurant," Lily told Danielle after she helped her clean up the kitchen.

"Yeah, right," Danielle said with a snort. "I like to cook, but this is all I want to do. Although, sometimes I think the real reason I opened the B and B was so I'd have an excuse to bake cookies and cake."

"I for one appreciate your cakes and cookies."

"Of course, if I stopped baking, maybe I could finally lose those fifteen pounds."

"If you stopped baking, that would just mean more trips to Old Salts."

Danielle sighed. "True. Which reminds me, I need to stop at Old Salts and pick up some cinnamon rolls."

Lily folded the dishtowel she had been using and hung it on a hook. "I'm glad Joanne worked out so well. It's nice to have an extra person help with the cooking."

"When I first talked to Joanne about staying on as a housekeeper, I had no idea she'd be able to fill in in the kitchen so well."

"Neither did I."

"You know, Joe could never understand why I wanted to keep running Marlow House as a bed and breakfast. Especially after the inheritances. He's right, I certainly don't need the money."

"I understand. It's fun meeting new people."

"Exactly!" Danielle nodded emphatically.

"And I've come to realize we all need to do something constructive."

Danielle glanced over at Lily. "You thinking about going back to teaching?"

"As much as I loved teaching, now that I don't have to do it, I honestly don't know if I want to. Oh, I want to do something with kids again. I need to start being productive again, but I don't know if I want to deal with all the political BS that comes with being a teacher. Not to mention the paperwork these days." Lily paused and looked directly at Danielle. "Do you understand?"

"Completely."

"But I can't keep spending my days following Ian around, being nothing more than his sidekick while he's doing research and writing. I'm sure he likes having someone around to make him coffee when he's deep in research or making him a sandwich when he's hungry, but that's not how I want to spend the rest of my life. I need to find something constructive, positive, to do with my time."

"You'll figure it out." Danielle reached into the overhead cabinet and removed a cup. She looked at Lily. "You want some coffee?"

"Sure. If we can have some of that crumb cake you made."

"We just finished breakfast," Danielle teased as she removed a second cup.

"So?" Lily removed the lid from the cake pan and picked up the plate, carrying it to the table. She set it down and then glanced around the room. "Have you seen Walt this morning?"

"He was with us at breakfast." Danielle carried the now full cups to the table. "But then he said something about going up to the attic to finish that book he was reading."

Lily cut a piece of cake for Danielle and one for herself, setting each one on a napkin. She then took a seat at the table. "When are we going to get Walt a Kindle? I think he'd get a kick out of downloading books. Look how much he loves the Netflix subscription you gave him for Christmas."

Joining Lily at the table, Danielle shook her head. "I'm not sure Walt is ready for eBooks."

"What, you think I'm incapable of mastering technology a child Evan's age can handle?" Walt asked indignantly when he appeared, standing by the table.

His abrupt appearance startled Danielle, and she splashed coffee on the table. She glared at Walt as he sat on one of the empty chairs. "I wish you wouldn't sneak up on me."

Lily glanced over at the seemingly empty chair next to her and watched as it repositioned itself. "Morning, Walt," she said before taking a bite of her coffee cake.

"And anyway," Danielle said as she wiped up her spilled coffee with a napkin, "I just meant that with older people, figuring out computers and reading tablets is often more challenging than for children."

"Older people? Might I remind you I am younger than both you and Lily."

Danielle shrugged and tossed her now crumpled and soaked napkin aside. "In your estimation you're in your late twenties, and I see you as a little over a hundred and twenty. About a century discrepancy there, wouldn't you say?" Danielle wrinkled her nose at Walt and took a bite of her cake.

"You know what is really strange?" Lily said as she broke off a small piece of cake.

"What?" Danielle asked.

"I actually know what you two are talking about, and I'm only hearing one side of the conversation."

THIRTY MINUTES LATER, Danielle and Lily were in the library, where Lily was busy surfing on her iPad while Danielle sat at her desk, working on her computer.

"Oh, Dani! You are not going to believe this!" Lily abruptly sat upright on the sofa, placing her feet on the floor. Still holding the iPad in her hands, she hastily scrolled through whatever website she was viewing.

Danielle looked up from the computer. "What is it?"

Holding the iPad with her right hand, Lily used her left hand to wave dismissively in Danielle's direction. "Just a minute." Still staring at the tablet, Lily muttered, "I don't believe this? Who is this person? How did they get that picture?"

Sounding bored and slightly annoyed, Danielle looked over to Lily. "What are you going on about? I'm trying to post these invoices, and I really need to focus."

"It's about you, Dani!"

Danielle frowned. "What's about me?"

"This blog! There's an entire blog dedicated to you and Marlow House!"

"What are you talking about? What blog?"

Lily leapt up from the sofa and carried her iPad to Danielle, who continued to sit at her desk. "The blog is called Mysteries of Marlow House. It even has its own URL."

Danielle took the iPad from Lily and stared at it. "That's a picture of me? Where did they take that?"

"It was obviously taken last year at the open house. You're wearing the Missing Thorndike and your vintage dress."

Staring at the image, Danielle shook her head. "I don't remember that picture. It wasn't the one in the newspaper or on the B and B website. It was obviously taken in the backyard. Who took it?"

Lily took the iPad from Danielle and looked at it again. "I don't know. But go to the website on your computer, and you can see for yourself."

Danielle turned her attention back to the computer. "What did you say the URL was again?"

"All one word, Mystery of Marlow House dot com."

Sitting on the arm of the sofa with her iPad, Lily faced Danielle. "It appears the blog started after you went missing. And since then, they've been making regular entries."

Staring at her monitor, Danielle frowned. "This is weird. Whose blog is it? I can't find any name."

"I couldn't either. But whoever it is, they seem to be fixated on you."

"That is just creepy," Danielle said as her fingers danced over the keyboard.

"What are you doing?" Lily looked over her iPad to get a better look of what Danielle was doing on the computer.

"I'm doing a WHOIS search to see who owns the domain."

"Playing Jessica Fletcher again?" Lily teased.

"I told you it's Nancy Drew," Danielle reminded her, her eyes never leaving the monitor. "Jessica is too old."

"Hmm…does that make Walt a Hardy Boy?"

"Hardy har har," Danielle said dryly. "Whoever it was hid their identity. But you're right, it was started the day after we went missing, at least according to the domain information. That's when it was registered." Danielle looked up from the computer.

"I wonder if it is someone we know," Lily said.

"If the blogger took the photo, not necessarily. There were a lot of people in and out of here on the day of the open house. There were a lot of people there that I didn't know and never saw again."

Lily stood up, setting her iPad on the sofa cushion. She began to pace the room. "Then whoever it is, maybe they'll return to the scene of the crime." Pausing, she faced Danielle and made a poor attempt at wiggling her eyebrows.

"What are you talking about? And stop doing that with your eyes. Makes you look like a geek."

Lily started pacing again. "Just saying, if the blogger did take that picture, then perhaps they'll come to your anniversary open house. We're having it, right?"

"I told you. No anniversary celebration." Danielle looked back at her monitor. "Now hush, I'm going to read what my cyber stalker has been writing about me."

TEN

P astor Chad took her gloved hands in his and gave them a gentle
squeeze. He continued to hold them as he looked into her eyes
and said, "I am so pleased to see you here today, Mrs. Nichols."

Pastor Chad and Marie Nichols stood outside on the steps of the
Frederickport Community Church as the parishioners made their
way inside for the Sunday service. It had been months since Marie
had attended church, but after she opened her birthday gift from
Danielle several weeks earlier, she knew she had to go, in order to
show off the lovely dress Danielle had given her. It was obvious Lily
and Danielle had conspired when selecting their gifts for her ninety-
first birthday, considering the lovely little hat Lily had given her
perfectly matched the dress. Marie wore them both today, along
with her white gloves. *Women rarely wear gloves anymore*, Marie thought.

"I figured it was about time I made an appearance," Marie said
as she removed her hands from his, yet not before giving the minister's hands a friendly pat. "At my age I can be called up at any
moment, and I figure it might give me some points if he knows I've
made a recent visit to his house."

The reverend smiled and said, "I do understand it's not always
easy for you to get here every Sunday. I've told you before if you
ever need a ride—"

Reaching out and patting his hand again, Marie interrupted him
by saying, "Yes, yes, I know. But frankly I'm a little too old to do any

significant sinning these days to warrant weekly sermons, and I don't imagine there is much you can tell me that I haven't already heard. But I do appreciate your offer."

Marie didn't wait for Pastor Chad to respond, but instead abruptly excused herself and moved to the doorway into the church, leaving the minister to greet his other parishioners. A few moments later she stood inside the church, the leather strap of her white handbag draped over her right forearm. Glancing around, deciding where to sit, she heard several people call her name in greeting. Responding with a friendly wave and cheerful smile, Marie made her way down the aisle.

One friend, who called out, pointed to the empty space next to her on the pew, yet before Marie took a step in that direction, someone else claimed it. Just as that happened, Marie noticed Beverly Klein sitting alone just two pews down. Picking up her step, Marie bustled in Beverly's direction.

"Marie," Beverly greeted her in surprise when the elderly woman took the space next to her.

Making herself comfortable, Marie set her purse on the floor by her feet and said, "I'm beginning to feel like a sinner the way everyone seems so surprised to see me here this morning."

Beverly tittered and patted Marie's arm. "Not at all. Goodness, I haven't come for months myself. But after Steve…" Beverly didn't finish her sentence, but instead let out a sigh.

Marie turned to Beverly, a concerned expression on her face as she studied the much younger woman's delicate profile. "How are you doing, dear?"

Beverly shrugged and then smiled at Marie. "Taking one day at a time. It's hard getting used to being alone."

Marie patted Beverly's knee and then turned to face the front of the church. "It will get easier over time. I promise you. It was rough after my husband died, but can I tell you a secret?"

Looking at Marie, Beverly cocked her head slightly. "Sure, what?"

"Sometimes living alone can be rather nice. No one's messes to pick up after. If I don't want to cook dinner, I don't have to. Of course, with my husband, it wasn't just dinner. It was breakfast, lunch, and dinner. But from what I understand with the younger generation, the husbands seem to help more around the house."

"Not Steve," Beverly said under her breath, and then added in a conspiratorial whisper, "Can I tell you a secret?"

"Certainly."

"I feel that way now."

Marie laughed. "Well, I understand. But you're still young. I'm sure you'll find someone else."

"I imagine your grandson has told you I'm thinking of leaving town."

"You are? He never mentioned anything," Marie lied.

"Really? I just assumed he would have."

"Oh no," Marie said seriously. "Adam is a professional. He never discusses his clients' private business."

Beverly smiled. "That's nice to know."

"But you know, dear, Frederickport has some eligible bachelors you should first consider before you go running off."

"You mean like your grandson?" Beverly asked with a grin.

"Oh no!" She quickly added, "I didn't mean that as it sounded. It's just that you have grown children, and I can't imagine you would want to have any more, whereas when Adam finally settles down, he'll want to start a family—children of his own."

Suppressing a smile, Beverly asked, "Who exactly did you have in mind?"

"Why, the police chief. Of course, he does have young boys at home, but they seem to be good boys. The poor man."

"I still can't believe Carol Ann was involved in that hijacking. And then a kidnapping! I would have never guessed in a million years she would do something like that."

Marie nodded her head in agreement. "I was in total shock. Of course, I always say you never really know someone. For example —" Marie lowered her voice and leaned close to Beverly as her gaze darted about the church, looking at the people sitting on the pews around them "—someone sitting under this roof could very well be a killer, and we would never know."

Beverly smiled and glanced around the room. "You're right, Marie. Nothing surprises me anymore."

Marie nodded emphatically. "Isn't that the truth."

"Which reminds me, I suppose you know what happened at the bank yesterday. After all, you are close with Danielle Boatman."

Marie frowned. "No, I don't know. What happened?"

"Apparently, Danielle went to the bank yesterday morning to

remove those gold coins from her safe deposit box—the coins she found at your house—and they were gone!"

"Gone?" Marie gasped.

Beverly nodded. "Yes. They have the FBI looking into it. I understand they've been going through the surveillance videos of the vault. Something like this would not have happened had Steve still been alive."

Marie started to ask Beverly how she knew, but then thought the question foolish, considering Beverly's late husband had been the bank's manager for a number of years. She imagined the widow kept in close contact with her associations from the bank.

"What all did the thieves take?" Marie asked.

"From what I was told, the only thing they know that's missing is the gold coins. From what I understand, Danielle opened her other safe deposit box and removed the Missing Thorndike and took it home with her."

"Took it home with her?" Marie gasped. "That seems a little dangerous, keeping something so valuable at her house."

Beverly shrugged. "She does run an inn; I would imagine she has some sort of safe there."

"She does, but still…"

"You can hardly blame her. If my deposits weren't federally protected, I'd be tempted to close my account myself," Beverly said.

"Do you know if the bank is liable for those coins?"

"From what Steve always told me, safe deposit boxes aren't insured per se. Of course, if the bank could be proven negligent in some way, I would imagine they might be held liable for some damages. Yet from what I'm hearing, Alan Kissinger—that's the new bank manager—insists the only person who was ever in that safe deposit box was Danielle. According to him, it's her word against the bank's."

"Danielle would never lie about something like that!"

"I'm not saying she would. In fact, Susan Mitchell insists the gold coins were in the box the last time Danielle was in it."

"Then why is the manager trying to say Danielle lied?"

"I imagine to save his own hide."

ADAM NICHOLS HAD DROPPED his grandmother off at church

that Sunday morning. He had been a little surprised when she had called him up the night before and had asked him for a ride to church. But when he picked her up that morning and saw her all dressed up in the new outfit Danielle and Lily had given her, he had a good idea the real reason she wanted to go. These days, his grandmother didn't have many opportunities to dress up in all her finery. He made himself a mental note to take his grandmother to Pearl Cove for dinner in the near future.

After she had asked him for a ride, she tried to talk him into attending services with her. He respectfully declined, telling her he already had an appointment with a client on Sunday morning. It wasn't exactly the truth. His appointment was in reality breakfast at Pier Café with Bill Jones, who was an old friend and part-time employee—not a client.

At breakfast, Bill told him an interesting story about someone stealing Danielle's gold coins from the bank. Initially, Adam didn't believe the story. For one thing, he knew Bill was still annoyed over the gold coins, believing the two could have ended up with them had Adam been more cooperative and arranged for Bill to search his grandmother's rental property. Yet by the end of breakfast, Adam was beginning to believe Bill was telling the truth.

Adam finished breakfast and left Pier Café before Bill, as he needed to head back to church and pick up his grandmother. She had been fairly cheerful when he had initially dropped her off that morning, but when she climbed into his vehicle after services, she was clearly agitated.

"What's wrong, Grandma?" Adam asked as he put his car in gear and pulled back into the street.

"I just heard the most troubling news," Marie said as she fastened her seatbelt. She then went on to tell Adam what Beverly had told her.

"Bill mentioned that at breakfast," Adam said without thinking.

"Bill? Breakfast? I thought you had an appointment with a client?"

"Uhh…well, I did. But right when I got to the office this morning, the client called and cancelled. And a few minutes later Bill called and asked me for breakfast."

"Right…" Marie said, unconvinced.

Adam shrugged guiltily.

"So how did Bill know about what happened at the bank? From

what Beverly told me, they're trying to keep it hushed up while the FBI investigates."

"Beverly told you, didn't she?"

"What is that supposed to mean?"

Adam laughed. "Grandma, you know as well as I, this is a small town. Things get around fast. Bill knows people, just like Beverly obviously knows people. Never can keep a secret in Frederickport."

"You're right, which makes me even more concerned. Before this evening I imagine everyone in town is going to know the Missing Thorndike is sitting over at Marlow House, unprotected."

"Last thing I heard, Danielle has a very secure wall safe."

"And would that stop someone from holding her at gunpoint and demanding she open that safe? Oh, goodness gracious, look what happened to them all when they got on that plane!"

"Don't get yourself all worked up. I suspect that necklace is going to be back in the safe deposit box by Monday."

"Why do you think that?"

"I imagine those surveillance tapes are going to help them figure out what went wrong and fix it, and then Danielle can put the necklace back."

"And if they don't, I imagine everyone in Frederickport will be waiting for the bank to open on Monday so they can clear out their safe deposit boxes before the thief does!"

ELEVEN

After dropping his grandmother off at her home, Adam decided to take a drive over to Marlow House. He was curious to find out the latest news regarding the missing gold coins and assumed if anyone knew anything, it would have to be Danielle. After all, it was her gold. *It could have been my gold*, Adam told himself. But as he pulled the car away from his grandmother's house and glanced back and saw Marie waving goodbye, he thought, *Nahh, it would have never been mine.*

Turning on the radio, he listened to the music as he drove toward Beach Drive. Just as he pulled up in front of Marlow House and parked his car, his phone rang. He turned off the radio and then the ignition before picking the phone up off his console. It was an incoming FaceTime call from Melony Jacobs.

Before answering the call, Adam quickly looked up into the rearview mirror and inspected his appearance, hastily using one hand to straighten his hair.

"Hey, Mel!" Adam said with a smile when he answered the call, holding the phone not quite an arm's length from his face.

"Hi, Adam." Melony's face smiled out at him from the phone's small screen. She appeared to glance around. "Hey, where are you?"

Adam laughed. "I'm in the car."

"Oh my god, please tell me you aren't driving!"

He laughed again. "No, I just parked the car. What's up? You look terrific, by the way."

She grinned back at him. "Thanks. I just wanted to let you know you'll be seeing more of my face."

He arched his brow. "Are we talking an increase in FaceTime calls, or are you coming for a visit?"

"I turned in my resignation two weeks ago. I'm moving back to Frederickport." By her smile, it was obvious she was excited with the change.

Adam sat up straighter in the seat and looked into Melony's face. "Are you serious?"

"Pretty serious considering I moved out of my place last week and moved into a motel. I needed to get things wrapped up before I take off for Oregon."

"Why didn't you say anything before?" Adam asked.

"I didn't want to say anything until I got everything square here. That's why I told you I didn't want to rent or sell Mom's house."

"So you're moving into her place?" he asked.

She nodded. "For now. Not sure if I'll stay there or sell it and get something smaller. But we'll see."

"What are you going to do about a job?"

"That's one of the things I've been working on. When I arrive in Oregon today, I'll be able to legally practice law in the state."

"*Today?*"

"Portland, anyway. I probably won't get into Frederickport until Tuesday morning."

"Do you need a ride?" he offered. "I could pick you up tomorrow. No reason to stay over in Portland."

"Thanks, Adam, but no. Dad's law firm's remaining files were transferred to storage in Portland, and I'm spending tomorrow sorting through what's left of them. I don't expect to go through everything, but it's a start."

Adam squinted his eyes and took a closer look at his cellphone's screen. "Are you at the airport?"

Melony laughed. "I was wondering when you'd notice. Yes. My plane boards in a few minutes for Portland."

Adam shook his head. "I can't believe you never told me."

"I wanted to surprise you."

Adam grinned. "You did."

"How's Ed?" she asked.

"Ed? Ahh…you mean since the hijacking?"

"I've talked to him a couple times in the last few weeks, and he sounded so down. That monster really messed up his head."

"He seems okay. I get the feeling he's not anxious to jump back into dating."

"And those poor boys! To have to worry about their dad like that after losing their mom. I'd like to smack her good."

"Well, I think she might be regretting her actions about now. Even with the plea deal she made, I understand she's looking at something like five years. That can't be easy for someone like her."

"It should be longer," Melony said angrily.

"Does the chief know about you moving back?"

"Yeah, I told him last week."

You told him, but you didn't tell me.

"Ed and I go back a long way."

Not as long as us.

"I didn't want to just pop back in town unannounced."

"He never mentioned it," Adam muttered under his breath, annoyed.

"What did you say?"

"I said he never mentioned it," Adam said in a louder voice.

"I asked him not to say anything to anyone." Melony paused a moment and glanced to her right. She then looked back to her phone. "I need to say goodbye, Adam. They just called our flight."

"Where are you staying tonight?"

"I'm not sure yet."

Adam could tell she was standing up.

"Call me when you land," Adam told her.

"Okay. But I need to go." She flashed him a smile.

"Fly safe!"

A knock came at the car window just as the iPhone screen froze. The FaceTime call had ended. Adam looked up. Chris stood outside his car, looking in the passenger window, wearing a grin and holding Hunny in his arms.

"I was wondering if you were going to sit in your car all afternoon," Chris said when Adam got out of his vehicle.

"I was talking to Mel," Adam explained as he slammed his car door shut. He noticed Chris's vehicle parked in front of his. It hadn't been there when Adam had pulled up.

"How is Mel?" Chris asked as he walked to Adam. Once on the sidewalk, the two men started toward Marlow House's front gate.

"She's moving to Frederickport—" Adam abruptly stopped talking when he noticed the front of Chris's new car was smashed in. He let out a low whistle and walked toward the vehicle. "What happened?"

"Heather plowed into it yesterday. So what is this about Melony moving to Frederickport?"

Not answering Chris's question, Adam stood over the smashed car hood, hands on hips, and shook his head. "Wow, she did a good job. How did she do this?"

"Ahh, you know Heather," Chris said dismissively, waving his free hand as if to brush away the subject. "Easily distracted. So tell me about Melony."

Adam looked up from Chris's car and shrugged. Stepping away from the vehicle, he joined Chris on the sidewalk and the two men made their way toward Marlow House.

Before he answered the question, he glanced at the pit bull puppy squirming in Chris's arms. She wanted desperately to greet Adam.

Adam reached over and scratched the puppy under the chin, yet not before Hunny licked and playfully chewed his fingertips.

"You have a real killer there," Adam said dryly.

Chris glanced down at the squirming pup. "You're telling me. So what's this about Melony?"

"I don't know much. This is the first I've heard about it. She FaceTimed me a few minutes ago, announcing she was on her way to Oregon."

"I BET YOU'RE EXCITED," Danielle told Adam after he recounted his recent call from Melony. He sat with Chris and Danielle in the parlor. Walt stood nearby, a fact Adam was unaware of. He could smell Walt's cigar, but assumed—as he always did—that it was just one of those odd smells an old house sometimes gets.

"Not sure how I feel about her telling the chief first," Adam grumbled.

"Well, they are old friends," she reminded him.

"And I'm not?" Adam snapped.

Danielle studied Adam and wondered, *Perhaps Marie will be getting her wish after all, and Adam will settle down and start a family.*

They continued to discuss Melony's impending move to Frederickport when the conversation shifted to the missing gold coins.

"Grandma is not thrilled you're keeping the Missing Thorndike here," Adam told her.

"I can't believe she already knows—wait a minute, what am I talking about? I'd be surprised if she didn't know." Danielle chuckled.

"I have to say I can't blame Grandma," Adam told her.

Danielle glanced over to Walt and smiled. She looked back to Adam and said, "I'll be fine here. We have a perfectly good safe and locks on the doors."

"Not to mention those security cameras of yours," Adam muttered.

"Security cameras?" Danielle asked.

"Oh, come on, I know you have this house wired with cameras." Adam glanced around the parlor, looking for signs of hidden cameras.

Danielle started to say something, yet decided not to. Settling back in her chair, she smiled and thought about that long-ago time when Adam had broken in to Marlow House. It was Walt who had caught Adam and Bill in the act, not some hidden cameras. Of course, Adam didn't know that. Danielle also knew Adam believed her antique croquet set was rigged with some remote control device. She chose not to bring up that subject.

"Hidden cameras or not, I'm not thrilled with Danielle keeping the Missing Thorndike here," Chris said.

Walt let out a sigh and shook his head. "You have no faith in me." He took a puff off his cigar as he sat along the edge of the small parlor desk.

"July fourth is just around the corner—Marlow House's first anniversary. Since you have the necklace here anyway, are you going to wear it again?" Adam asked.

Sitting on the sofa next to Chris, Danielle uncrossed and recrossed her legs, repositioning herself on the sofa as she stubbornly shook her head. "I told you before, I'm not having any sort of celebration this year."

They all remained silent for a few minutes.

Adam was the first to speak. In a soft voice he said, "Don't let Renton spoil everything."

Walt spoke up. "Adam has a point. You said yourself you no longer believed the Missing Thorndike was responsible for Cheryl's death. Same for the July fourth party."

Danielle shrugged. "I would just feel strange celebrating the anniversary of the opening, knowing it was the anniversary of Cheryl's death. Although…technically speaking, she was killed the next day."

Adam let out a sigh. "I have my share of regrets about all of that. If Cheryl hadn't come with me, maybe Renton would never have had the opportunity he did."

Danielle looked over at Adam and smiled sadly. "Oh, let's face it. Cheryl did exactly what she wanted to do. Looking back, she was really the only one who could have prevented it. But the fact is, maybe she actually saved my life."

"What do you mean?" Chris asked.

"Renton had stolen from my aunt's estate. Had Cheryl not stirred things up when she did, I might have eventually figured something out, approached Renton wrong, and gotten myself killed. Who knows?"

"If you will remember, you almost did get yourself killed," Walt reminded her.

"Then maybe you should do this for Cheryl. Your cousin loved a good party." Adam grinned.

"Considering all that we've gone through, maybe we deserve a good party just to celebrate surviving this past year," Danielle said with a laugh.

"I'm always up for a party," Chris said.

"With Melony here, I suppose that will keep Adam out of trouble," Danielle teased.

Before Adam could respond, the doorbell rang. In the next moment Walt was by the parlor window, looking outside.

"It's those G-men," Walt told Chris and Danielle.

Danielle looked from Walt to Chris and then stood up. "I'll get the door."

After Danielle left the parlor, Walt by her side, Chris sat alone with Adam.

"So, Adam, what's the deal with you and Melony?"

"Honestly? I'm not really sure. Since I saw her last, we've been keeping in touch on the phone. But she never said anything about quitting her job. She's giving up good money in New York. I don't see how she can make near as much in Oregon, especially in Frederickport. It's not like she has any family money to fall back on. All Jolene left her was debt."

"Money isn't everything," Chris reminded him.

Adam laughed. "Says the multibillionaire."

TWELVE

There was nowhere to park in front of Marlow House. Chief MacDonald recognized three of the vehicles in front of the bed and breakfast. Adam Nichols was parked between Chris's vehicle and the dark sedan driven by Special Agents Wilson and Thomas. For a brief moment MacDonald entertained the idea of driving on and returning later, after Wilson and Thomas were gone. Instead, he made a U-turn and parked in front of Ian's house.

Sitting in the backseat of MacDonald's car was his youngest son, Evan, who waited for permission to unhook his seatbelt. Just as MacDonald got out of his car and made his way to the sidewalk, to let Evan out of the backseat, he heard someone calling his name. It was Lily. She was walking toward him from Ian's house.

"Looks like they're having a party over there," MacDonald greeted her with a nod toward Marlow House as he opened his back door.

"Did you come to visit Ian and me?" Lily asked with a grin, now standing on the sidewalk. She leaned down and waved into the car at Evan, who remained sitting in his booster seat while wrestling with the latch on his seatbelt.

"I'm here to see Walt!" Evan announced when he climbed out of the car.

Lily grinned and then placed a finger across her lips and said in a hushed voice, "You don't want to say that too loud; Ian might come out here at any moment."

"Oh, sorry." Evan blushed. He now stood on the sidewalk.

MacDonald slammed the car door shut. "I hope Ian doesn't mind if I park here."

Lily waved a hand dismissively. "Don't be silly." She glanced across the street. "But I am trying to figure out who the black car belongs to."

"Agents Wilson and Thomas, I'm pretty sure," MacDonald told her.

Lily looked back across the street at the dark sedan. "You mean those FBI guys?"

"Yes."

"What are they doing here?"

"I assume to question Danielle about the missing coins."

"That makes sense." Lily then pointed across the street. "Did you see what happened to Chris's car?"

Standing between Evan and Lily on the sidewalk, MacDonald looked across the street. He saw the smashed-in hood. "When did that happen?"

Evan spied an interesting bug along the edge of the sidewalk and knelt down to inspect it.

"Happened yesterday. It was parked where Adam's is now. Heather was driving down the street and plowed into it. The official story, she was dodging a dog who ran in front of her car."

"Official story?" MacDonald asked.

Lily glanced briefly to Ian's house to see if her boyfriend had come outside. She looked back to MacDonald and whispered, "Heather saw something on our roof."

"And?"

"The kind of thing she and Dani and Chris—" Lily glanced down at Evan, who was still on his knees, paying no attention to their conversation "—and Evan sometimes sees."

"A ghost?" MacDonald whispered.

"Either that or a leprechaun."

"SHE'S in the parlor with those FBI agents," Chris explained when

68

he opened the front door and let MacDonald and Evan into the house.

MacDonald glanced to the closed parlor door. "How long have they been here?"

"About twenty minutes. Adam's in the library. You want to go in there with us and wait, or are you going to barge in on them?" Chris asked.

"I'll go in the library with you guys."

"Where's Walt?" Evan asked Chris.

"I'm pretty sure he's in the parlor with Danielle," Chris answered in a whisper.

Evan let out a disappointed sigh.

Chris reached out and rustled Evan's hair. "But I understand there's a puppy in the library that just loves little boys."

Evan perked up. "Hunny's here?"

Chris nodded. "In the library."

Evan dashed off in front of them.

"Hi, Adam," MacDonald greeted when he walked into the room. Adam waved from his place on the sofa. Evan was already on the floor, playing with Hunny. MacDonald glanced to Chris and asked, "Where's all the guests? Joanne?"

"Joanne's in the kitchen, and I know a couple of the guests said something about going up to their room and packing. I think one group went down for a final walk on the beach. According to Danielle, all the current guests will be leaving by tomorrow," Chris explained.

"I guess you know Melony is moving back to town," Adam said when MacDonald took a seat near the desk.

"Can Hunny and I go see Joanne?" Evan interrupted.

MacDonald looked down at his son. "It's really cookies you're after, right?"

Evan grinned.

"Just don't give Hunny any cookies," Chris told him. "But Joanne has some dog treats out there. You can give her one of those."

MacDonald waved his hand toward the door. "Go."

Just as Evan reached the doorway, his father called out, "No more than two!"

Once Evan was out in the hallway, MacDonald looked at Adam and smiled. "That's what I hear. Have you heard from her?"

"I spoke to her about an hour ago. She was just getting on the plane. But she doesn't plan to get here until sometime Tuesday."

"She did mention something to me about staying over in Portland so she could go through some of the files from her dad's law firm," MacDonald said. They discussed Melony's move back to town, and then the conversation changed to the missing coins and the FBI agents now interviewing Danielle. They were discussing Chris's recently smashed car when the FBI agents were finished with Danielle.

"Hey, Chief, when did you get here?" Danielle asked when she entered the library.

MacDonald stood up and glanced at his watch, and then looked to the doorway Danielle had just walked through. "About twenty minutes ago. I should check on Evan—"

"Evan's okay." Danielle smiled. "I just ran into him in the hall. He and Hunny just went up to the attic—with Max." Chris didn't point out that the last time he had seen Max, the cat was napping in the living room. Plus, he seriously doubted Hunny would willingly go upstairs with Evan if Max was tagging along. He understood Evan and his pup were in truth going up to the attic with Walt.

MacDonald sat back down.

Adam cringed. "No offense, but that attic of yours creeps me out. Can't believe that kid likes it up there."

Danielle stifled a grin and sat down on the empty chair.

"Did Thomas and Wilson leave?" MacDonald asked.

"Yeah. I didn't realize you were here until right after they left and I ran into Evan coming out of the kitchen."

"So how did it go?" Chris asked. "Any news on the missing coins?"

Danielle shook her head. "Not really. They asked me a bunch of questions—like if I had insured the coins and the last time I saw them. They also grilled me about Susan Mitchell and how close we are."

"Susan? Why?" Adam asked.

"I think they wonder if Susan and I faked the robbery, but they haven't figured out our motive."

"They have to look at every angle," the chief pointed out.

"I suppose." Danielle let out a sigh. "But whenever I inherit anything, it always turns into a major pain in the butt."

"Well, I told you, you should have just let me keep the gold coins," Adam reminded her.

Danielle glanced over to Adam and smirked. "Well, they also asked me about you."

Adam's eyes widened. "Me? Why? What do I have to do with this?"

"They wanted to know about the people who felt they should have gotten the coins," Danielle explained.

"And you tossed me under the bus?" Adam fairly squeaked.

Danielle rolled her eyes. "No. In fact, I didn't even bring up your name. The only one I mentioned was Jolene, and she's dead. Then they brought up you and Bill."

"Bill?" Adam asked.

"They must have done their homework. They knew Bill was treasure hunting at Ian's house for the coins, and they knew you expressed an interest in them. But I explained your grandmother was the one who owned Ian's house, and she made her feelings about the coins very clear. I told them we were friends, and you wouldn't steal from me."

Wide eyed, Adam stared at Danielle. "You told them that?"

Danielle shrugged. "Well, I said I didn't think you would steal from me...*now*."

"Danielle, do you think we could talk in private for a minute?" MacDonald interrupted.

Curious, Danielle looked at the chief. "Sure. I guess..."

After Danielle and MacDonald left the parlor for the library, Chris said, "I wonder what that was about?"

"I just hope it's not about me," Adam grumbled. "Like I would know how to break in to a safe deposit box."

"SO THIS WASN'T JUST a friendly visit?" Danielle asked as she closed the door to the parlor.

"It's about the missing coins." MacDonald took a seat on the sofa and watched as Danielle sat on the chair across from him.

"I sort of figured."

"I assume Wilson and Thomas didn't tell you anything new?"

Danielle shrugged. "Not really. We talked a little bit about the security footage and how the camera moved off my safe deposit box for several minutes and then went back to its normal position. According to Thomas, this happened in the middle of the night, and they speculate there might have been an earthquake or something that caused it."

"Excuse me? An earthquake?"

Danielle's right hand absently toyed with her chair's arm as she explained her recent meeting with the FBI agents. "They said according to the footage captured from the other cameras, no one was in the vault at the time the camera moved. So they figure there must have been some movement under the bank, like an earthquake, that caused the lens to move."

"That's the most ridiculous thing I've ever heard. There was no earthquake that night."

Danielle's hand stopped fiddling with the chair's arm. Looking up at the chief, she folded her hands on her lap. "I know that. But I think they're just trying to figure out what happened to that camera. I got the feeling they're having the video analyzed to see if anyone manipulated it—the one aimed at the entrance to the vault area. But in the meantime, they're taking a closer look at me. I get it. It is annoying. But I suppose I understand. This entire thing makes no sense."

"The reason I wanted to talk to you alone—I couldn't really ask you this in front of Adam."

"What?"

"This may sound crazy, but is there any chance a ghost might be responsible for the missing coins?"

Danielle cocked her head. "Ghost? You think a ghost cleaned out the safe deposit box?"

MacDonald slumped back on the sofa. "I know it sounds crazy. But something moved that camera, and I don't believe it was an imaginary earthquake. And there was nothing captured on the other cameras for that time frame."

"I suppose—technically speaking—a ghost could do that. Walt can move objects, so I don't see why a ghost couldn't turn a lock without a key and even levitate the coins. But why bother moving the camera? It's not like you can film a ghost. And even if you could, what are you going to do, put him in jail?"

"Maybe he doesn't know he's a ghost?" MacDonald suggested.

"That is entirely possible." Danielle considered it a moment. "Can you imagine if a ghost really is responsible for emptying that box, and they didn't bother moving the camera? Imagine what Wilson and Thomas would be thinking right now if they saw that box open on its own and gold coins floating out."

With a quiet yet serious voice, MacDonald said, "The problem is, Danielle, I don't doubt for a moment you put those coins in the safe deposit box, just like you said you did. But if I didn't know you, quite frankly, you'd be my prime suspect."

No longer smiling, Danielle stared at the chief. "Are you serious?"

"Think about it. Unless they discover the video to the entrance to the vault was tampered with, then no one could have possibly emptied that box. Even if someone at the bank had a copy of your safe deposit key along with the bank's, there is nothing on those videos that indicates anyone opened your safe deposit box from the time you rented it to yesterday."

"But you said yourself someone moved the camera. It's possible the gold was taken then."

"True. But only if it was something like a—ghost."

Danielle considered his words for a moment. With a frown, she looked squarely at MacDonald. "It can't be a ghost. Someone obviously tampered with the video."

"Why do you say that?"

"For one thing, even if the camera couldn't record a ghost, the same isn't true for the gold. None of those cameras captured the gold mysteriously floating out of the vault. And then there is the shamrock. Whoever took the gold left a shamrock. How did they get the shamrock through the door into the vault without being detected?"

THIRTEEN

Danielle stood with Lily by the front gate of Marlow House as the last of the guests drove away. Behind them the front door was open, and just inside the house stood Walt, who smoked a cigar and waited for Lily and Danielle to return to the house. Max had followed the two young women outside and now wove back and forth around their feet, gently nudging each of their legs.

"It was a good group," Danielle said as she reached down to stroke Max's ears. He stopped, started purring, and leaned into her hand.

"Yes, it was, but I really thought we were going to have a break until Friday. I didn't expect a last minute reservation, much less two of them."

"Hey, was that your last guest leaving?" a voice called out.

Danielle and Lily looked up the sidewalk. It was Heather, walking in their direction.

"Yes, everyone's checked out," Danielle said when Heather reached them.

"Do you know if Chris is home?" Heather asked, looking down the street toward his house.

"No, he's at his office," Danielle told her. "He stopped by earlier and had coffee on his way there. He has some meeting this morning. But I'm glad you stopped by. He wanted me to talk to you about the car."

74

Heather groaned and slouched dejectedly. "That's what I wanted to talk to him about."

"When he was here this morning," Danielle began, "he told me to tell you to take your car to that body shop downtown across from the grocery store. He's already talked to them. Just take it down there, and say Chris Johnson sent you."

"Danielle, I can't afford to get my car fixed. I'm just going to have to live with it that way for a while. But I wanted to ask Chris if there was any way we could work out some sort of payment plan for his car." Heather shifted her weight from her right foot to her left. "If I file an insurance claim, they're going to drop me."

"Chris is paying for the repairs," Danielle told her. "Just take your car down there, and they will take care of you."

Heather frowned at Danielle. "Why in the world would he do that? I'm the one who ran into his car."

"Well, for one reason, you did sort of save our lives," Danielle reminded her.

"Yes, there was that." Lily laughed.

"Not to mention the accident really wasn't your fault," Danielle pointed out.

Standing up straighter, Heather looked from Lily to Danielle. "Are you serious? He really wants to do this?"

"Sure. Frankly, I was going to offer to fix your car for you if Chris hadn't," Danielle told her. "After all, that annoying ghost was on my roof."

"Oh, thank you, Danielle!" Heather impulsively grabbed Danielle in a bear hug and squeezed, stepping on poor Max's tail as she did. The cat let out a loud screech and then took off running to the front door.

Heather released Danielle and looked up to where Max had run off to. Sheepishly she said, "Oh, sorry about that. I hope Max's okay."

Danielle glanced to the house and then back to Heather. "I'm sure he's fine."

Heather looked up to Danielle's bedroom window. "Any more ghost sightings?"

"Hush, you two," Lily hissed under her breath. "Ian is on his way over here. No ghost talk." Lily waved to Ian, who was now jogging across the street in their direction, Sadie by his side.

CROUCHED BEHIND A ROSEBUSH, concealing himself, he watched as the man ran across the street with the big yellow dog. *That dog.* It was the dog's fault he had been separated from his gold. Since the pair had moved into the house, he was unable to come and go as he had always done. And now, the gold was missing. But not for long. He would return it to its rightful place, but first, he needed to do something about the dog. What exactly, he didn't know.

Looking across the street, his gaze moved to the upstairs window of Marlow House. He thought of the woman he had found sleeping in Walt Marlow's bedroom.

"I wonder who she is? What is she doing there?" he asked himself. He then remembered how the same woman had removed a necklace from a wall safe.

"The necklace," he murmured. "Where have I seen it before?"

He thought about it a moment and then smiled. "I suppose it doesn't matter. I'll get it too and keep it with my gold." Looking to the house where the man now lived with his dog, he thought about his hiding place.

Moving from outside into the house, he went to the guest room and watched as the closet door slowly opened. Kneeling down, he pulled a tool from his leather apron and used it to pry open the floorboard, exposing the empty space.

"This was a good hiding place for many years, but they'll just find it again if I put it here. And now, now I need to find somewhere suitable for the necklace." Returning the floorboard to its place, he used the tool to hammer the nail back into its hole. Standing up, he looked around the room.

Returning the tool to his leather apron, he said, "I suppose if I can't figure out how to get rid of that dog, I might as well find another hiding place." In the next moment he vanished.

DAVE WATCHED as Stephanie fitted the wig on her head. After she turned to him, he let out a low whistle. "Damn, your mother wouldn't recognize you."

Stephanie smiled and made a quick model's turn to show off her entire transformation.

Again Dave whistled, his attention on her backside. "That's an impressive bootie you have there."

Stephanie laughed and then reached back and gave her padded buttocks a pat. "Anyone can pad a bra, but no woman really wants a butt this size. But the trick is really in the makeup. My real complexion would never go with this wig color."

"I don't really care how you do it, but you're the best."

Leaning to Dave, she dropped a kiss on his lips. When she pulled away, he frowned.

"Are you taller?" he asked.

She giggled and lifted up one of her feet, twisting it at the ankle so he could have a better look at the jogging shoe. "It's these shoes. Makes me two inches taller. And with the length of these jeans, no one will notice." She put her foot back down on the floor.

He shook his head, still looking down at her feet. "They have jogging shoes that make you taller?"

With a shrug she said, "Technically speaking, these are not really for jogging. Not unless I want to break my ankle. But they are supposed to look like athletic shoes—for short women who want to look taller."

"Where do you come up with this stuff?"

Stephanie grinned and gave him another quick kiss. "You don't tell me how you open safes, and I don't tell you my secrets. That way you'll need me."

Dave laughed as he reached out and pulled her to him. Wrapping his arms around her, he kissed her mouth. When the kiss ended, he whispered against her cheek, "I will always need you, baby."

When he finally released her, he walked over to the desk and pulled out the top drawer, removing a tattered cigar box. Setting it on the desk, he opened it. Inside were several fake IDs, along with a credit card.

Picking up the credit card, he said, "We know what aliases we need to use this time." He briefly held up the card, then dropped it back on the desktop.

"Are you sure the credit card is still good?"

Dave nodded and picked it up again, looking at it. "I used it to rent the room at Marlow House. And I called Alan this morning to double-check on the available balance. We only need to use it one more time, to rent the car. After that, we can just use cash."

"Then let me do my magic on you, and then we can take the pictures and you can finish making the IDs. You know, you really don't need to make one for me. After all, the only time we're going to use it is to rent the car."

Dave stood up and tossed the credit card back on the desk. "No, we're going to do this right. And it's entirely possible we'll both be asked to show our IDs when we check into that bed and breakfast. I don't want to give this Boatman any reason to be suspicious of us. If she is, she'll never let her guard down."

SPECIAL AGENT WILSON sat across the desk from the bank manager, Alan Kissinger.

"Our people have finished going through the security videos," Wilson told him.

"And are you confident now they haven't been tampered with?" Kissinger asked.

"Let's assume for a moment they weren't tampered with. Do you have any idea what might have happened to the contents of Ms. Boatman's safe deposit box?"

"Like I said before, I have no personal knowledge of what she left in that box when she rented it."

"So you are saying you believe the gold coins were never in the box?"

"I'm just saying they weren't there when she opened it on Saturday. And I wasn't even at the bank on the day she rented the box, so I can't say if she put anything in there or not."

"Let's assume she did put the coins in the safe deposit box. After all, your own employee was adamant that the box was quite heavy when she locked it in its vault. Since none of the security videos we reviewed showed anyone leaving the vault area with a package large enough to hold those coins, in the timeframe beginning from when Ms. Boatman first rented it to Saturday, I have to wonder, could they perhaps have been moved into another nearby safe deposit box?"

"Are you suggesting someone in the bank found a way to access that box, opened it, and then moved its contents?"

"I'm simply considering all possibilities. Do any of your bank employees have a safe deposit box in that area?"

"If something like that happened, exactly how did this employee get into the vault undetected?" Alan asked.

"We know the camera mysteriously moved for several minutes, leaving that area near Boatman's safe deposit box no longer in view. It could have happened then, which is why I asked if any of the bank employees have a safe deposit box in that area."

"You also said none of the cameras detected anyone coming in or out of the vault area during the time frame."

"Something moved that camera," Wilson reminded him.

"I'm sure it was something like a minor earthquake tremor," Alan suggested.

"We have considered that."

"Then why all these questions? I thought you already determined none of the other cameras or videos were tampered with?"

Wilson arched his brows. "Did I say that?"

Alan stared at the special agent for a few minutes. Finally, he asked in a quiet voice, "What do you want from me?"

Wilson smiled. "You could start with the information I asked about; do any of the bank employees have a safe deposit box in that area?"

FOURTEEN

"The anniversary celebration is less than two weeks away," Lily reminded Danielle on Tuesday morning. "This isn't like you to put things off."

Danielle poured herself a cup of coffee. It was her third cup that morning. She paused for a moment, asking herself if filling up with caffeine was a terrific idea. But then she shrugged and added milk to the cup. "I didn't even agree to have one until this past weekend."

"Exactly. And it's Tuesday already. We don't have much time. And when I ask you about the plans, you say, *I haven't thought about it.*"

Danielle shrugged and took her cup to the kitchen table and sat down. "Well, I haven't. Whatever we do, it won't be as big as last year's. More low key. And anyway, technically speaking, we missed our first-year anniversary. We moved in June tenth."

"You know it isn't the same thing." Lily grabbed the last piece of coffee cake, set it on a napkin, and poured herself a glass a milk. She took them to the table and joined Danielle. "I have an idea for the open house, but we'd need to get an ad in the paper this week."

"What is it?"

After Lily shared her idea, Danielle said, "I like it. Sorry I've been such a flake about this. Too many distractions lately."

"The gold coins?"

Danielle wrinkled her nose. "Partly. But it's not like losing the coins impacts my standard of living. I mean seriously, those sorta fell out of the sky and have been nothing but a pain in the butt. It would have been nice to donate the money to a good cause. I suppose if anything, I'm curious about what happened to them."

"What else is distracting you?" Lily asked.

"I bet it's the leprechaun," Walt said when he suddenly appeared by the table.

Danielle looked up at Walt and smiled. "I thought you said there were no such things as leprechauns?"

Walt shrugged and took a seat. Lily watched as the seemingly empty chair next to her moved out from the table and then scooted slightly back in.

"Morning, Walt," Lily said as she nibbled her coffee cake.

Walt reached over and lifted Lily's glass of milk up off the table, as if to say hello. She watched the glass rise and set back down. Grinning at Walt's place, she put another piece of cake in her mouth.

"No, I don't believe in leprechauns. But you know I'm not fond of the term ghost. So for this palooka, we can agree to call him a leprechaun."

"Does Walt think this guy is a leprechaun now? What next? Are unicorns real too?"

Walt shook his head at Lily. "Did she just compare me to a unicorn?"

"No, Lily, Walt didn't say they're real. He just has that ghost fetish." Danielle reached over and snatched a hunk of coffee cake from Lily's napkin.

"Doesn't fetish mean he likes something?" Lily asked.

"Then a fetish for loathing the word," Danielle suggested. "Whoever this character dressed up in a Saint Patrick's Day costume is, I'd like to figure out what his deal is so he would move on."

"When are your guests arriving? You said there are two couples?" Walt asked.

Danielle set her cup on the table and leaned back in the chair. "They're supposed to be here by noon. I told Joanne she didn't have to come in today, since their rooms are ready."

"So what's the deal with these two? Typically, our guests don't make reservations on a Sunday for a Tuesday," Lily asked.

"One of them told me they had already made a reservation through a private party to rent their house for the week. But then on

Friday they had some plumbing issue, and it won't be fixed until next week. They didn't want to cancel, since they already put in their time at work."

"You said both couples are from Portland?" Lily asked.

"Yes." Danielle picked up her cup and finished the last of her coffee. She then set it back down on the table. "The other couple is celebrating their anniversary, and it sounded like they're not big on planning ahead."

"Like you and the open house?" Lily smirked.

IT WAS NOT QUITE ELEVEN a.m. when the doorbell rang. Danielle assumed it was probably the first of her guests to arrive. But when she swung the door open, she was pleasantly surprised to find Melony Jacobs standing on her doorstep, holding a cardboard file box in her arms.

The attractive blonde's hair was carelessly clipped atop her head, and she didn't appear to be wearing a smidgen of makeup. In spite of that, she looked utterly lovely, and if Danielle wasn't a self-confident woman, she might have experienced a flash of jealousy.

Instead, Danielle quickly ushered Melony inside, and as soon as the woman set the box on the floor, the two hugged in greeting.

"Adam told me you were moving back," Danielle said with a smile. "Welcome home. You just missed Lily. She and Ian drove over to Astoria today."

Melony leaned down and picked up the box. "There will be plenty of time to visit with them later, since I'll be staying," Melony said with a grin, now holding the box in her arms again.

Danielle nodded to the cardboard container. "What's in there?"

"It's for you. It belonged to Brianna Boatman."

Five minutes later, Melony and Danielle were in the library, with Walt watching silently from the sidelines. The cardboard box sat on the library desk.

"Adam mentioned you were going through boxes from your father's law firm. But I thought everything to do with my aunt's estate was already removed from storage."

"That's what I thought too," Melony said as she removed the box's lid. "I don't really think you're going to find anything significant in here—I mean nothing like information on secret bank

82

accounts or property she owned. I already looked through it. It appears to be personal stuff. There are some photographs and a few letters from your aunt to Clarence. I just skimmed the letters, but they didn't really say much. Not even sure why Clarence held onto this. I have to assume he got some of it after she died, like the photographs."

Danielle reached into the file box and pulled out a small white cardboard box with a flapping lid. She opened it. The box was empty save for a slip of paper. Closing the box, she took a second look and noticed *AncestryDNA* printed in green type across the lid.

"Now that was the strangest thing in your aunt's box. I almost tossed it out, but then I noticed the email address and what appears to be a password written on that piece of paper." Melony took the box from Danielle and opened it. After removing the slip of paper, she handed it to Danielle to show her what she was talking about.

Taking the paper in her hand, Danielle read the email address. She didn't recognize it. But the second word could possibly be a password, as Melony suspected. It read *Brianna1234*.

"Whenever I see an email address next to a word with numbers attached, I automatically think it's for some Internet account," Melony told her. "I could be wrong. But I do know what the box is." She handed it back to Danielle, who looked at it again.

"What?"

"It's the box Ancestry.com sends you when you order one of their DNA tests. I know. My mother did one. She told me about it. After she died, I found it in her things. You see, they send you this little box with some kind of bottle that you spit in. Then you mail it back, and they run your DNA test."

"Sounds gross. But actually, I've considered doing one of these myself. Do you think my aunt had a DNA test done before she died?"

Melony shrugged and then sat down on the desk chair. "If it wasn't for the paper inside, I would assume it was just a box. Maybe someone in Clarence's office had it sitting around and used it to store something in. But the fact it held a piece of paper with an email address and what appears to be a password—one using your aunt's first name—I do wonder if it's the password to your aunt's Ancestry.com account."

"I don't think these things have been around that long, have they?" Danielle asked.

"What do you mean?"

"My aunt's been gone for almost a year and a half now. And before that she had Alzheimer's. I can't believe she'd be capable of ordering something like this online. Was the site even offering DNA tests back then?"

"Well, all you can do is try logging into Ancestry.com using that email address and password. If you can't log in, then maybe it's just a cardboard box and someone's random email address. All this is an educated guess on my part."

"You didn't happen to ask Gloria Comings about the things in this box, did you?" Danielle asked.

Gloria Comings had worked for Clarence Renton and had left the state after his arrest. Melony's father, Doug Carmichael, had been Renton's business partner. After Doug passed away, his widow, Jolene Carmichael, continued to own a share in the law practice. But now, both Jolene and Renton were dead—both murdered. Melony was now responsible for sorting through what remained in storage.

"Gloria?" Melony scoffed. "She refuses to answer my calls anymore. The last time I spoke to her she was pretty short with me. Said she had no idea what Clarence had been up to and told me to stop calling her."

"According to Adam, Gloria was always pretty conservative. He never felt she knew what Renton had been doing."

"Like Adam, I went to school with Gloria. We ran in different crowds. But Adam is right, back then she was pretty uptight." Melony giggled. "I was the wild child."

Danielle put the slip of paper back in its box and closed the lid. She returned it to the larger cardboard container. "I'm not sure what I will do with all this, but it will be interesting going through it, especially the photographs. Thanks for bringing it to me."

"No problem. I didn't want to just toss it."

"So tell me, how did your mother's DNA test work out? Did you find out you're related to royalty?" Danielle teased.

"You mean as opposed to having a great-grandfather responsible for massacring a boatload of innocent people?"

Danielle cringed. "Oh, sorry, Mel, I wasn't thinking."

Melony smiled and reached out, gently patting Danielle's arm. "Oh, that's okay. I figure we probably all have a monster in our family tree. Mine just happens to be someone my mother adored."

"Maybe that's why your mother did the DNA test, to see if she could find something to offset her grandfather's legacy."

"You may have a point. I know she had it done after all that happened. But I don't think she lived to see the results. I remember her telling me about taking the test, and finding the empty box in her things after she died."

"That's kind of sad, she took the test and you can't see the results?"

"Well, I can if I want, I just haven't bothered."

"What do you mean?" Danielle asked.

"It's why I suspect that email and password is for an Ancestry.com account. That's how it works. You log in to your account to get your results. Mom's results are probably sitting there in her account, but I just haven't looked yet. I will someday. But I just haven't gotten around to it."

The doorbell rang. Danielle looked up at Melony. "That's probably some of my guests arriving."

Melony stood up. "Well, I need to get going anyway. I came straight here when I got into town. I promised Adam I would stop by his office when I got in Frederickport, so if I hurry up, maybe I can get him to buy me lunch."

FIFTEEN

Danielle woke up early on Wednesday morning to prepare breakfast. The previous evening, when chatting with her guests, she asked them how they felt about quiche. None of them objected to a breakfast of quiche and fresh fruit, so that was what she decided to prepare the next morning.

After all the breakfast food was set on the dining room table, Danielle took a seat on one end of the table while Lily took a seat on the opposite end. On one side of the table sat the Hortons, and on the other side sat the Spicers.

It was not unusual for Marlow House guests who arrived as strangers to strike up a friendship. Over Christmas, the guests had become family. Danielle suspected a friendship might develop between the two couples now staying under her roof, considering the fact they appeared to be about the same age, and if Danielle didn't know better, she would wonder if the two women were sisters. Both were redheads, about the same height, and both had a prominent backside. Danielle glanced down the table at Lily, who was also a redhead. However, she did not have a prominent backside; her prominence was more along the bustline.

"Did you make this from scratch?" Nola Horton asked as she took a second helping of quiche.

Danielle smiled at Nola. "Yes. I hope you like it."

"I must," Nola said with a laugh. "I'm having a second helping."

Danielle flashed her another smile and picked up her glass of juice. "I'm glad you're enjoying it."

"It's just delicious. But I've been wanting to ask you, are you a socialist?"

Danielle almost choked on her juice. After surviving the drink, she paused and looked back to Nola. "Excuse me? What do you mean a socialist?"

Nola shrugged. "I was just wondering since your blog talked about how you've given away so much of your inheritance, but you're still running a B and B and making breakfast for your guests. I just wondered if it was some sort of political ideology of yours." Nola took a bite of her quiche.

"What blog are you talking about?" Danielle asked with a frown.

"Your Mystery of Marlow House blog, of course," Nola said after she swallowed her food.

Danielle and Lily exchanged quick glances.

"You've read that?" Danielle asked.

"Of course, why do you think we wanted to stay here?"

"Very clever marketing," Albert Horton noted, raising his cup of coffee in salute to Danielle before taking a sip.

"I agree. We read it too. Very interesting. I wondered if it was all true," Jeannie Spicer said.

Danielle set her juice glass on the table and picked up her napkin. She wiped off the corners of her mouth and then said, "Actually, it's not my blog. In fact, I just recently became aware of it. I have no idea who's behind it."

"So none of it's true?" Jeannie asked.

"What do you mean?" Danielle asked.

"About being trapped in a house on Halloween and just escaping before it burned down. Or being falsely accused of murdering that man?" Jeannie asked.

Lily spoke up. "I came across the blog the other day. I read through it. I don't know who's behind it, but the information posted is fairly accurate."

"Then you have a fan," Blake Spicer said with a chortle. "Or a stalker."

Danielle cringed. "It is a little creepy."

"So back to my original question," Nola said. "Are you a socialist?"

"Nola," Albert hissed under his breath, "it really isn't any of your business."

Nola looked at her husband and frowned. "Why?"

"I don't mind answering the question if you don't mind telling me why you would wonder if I'm a socialist," Danielle asked.

"Just the fact you don't seem to like money," Nola explained.

"What makes you think that?"

"You said that blog was accurate, and they talk about how you keep giving all your money away. I just wondered if you were a socialist. Maybe you find capitalists sinful?"

Danielle chuckled. "Actually, I have a degree in marketing—and my late husband and I owned our own marketing agency. I'd have to say that tends to give me a capitalist bent. But I like to think of myself as a compassionate capitalist. And frankly, I didn't do anything to earn my inheritances. And there is only so much money one person really needs. As for running Marlow House, I enjoy meeting new people, and I enjoy cooking."

"A woman's place is in the kitchen," Blake blurted.

Danielle smiled at Blake. "Only if that's where she wants to be."

"AT LEAST WE won't upset Ms. Boatman when we take her necklace," Dave said in a whisper when he and Stephanie returned to their room after breakfast.

"What are you talking about?" Stephanie stood by the dresser mirror and turned to the side, looking at the reflection of her body's profile. Reaching back, she grabbed hold of the portion of her blue jeans covering her buttocks and repositioned it.

"She just told us she doesn't care about money. That there's only so much she really needs. So she won't be too upset when we relieve her of that necklace. We might even be doing her a favor." He laughed.

"The Missing Thorndike. You think it's cursed?" Stephanie turned to face the mirror. Leaning forward, she looked at her reflection and began repairing her makeup.

"Missing Thorndike?"

"Yeah. I told you that's what it's called. I read about it online. The necklace you're stealing."

"Keep your voice down," he snapped.

"Hey, you brought it up," she reminded him, still fussing with her makeup.

Dave sat down on the edge of the bed. "I know. But we need to keep our voices down. You don't need to scream."

"I wasn't screaming," she snapped. "But you didn't answer my question. Do you think it's cursed?"

"Why would you ask that?"

Stephanie turned from the dresser and faced Dave. "Well, think about it. According to the stories, that actress died not long after someone stole its original diamonds and emeralds. And then that Marlow dude stole the necklace and he was murdered. And Danielle's own cousin was murdered after she stole the necklace."

"Are you suggesting I could get murdered when I take it?"

Stephanie shrugged. "I don't know. But it does make one wonder."

"WHAT ARE you doing in here on such a beautiful day?" Walt asked when he appeared in Danielle's bedroom later that morning.

She sat on her bed with the laptop on her knees. "I wanted some privacy."

"Should I leave?"

Danielle looked up at Walt and smiled. "No. I meant from our guests." She scooted over on the bed, silently extending an invitation for Walt to join her. In the next moment, they sat side by side on the bed, each leaning back on the pile of pillows at the headboard.

"You couldn't find privacy outside in the sunshine? I was just looking out my window and it truly is a magnificent day. I envy you the ability to go outside and feel the sunshine on your face."

"You're sounding a bit like a romantic right now."

"Perhaps." Walt kicked off his shoes. They disappeared before dropping to the mattress. "So what are you looking up?"

"Remember that box from the DNA test?"

"Of course. That was just yesterday. I find the science of DNA fascinating. I am constantly amazed at the strides taken in science since I died."

"You know how I told you I wanted to see if Brianna had taken a DNA test?"

Walt nodded. "Yes."

"Yesterday, I didn't get a chance to go online and try logging in using the email and password from the box."

"Our new guests did keep you occupied most of yesterday afternoon and evening."

"And when I finally got to bed, I was too exhausted, so I thought I'd do it today when I had a chance. And here I am."

"Ahh, you're doing some sleuthing? Continue. I'm curious to see what you find out."

"Actually, I'm done. I was just about to put my laptop away and track you down so I could tell you what I found." She closed her laptop.

Walt glanced down at it. "Are you finished with your computer?"

"Yes, why?"

Instead of answering the question, the laptop lifted up from the bed and floated to the table next to the bedroom sofa.

Danielle grinned. "Gee, thanks, Walt."

He shrugged. "No problem. So tell me, what did you find?"

Danielle turned so she could look at Walt. "Melony was right. Brianna1234 was a password. I went to Ancestry.com and was able to log in to an account using the email address on that piece of paper."

"So your aunt had an account at this Ancestry dot com site?"

"No. The account was registered to Clarence Renton. But the only family tree in the account was my aunt's. The only people on her tree were Brianna and her mother."

"Really?"

"It appears the test kit was ordered after Aunt Brianna was in the care home, already diagnosed with Alzheimer's. In fact, from what I know about her illness, she was pretty out of it by then. According to the site, Aunt Brianna's saliva was received at the lab the same week she died. So she never saw the results. But even if she had, she wouldn't have understood them."

Walt frowned. "Why would Renton have her DNA tested?"

"I have no idea."

"If we're trying to figure out Renton's motive for having Brianna's DNA tested, perhaps we should first ask why do most people have their DNA tested?" Walt asked.

"To build their family trees. To find family members."

"Perhaps that's it."

Danielle frowned. "What do you mean?"

"Remember when Renton was surprised you had a cousin? He thought you were her only family?"

"Sure. But I don't know what that has to do with anything. Cheryl and I were only related to Aunt Brianna by marriage. Even if we had our DNA tested and were in the data bank, it wouldn't have showed up as possible family members in Aunt Brianna's results." Danielle paused a moment, and then added, "That's not entirely true. If Renton had included Aunt Brianna's husband on the tree, it could have led to Cheryl—and to me. But he already knew about me. So obviously, he was only concerned with blood relatives."

"I suspect Renton wanted to make sure there weren't other family members who were going to suddenly appear and make a claim on the property. He obviously felt he could deal with one niece, but more than that—especially a blood relative—it would complicate his plans. Look at what he did with Cheryl when she showed up."

Danielle leaned back against the pillows and stared up to the ceiling. "It could possibly help him find some cousin or maybe a sibling."

"You're suggesting Renton was looking for any children from her father—half siblings?"

Danielle looked at Walt. "It's entirely possible she had some. I would be surprised if she didn't. Unfortunately, nothing showed up on her results that might lead to possible siblings."

"Does that mean she doesn't have any?" Walt asked.

"Not necessarily. Just means no one from that branch of the tree is currently in the data bank. It would have been kind of neat had the test results led to her father." Danielle sighed and leaned back against the pillows.

"Old Sullivan knew who the father was. I would bet on it," Walt murmured.

"That's right, Sullivan. With all that's been going on lately, I forgot about him."

SIXTEEN

"I really don't have time, Mother," Joyce Pruitt insisted.

Joyce's mother, whom her children referred to as Gran, angrily smacked the side of her wheelchair with a cane. While she no longer used her cane to help her walk, she liked to keep it handy so she could give her chair a good whack should the occasion arise. This was one such occasion. "What do you mean you don't have time? It will take you maybe ten minutes out of your *busy* day."

Joyce groaned. "I have two houses to clean today."

"And I want you to empty that safe deposit box today! If someone hasn't already done it."

"I don't think anyone wants your papers, Mother."

"What about my father's iron bookends? He made those himself!"

"No one wants those ugly things."

"How do you know what they want? And if you think they're so worthless, then why pay to keep them in a safe deposit box?"

"Because, Mother, that's what *you* wanted."

"And *now* I want them here, with me."

"Fine," Joyce said as she angrily snatched her purse from the coatrack.

"Don't you forget the key!" Gran shouted at Joyce, who was now heading to the door.

"I already have it, Mother."

"I HAVE TO SAY, I haven't opened so many safe deposit boxes in my entire time at the bank as I have in the last two days," Susan whispered to Joyce as she watched her sign the ledger.

Joyce handed Susan back her pen. "I bet, since that article came out in the paper on Monday."

"Yep."

"Has anything else been reported missing?" Joyce asked.

"Well, if anyone had reported anything, I couldn't say." Susan glanced around the bank and then leaned closer to Joyce and whispered, "But since nothing else has been reported missing, I guess I can tell you that." Both women giggled.

"So just Danielle Boatman's gold coins?" Joyce asked in a hushed voice as she followed Susan into the vault area.

"Apparently." Susan shrugged. "It's a mystery for sure."

A moment later Joyce handed Susan her key. She watched as the other woman opened the safe deposit box. After handing Joyce the key back, Susan slid the box from the vault.

With a grunt, Susan said, "Lord, this is heavy!"

"It's those stupid iron bookends."

"They weigh a ton," Susan said as she handed Joyce the box. "Those must be some hefty bookends."

"They are." Joyce frowned after Susan handed her the box. It felt much heavier than she remembered, but she said nothing.

Joyce followed Susan to a private room, where she left her to sort through the safe deposit box alone. What Joyce didn't realize, she was not alone. Standing next to her was what appeared to be a man wearing a green derby hat. However, Joyce could not see him any more than Lily could see Walt.

"What a pain, Mother," Joyce grumbled. "I hope you don't expect me to put these things out on the bookshelf."

Flipping open the safe deposit box lid, Joyce let out a startled gasp when her eyes fixed on its contents. Instead of just her mother's iron bookends and small stack of papers filling up a fourth of the container, gold coins packed the metal box, filling it to the rim. Joyce knew instantly they were the missing gold coins from Danielle Boatman's safe deposit box. *But how did they get in here?* she wondered.

Nervously looking over her shoulder to the entrance of the small room, she moved quickly and closed the door completely, securing her privacy. Returning to the box sitting on the table, her eyes widened as she gazed at the glittering coins—which from all accounts were valued at over a million dollars.

Taking a deep breath, she dipped her hands into the unexpected treasure, scooping a handful of the coins from the box and then letting them slip through her fingers.

She began to laugh and then asked the room, "Can you imagine if Mother had insisted I bring her today? She'd already be stuffing them in her purse. As if Mother needs any more money. Hell, she doesn't spend a dime of what she already has."

She stared at the coins. "Danielle doesn't really need this any more than Mother does. I don't even think she cares it went missing. I bet she had it insured," Joyce murmured.

Removing one of the gold coins, she held it up to have a closer look. "And to think, if that guy hadn't hidden this in the Hemming house, it would have been melted years ago."

Dropping the coin back in the box, she glanced behind her at the closed door. Susan would be returning soon. Joyce looked down at the large canvas bag. It was her bag she normally used for hauling groceries, and she kept it in her car. She had brought it in the bank with her, not because she felt she needed a bag to carry a few papers and the bookends, but she didn't want anyone seeing her carrying the ugly things. She wondered, *Will the canvas bag be sturdy enough to carry the coins? Can I fit them all in?*

Closing her eyes, Joyce thought about her mother, Agatha Pine. Since Joyce's divorce, her mother had lived with her. After Joyce's husband had taken off, Agatha had talked her into moving to Frederickport—Agatha's home town. Agatha had moved from Frederickport after marrying Joyce's father, and she had always wanted to move back.

Joyce assumed the arrangement would provide her with child care while she sought work. She was also hoping her mother would help with the household expenses. She would need help, since her deadbeat husband had disappeared, never making one child support payment.

The living arrangement had not worked out as Joyce originally imagined. Once Agatha moved in, she made it very clear she didn't intend to do any of the cooking or cleaning.

"I've cooked and cleaned all my life, and it's time someone else did it for me," Agatha had told her daughter.

When asked to chip in and help pay some of the household expenses, Agatha had said, "Why should I do that? You'll be getting all of my money soon enough. It's not as if having me live with you is costing you extra."

Joyce's children were all grown now and living on their own. The only time they visited was to placate Gran, who was adept at keeping her grandchildren in line, frequently reminding them all how easy it would be to write them out of the will should any of them step out of line or take their grandmother for granted.

In their attempt to stay on the good side of their grandmother, Joyce's children—three sons and a daughter—often neglected their mother. The house they had grown up in—which Joyce had slaved long hours to keep—was in dire need of repair, which she could not afford to do.

Joyce had no savings. Any extra money had been spent helping her oldest three children attend college, and her youngest to get out of jail. Whenever she asked her mother for any assistance, it was always the same response: *You will get my money soon enough.*

Opening her eyes, Joyce looked at the coins. She imagined herself simply disappearing. She could go to Europe. Joyce always dreamed of traveling abroad. Or perhaps Hawaii? All Joyce's friends had been to Hawaii. The farthest Joyce had ever traveled was to Anaheim, California, when she had saved to take her children to Disneyland. Agatha had insisted on going along, yet it was Joyce who had paid for the entire vacation.

Joyce imagined her mother would be okay. After all, her grandchildren would eagerly be waiting on the old woman hand and foot, especially now that Joyce was no longer in the will. And Joyce had no doubt her mother would quickly write her out of the will. But what would she care? She would have over a million dollars.

Smiling, Joyce opened the canvas bag and quickly filled it with the gold coins. When she got to the bottom of the box, she found her mother's papers and the iron bookends. Reluctantly, she added the bookends and papers to the bag. Joyce understood she couldn't disappear right away. First, she needed to find out how to sell the coins. Perhaps she would sell them a little bit at a time, disposing of them at coin shops.

HE FOLLOWED the woman out of the bank. No one paid any attention to her as she protectively clutched the large canvas bag to her chest. At one point, she almost dropped it when opening the trunk of her car. Had that happened, coins would have spilled out and rolled into the street, causing a spectacle. He managed to intervene, and she lost not a single coin as she put them in her car. She stood at the back of the vehicle for a moment, the trunk still open, and removed two iron objects from atop the coins, along with some papers. She set them next to the canvas bag on the floor of the car and then closed the trunk.

After she got into the driver's side of the vehicle, he sat on the passenger seat. Together they drove around town. After about thirty minutes, he thought, *She has no idea where she's going. She must be looking for somewhere to hide the gold.*

When she finally stopped, it was in the driveway in front of a residential house. He assumed it was her home and wondered why she left the gold in the back of her car. But when he followed her inside the house, it didn't look as if anyone lived there. While there was furniture, it was covered in sheets, and in the kitchen, cabinets were torn up, as if under construction. He watched as she removed a key from a hook on the wall and then dashed out of the house and climbed into the car again. She backed out of the driveway and drove down the street.

Not far from the house, she pulled over and parked the car. Turning off the ignition, she sat there a moment, seemingly contemplating her next move. He looked out the front windshield. They were not far from the beach. After a few minutes, she got out of the vehicle.

He followed her as she removed the bag from the trunk of the car and then headed toward the ocean.

"Please tell me you don't plan to toss it in the sea," he said. She didn't hear him.

He followed her down a winding path from the road, leading toward the ocean. Halfway down the path, he spied a row of six shacks along the edge of the beach. By their size, he doubted anyone lived in them, they were too small. He imagined they were used for storage.

When the woman reached the sixth shack, she set the canvas bag on the ground and removed a key from her pocket. It was the key she had taken from the house. She quickly unlocked the shack's padlock and then picked up the canvas bag before entering the hut.

He followed her inside the modest building. Sunlight spilled into the small window facing the ocean. In one corner was what appeared to be a trunk of sorts. It was bright red with a white lid. He watched as she removed the lid. The box was empty. But not for long. She dumped the coins into the red box, filling it. When the bag was empty, she looked inside, he assumed to make sure there were no coins left behind. Placing the lid back on the box, she stood there a while and stared at it.

"I suppose this is as good a place as any," he said. "At least until I find somewhere better to hide them."

SEVENTEEN

When Danielle opened her bedroom door, preparing to step out into the hallway, she practically ran into Nola Horton, who she found lingering just outside her doorway. Surprised at Danielle's sudden appearance, the middle-aged woman let out a startled gasp.

"Oh, you scared me!" Nola laughed nervously, her face reddening.

"Were you looking for me?" Danielle asked, thinking the guest was preparing to knock on her door—*or open it.*

"I-I was just having a look around the house. I hope you don't mind."

Danielle smiled. "No, that's fine. Marlow House has a lot of history."

"Are you on your way out?" Nola asked.

"No, did you need something?"

Nola stood in silence for a moment, as if trying to decide what to say. Finally, her eyes darted to the stairway leading to the attic. "Would it be okay if I had a look in the attic?" She lowered her voice and whispered, "I understand that's where he was killed."

"I assume you're speaking of Walt Marlow?"

Nola's eyes widened. "Are you saying he's not the only one to have been killed in this house?"

"Let's just say, as far as we know, Walt Marlow is the only one we know of who was murdered in the attic." *I guess she didn't read all the blog entries*, Danielle thought.

Closing her bedroom door and locking it, Danielle headed for the attic, Nola following her.

Nola glanced back to the bedroom door for a moment and then asked, "Do you always keep your bedroom door locked? I guess I never really thought of this as a regular motel—more like someone's home."

Starting up the stairway leading to the attic, holding onto the handrail, Danielle looked back to Nola, who continue to follow her. "I think it's always a good idea for all of us, the guests included, to keep our bedroom doors locked."

Nola continued to follow Danielle. She glanced briefly over her shoulder at the door to her room.

"Why did you bring her up here?" Walt asked when Danielle walked into the attic with Nola. He stood next to the spotting scope by the window.

Nola looked up to the ceiling. "Where did they find him hanging?"

Walt groaned. "Another one with morbid curiosity?"

Danielle flashed Walt a sheepish grin and then looked at Nola. "I'm not sure exactly."

Walt smiled and then waved his hand, summoning a lit cigar. "Good. Don't give in to her ghoulish requests."

Nola turned to Danielle and sniffed. She then looked around the room and sniffed again. "Has someone been smoking up here?"

Danielle shrugged. "I don't think so."

"You know, I think I smelled that last night. It smells like some-one's smoking a pipe…or maybe a cigar." Nola sniffed again.

"This is an old house. They often come with funny smells." Danielle flashed Walt a smile.

Walt frowned. "Are you calling me a funny smell?"

Nola glanced up to the ceiling for a moment and then stepped closer to Danielle and whispered, "Well, you know, maybe this house is haunted."

Danielle turned to face Walt. "I seriously doubt it."

In the next moment, the spotting scope swung around on its tripod. It made three full turns and then stopped abruptly.

Surprised at Walt's impulsive antics, Danielle found herself staring at him in disbelief, reluctant to face Nola, who was standing behind her.

Walt looked past Danielle to Nola and cringed. "Perhaps I shouldn't have done that."

Danielle glared at Walt.

"You better turn around quick! I think she's about to faint!"

Nola would have fallen to the floor had Walt not caught her first. She was still unconscious when he floated her to the sofa and laid her down.

"Why did you do that?" Danielle hissed at Walt.

"It seemed somewhat amusing at the time," he said with a hint of regret.

A moment later Nola opened her eyes and blinked. Danielle sat at her side on the sofa.

"Are you okay?" Danielle asked.

"I…I…" Nola sat up and looked nervously at the spotting scope. "It moved on its own."

"Oh, that?" Danielle forced a laugh. "The tripod is pretty wobbly. The slightest breeze sends it spinning."

Nola looked at the closed window.

"Drafts. The walls in here have horrible insulation. Drafty air coming in all the time," Danielle hastily explained.

Nola sat silently for a moment, her hands folded tightly on her lap as she considered Danielle's words. Finally, she laughed and shook her head. "That was silly of me. I actually thought for a minute there I was witnessing paranormal activity. Whatever you do, please don't tell Albert about this. He will never let me live it down."

Danielle smiled. "No problem. Sometimes being up here, considering what happened, one's imagination can take off."

Nola nodded her head in agreement and stood up. She started to take a step and then paused. "How did I get over here?"

"Excuse me?"

Nola pointed across the room. "We were standing over there when I saw the telescope move."

"It's not a telescope," Walt corrected.

"You fainted," Danielle explained.

"But how did you get me over here? No way could a little thing like you carry me."

Danielle smiled and said lightly, "You didn't actually fall when you fainted…more like you got woozy. I helped you walk to the sofa. Don't you remember?"

Nola frowned and then shook her head. "No. No, I don't."

WHEN DANIELLE and Nola returned to the second floor, Nola excused herself and went to her bedroom to find her husband, who she claimed had been taking a shower when she had stepped out into the hall.

Downstairs, Danielle ran into her other guests, Jeannie and Blake Spicer. She found the couple standing in the library, looking at the life-size portraits of Walt and Angela Marlow.

"I love the way they dressed back then." Jeannie let out a sigh and continued to gaze at Angela's painting.

"I think you might have a problem fitting into one of those dresses," Blake said as he gave his wife a quick slap on the derriere. In return she glared at him and swatted away his hand.

"I imagine she was wearing a corset," Danielle said. "Made them look unrealistically smaller back then."

"Wrong," Walt piped up when he appeared the next moment. "Angela never wore a corset. Most women stopped wearing them during the war." Walt studied his wife's portrait for a moment. "The steel used to make corsets was needed more for the war effort. But she did wear a girdle."

"I'd think a corset was more to hold in the waist and make the hips look larger?" Jeannie asked.

"Umm…I meant girdle, not corset," Danielle corrected. "Actually, corsets were no longer worn much after World War I because they needed the steel for the war effort."

"Hmm, I wonder where you got that?" Walt snickered under his breath as he took a puff of his cigar.

"Interesting," Jeannie murmured, still looking at the portrait.

Turning to Danielle, Blake asked, "Where are you off to this afternoon?"

"Me?"

"I assume you don't stick around here all day."

"Actually, I'm going to visit a friend this afternoon. What are your plans?"

"I'm a little tired after driving yesterday. I was thinking of maybe taking a nap," Blake told her. "And later, taking a drive around town, maybe go down to the pier."

"While he's napping, I intend to finish my book," Jeannie added. "Is it okay if I read in here? It looks like the perfect place to snuggle down with a book."

"I also have a book to finish," Walt said before he vanished.

"Certainly, none of the rooms are off-limits, aside from the bedrooms, of course."

"Does that mean I can't take a nap in our bedroom?" Blake asked with a snicker.

Danielle smiled. "I meant all the bedrooms except the one you're staying in."

Blake winked at Danielle. "I was just teasing you."

"Where is Lily? I haven't seen her since breakfast?" Jeannie asked.

"She volunteered to docent at the museum this afternoon. They're having a summer program for kids, and she's helping out."

"We should probably check out the museum while we're here," Blake said. "I haven't seen Nola and Albert since breakfast. Did they go out?"

Danielle glanced briefly to the ceiling. "No, I believe they're upstairs in their bedroom. Nola said something about Albert taking a shower. I have no idea what their plans are."

"They seem like a nice couple. I was wondering if they might be interested in joining us for dinner tonight," Blake said.

"If you like seafood, I'd suggest Pearl Cove. They have a wonderful view of the ocean and the best clam chowder." Danielle glanced at the nearby clock. "If you will both excuse me, I'm going to the parlor. I have a few things to attend to before I take off."

IT TOOK Walt less than thirty minutes to finish the book he had been reading. He decided to leave it in the attic and put it away later. If one of the guests spied the book floating down over the staircase toward the library, he imagined Danielle would get annoyed with him.

She hadn't come up to say goodbye yet, so he suspected she was still in the parlor. He knew she had a date with Marie this afternoon.

Instead of waiting for Danielle to come upstairs to say goodbye, he headed downstairs.

He found the guests who were staying in the Red Room blocking the staircase leading to the attic. Curious as to what they were whispering about, he lingered behind them as opposed to moving through them to continue on his way.

"Is she ever going to leave?" the woman whispered, glancing toward the staircase leading to the first floor.

"We need them all to leave, not just Danielle. I was really hoping we'd be the only guests, since we made the reservations for mid-week."

"There has to be some way to get them all out of the house so we can get the privacy we need," she said.

"Come on, let's go back to our room. We can have some privacy there." He sniggered and grabbed her hand, tugging her toward their bedroom door.

"ARE YOU ABOUT READY TO LEAVE?" Walt asked Danielle when he appeared in the parlor a moment later.

Danielle, who sat at the desk, looked up from the laptop she was working on. She turned it off and closed it. "Yes. I wanted to do a little research before I headed over to Marie's."

"Research?"

"I want to see if she knows anything about Sullivan. But before I asked her, I was doing a little search on one of the newspaper archive sites to see if anything popped up on him."

"Sullivan? Why?" Walt stood by the desk.

"After finding that DNA test and you telling me about Sullivan, I'm curious to see if I can figure out who Aunt Brianna's father was."

Walt glanced up to the ceiling. "While you're off solving ancient mysteries, we have one brewing under our roof."

"What do you mean?"

"Your guests staying in the Red Room seem awful anxious for you to leave." He then told Danielle what he had overheard and observed.

Danielle considered the conversation a moment and then made a cringe-like smile. "I hope it isn't what I think it is."

"What's that?" Walt frowned.

"You say they wanted us all gone for privacy—then he suggested they find it in their room for now?"

"So?"

"Think about it, Walt. Ewww, I hope they aren't going to…I mean…" She cringed again.

"Ahh…you think they intend to take their bedroom activities to other rooms in the house?"

"I suppose it's not as outrageous as the couple who paid the restaurant maître d' to dine nude in one of the little alcove rooms off the main dining hall."

"Where was this?"

Danielle grinned. "A restaurant in Arizona."

Walt arched his brow. "And you know this how?"

Danielle grinned. "I had a friend—a very conservative friend—who was a server there. She happened by the little alcove room and glanced in. She was quite shocked to find a nude couple sitting at the table, drinking wine. She told me all about it."

Walt laughed. "I'll keep an eye on our adventurous couple in case they are up to something else. But if their clothes start coming off, I won't stick around."

EIGHTEEN

Colorful flowers dotted the perimeter of the property, peeking out between the slats of the fencing. Beyond the gate, the cheery house, sunny yellow with white trim, stood proudly under the clear blue sky amidst a sea of freshly cut lawn, an example of what many believed an ideal beach cottage should be.

A car was already parked in front of the house when Danielle arrived. It was Adam's car, and Adam himself was just coming down the walkway when Danielle turned off her ignition.

"Grandma said you were coming over," Adam greeted Danielle when he reached the sidewalk.

"And you were hoping to slip away before I arrived?" she teased.

He grinned. "Well, I tried." His expression then grew serious and he asked, "Any word on the gold coins?"

Danielle shook her head and then glanced up at Marie's house. "Although you probably knew that. If there was any news, I would imagine Marie would be the first to know."

"True. But she hasn't heard anything either. I told you, you should have just let me have them."

Danielle giggled. "You're probably right." She shifted her purse from one hand to another and then hung its strap over her right shoulder. "Mel dropped by yesterday."

"Yeah, I saw her after she left your place."

"She brought me a box from Renton's storage."

"She told me about that."

"So she's really moving back?"

"Appears that way. She resigned from her job in New York, plans to practice law in Oregon," Adam said.

"Yeah, she told me."

"You know, she's considering changing her name back to Carmichael."

"Really? Does that mean the divorce is final? We didn't discuss her marriage."

Adam shrugged. "I guess it is."

"So tell me, you going to finally settle down? Marie would love that."

"Mel just moved back to town. Aside from seeing her when she came for Jolene's funeral, Mel and I haven't seen each other since we were kids."

"You two seem to hit it off pretty good when she was here the last time. I just figured—"

"So when are you and Chris getting married?" Adam countered.

"Me and Chris?"

"Sure, you two seem to get along great. You even went on a romantic rendezvous—at least you would have if someone hadn't hijacked the plane."

Danielle laughed. "Okay, okay. I get your point. And anyway, I wouldn't call it exactly a romantic rendezvous, considering we went with three other couples."

"Not to mention one of them was your old boyfriend. What was that about?" Adam teased.

"Oh, shut up. Joe is not an old boyfriend," Danielle scolded good naturedly.

"Not so much fun when someone is butting into your love life, is it?"

"Are you implying I'm butting into your love life?" Danielle asked with faux outrage.

"Aren't you?" he smirked.

"First you have to actually have a love life for me to butt into."

Adam groaned. "Brat. But you do have a point." He glanced at his watch. "I better run. Enjoy the visit with Grandma, but no plotting with her about me and Mel."

Danielle let out a sigh. "Okay. I promise."

Adam started for his driver's side door. Instead of heading toward the house, Danielle turned to his car and watched him open the car door.

"Adam, can I ask you just one thing?" Danielle asked.

About to climb into the car, Adam paused and looked to Danielle. "What?"

"You and Mel, I mean, you do care about her, don't you?"

Adam opened his mouth to say something and then paused. Finally, he said, "Yeah. Yeah, I do."

———

"I ASKED Adam to join us for lunch," Marie explained when she showed Danielle to the back porch. On the patio table lunch was already laid out, including two place settings and a vase of freshly cut flowers in the center of the table. "But he had an appointment with some client."

Danielle removed her purse from her shoulder and slipped it over the back of a chair before taking a seat at the table. "He didn't mention that."

"I suppose you heard about Melony moving back to town?" Marie asked as she sat down. She lifted the lid from a covered dish and removed a sandwich, its crust already neatly trimmed from the bread, and set it on Danielle's plate.

"Yes. In fact, she stopped by to see me yesterday on her way into town." Danielle picked up the glass of ice water and took a sip. "She brought me a box with some of Aunt Brianna's things."

"Really?" Marie set a sandwich on her plate. She then passed a bowl of potato chips to Danielle, silently offering her some.

"She's been sorting through the boxes that were put in storage after Renton was arrested. I guess after her mother was killed, they became her responsibility."

"I thought all the boxes holding information pertaining to Brianna were removed from storage already?"

Danielle shrugged. "That's what Melony thought too. But this box didn't really hold any legal papers, just personal items." Danielle then went on to explain what had been in the box, while Marie silently ate her sandwich and listened.

"Very interesting. You know, I've thought about taking one of those DNA tests. Adam doesn't seem to be very interested in genealogy research, but I think his brother might be."

"I tend to forget Adam has a brother." Danielle took a bite of her sandwich.

"Adam's the oldest, you know. When my son and his wife moved to California, Jason was still in high school. He went to Colorado for college and never moved back west. I don't think he sees his parents any more than he sees Adam and me. Sadly, the boys were never close."

"I've been here over a year and haven't met Adam's parents." Danielle popped a chip in her mouth.

Marie shrugged. "I wouldn't hold your breath. Adam had a bit of a falling out with his father, and since I took Adam's side, I haven't been on the best of terms with my son. To be honest, I was never on terrific terms with my daughter-in-law."

Danielle set her half-eaten sandwich on its plate. "I'm sorry."

Marie sighed. "Don't be, it happens."

Danielle nodded, picked up her sandwich again, and took a bite.

"Guess who I ran into at church?"

"Who?" Danielle picked up another chip and looked across the table at the elderly woman.

"Beverly Klein. I haven't seen her much since Steve's death. But I must say, she looks well. I always thought she was an attractive woman. She's probably relieved to be free of her cheating husband."

"Marie!" Danielle almost choked on her chip. She snatched her glass of water and took a quick gulp.

"Oh posh, you know I'm right," Marie clucked.

"I always thought Beverly was in love with Steve—in spite of his flaws."

"Some flaw, unable to keep his pants zipped up," Marie scoffed.

"To be honest, I never saw Steve as a player. He was always very professional with me, and back when I was having problems with Jolene, he seemed genuinely sorry. I was pretty shocked when I learned the truth about him."

"I suppose we never really know people. By the way, Beverly mentioned she might be leaving town," Marie told her.

"Adam mentioned that to me. Doesn't really surprise me. I wanted to move after my husband was killed." Danielle finished the last of her sandwich.

"Sometimes a fresh start is for the best. And sometimes, it is comforting to come home again."

Danielle looked up at Marie and smiled. "Are you talking about Mel moving back?"

"Yes. I admit I'm a little surprised she decided to. But now that she has…" Marie flashed Danielle a smile. "She's a spunky young woman. In spite of who her mother was. Although, I'm not sure how I feel about a mass murderer in the gene pool."

"Jolene's grandfather?" Danielle asked.

"Good lord, was there another one in her bloodline?"

Danielle chuckled. "Who knows. I imagine we all have some sketchy ancestors in our family trees."

"True." Marie nodded.

"Speaking of family trees, I've been thinking a lot of Brianna's. And who her father might have been."

"Ahh, because of that DNA test?" Marie asked.

"Yes. It got me to thinking about it."

"You said you have the results. Doesn't that tell you anything?"

"I looked at her results online. No close matches to indicate a parent, siblings or even cousins."

"Is there any particular reason why you're trying to find out who her father was?"

Danielle shrugged. "I'm just curious."

"If that test was really taken after she got sick, I suspect Renton had it done because he wanted to see if there were any close relatives floating around. Maybe a sibling she wasn't aware of."

"That's kind of what I was thinking too." Danielle wiped her hands on a napkin. "But there was something else I wanted to ask you, about Brianna."

"What's that?"

Danielle refolded her napkin. "Did she ever mention someone named Sean Sullivan to you?"

"Sean Sullivan?" Marie frowned and then shook her head. "No, I don't think so."

"He was a close friend of her mother's. He and Katherine grew up together. I have a feeling he might have known who Brianna's father was."

"Did Brianna tell you about him?"

"Yes," Danielle lied.

"Did she say he knew who her father was?" Marie asked.

"No. In fact, I never really talked to Aunt Brianna about her childhood—her parents. But she did mention him once in passing. That he had been a close friend of her mother's." Danielle felt bad about lying. But she couldn't very well say Walt had told her about Sullivan.

"So what is it exactly you hope to find out about this Sullivan?"

"I just figure, if he really was a close childhood friend of her mother's, someone who was still in contact with her after Brianna's birth, then maybe he knew who the father was."

"Do you think he was the father?"

Danielle shook her head. "No. I don't."

"Are you sure?"

"I can't really be sure, but I have this gut feeling." *More like Walt is that gut feeling.*

"I seriously doubt he's still alive," Marie teased. "What would he be, at least a hundred and twenty by now?"

"I was thinking, Katherine's death was pretty sensational at the time. If he got married, had kids, maybe he talked about Katherine to his kids. Maybe even mentioned something about who the father of her child was."

"Sounds like a bit of a long shot, dear." Marie reached across the table and patted Danielle's hand. "But if you really want to look into this, you might talk to Ben Smith. You know, his father was the court-appointed attorney for Brianna back then. It's possible his father mentioned something about this Sullivan. But I know my father never mentioned him to me, nor did Mother."

"Your mom was pretty fond of Katherine, wasn't she?" Danielle asked.

"I think she felt sorry for her. Katherine worked for Walt Marlow mostly, but she also worked a few hours each week for my mother. Katherine needed the money, raising Brianna on her own. But then, of course, she ended up inheriting Walt Marlow's estate. But that didn't turn out well for her."

Danielle shook her head. "No, no, it didn't."

"Oh! I almost forgot!" Marie stood up abruptly. "I'll be right back." She rushed into the house and then returned a few minutes later, carrying a stack of yellowed and tattered envelopes. Before sitting back down, she set the stack on the table in front of Danielle.

Danielle picked up the envelope on the top of the stack and

looked at it. There was a letter inside and the envelope was addressed to George Hemming.

"I had Adam take a box of photographs down from the attic for me to sort through, and I found those. I thought you might like them. They're letters from Walt Marlow to my father. It appears Walt wrote those when he was traveling in Europe."

"Really?" Danielle slipped one of the letters from its envelope and unfolded it. Walt's elegant cursive handwriting filled the page.

NINETEEN

With the late afternoon came the rain clouds, transforming the bright blue canvas a dull gray. In spite of the changing sky, there was no need to bring out an umbrella, even with the dampness permeating the air. However, should the rain start falling, it was doubtful many in Frederickport would reach for an umbrella.

The change of weather didn't bother him. It certainly didn't chase him off the roof, where he sat across the street from Marlow House. Shielded from view by the chimney, he peeked around the brick stack and watched the people come and go. Someone was standing at Marlow House's attic window, looking down at the side-walk and the couple getting into their car. He was fairly certain it was Walt Marlow at the window.

It wasn't until the man with the dog had arrived that he had been forced outside, which led him to explore his surroundings. He then took a closer look at Marlow House and the person frequently in its attic. It was indeed Walt Marlow.

But then more people started showing up and he went away for a while. He preferred a quieter place. He didn't need some human to capture him and demand their three wishes. But when he finally returned and was able to go back into the house, his gold was gone. It then became his mission to reclaim it.

He looked down at the street. The redhead getting into the car was one of the guests staying at Marlow House. It wasn't the redhead who lived there and frequently visited the Hemming house. He watched the car drive away, and then he glanced up at the attic window. The man turned away and was no longer in sight.

There were no vehicles parked in the driveway at Marlow House, just one car parked in front of it. By his estimation, the only people currently inside Marlow House was that other couple staying there. There was of course Marlow himself, yet he didn't consider him a person per se, and Marlow would pose his own challenges.

Moving swiftly from Hemming's roof to Marlow's, he peeked in the attic window. He spied Walt Marlow sitting on the sofa, reading a book. In a flash, he moved to the brunette's bedroom window. That was the room with the safe—and the necklace.

Looking in the window, preparing to enter, he froze. There, stretched out on the bed, was a black cat. The animal appeared to be sleeping, but the last thing he wanted to do was to wake the evil creature. He then noticed the bedroom door was closed, trapping the cat inside the room.

While the feline's presence meant he couldn't move forward with his plan to procure the lovely necklace, it would enable him to look through the house and see if there was anything else he might be interested in. All he had to do was stay out of the attic and away from Walt Marlow.

PUSHING the parlor blind to one side, Nola looked outside. She glanced back to Albert, who sat on the sofa, flipping through a magazine. "They're gone."

Albert looked up. "Are you sure? Can you even see the street from there?"

Nola released the blind, sending it swinging gently from right to left until it came to a rest. She turned to her husband. "I saw them go down the walkway and the top of the car drive away."

"Just the top of the car?" Albert flipped the page. "Must look pretty strange with just a bottom of a car sitting out there."

Nola groaned and stepped from the window. "That isn't even funny."

Never taking his eyes from the magazine, he said, "Probably why I never could make it as a stand-up comedian."

Hovering over Albert, Nola said, "Come on, this is our chance!"

He glanced up from the magazine. "Chance for what?"

"Everyone is gone. It's just you and me in the house! Our chance to check it out."

With a sigh, Albert closed the magazine and tossed it on the coffee table. "I guess you're right. Danielle and Lily could come home at any time."

———

WHEN HE APPEARED in the entry hall of Marlow House, the couple was just walking out of the parlor. He hadn't expected their sudden appearance. If he had been concerned they might see him, that fear vanished when the redhead walked through him, oblivious to his presence.

"Let's see how much we can explore of this place before Danielle and Lily get back," the redhead said.

"Don't forget, Danielle said something about a housekeeper," the man reminded her.

"She said the housekeeper was coming tomorrow morning. Not today," the woman told him.

Narrowing his eyes, he studied the couple as they poked their way down the hall, examining every inch of the wall's paneling. "Don't tell me you're looking for it too!" he said in outrage. "Well, you won't find the necklace downstairs."

He followed them to the library and watched as they stood before the giant portraits, examining each one.

"So that's Walt Marlow, I suppose?" the man asked.

"Yes. Lily told me the other one was his wife," she told him.

The man turned his attention back to Walt's portrait. "So, he's the one who was murdered in the attic?"

"You know, he isn't the only one who has been killed in this house," she whispered.

He glanced from the portrait briefly to his wife. "What do you mean?"

"Something Danielle said when we went up to the attic. I did a little searching on my phone. Did you know someone was murdered in the parlor just a few months ago? And after that, one of the guests died upstairs!"

"Was she murdered too?"

"No. It was natural causes."

"Which room upstairs?" he said.

"The article didn't say. But that's kind of chilling," she whispered.

"Did they catch the killer—the man who was killed in the parlor?"

"Yes…but still." She shivered.

"Still what?"

"Makes one wonder if maybe this place really could be haunted. I mean, with all these deaths. Who's not to say their ghosts aren't hanging around.

"Ghosts?" He let out a grunt. "Yeah, right, Nola. Ghosts."

He couldn't help it. In the next moment a dozen or more books shot from their places on the bookshelves. They ricocheted wildly around the room. Before they landed on the floor, the couple was already out of the library, heading down the hallway as fast as their feet would take them.

Now on the floor laughing wildly, unable to contain his mirth, he could hear them pounding up the stairs, and then he heard the door to their bedroom slam shut. Forcing himself to regain composure, he picked himself up off the floor and moved toward the window, preparing to make his exit. He couldn't stick around, Walt Marlow was bound to show up at any moment to see what the commotion had been about, and he wasn't sure he could prevent Marlow from seeing him.

WHEN DANIELLE RETURNED to Marlow House late Wednesday afternoon, Lily was still gone, her car was not parked in the driveway, nor was it across the street at Ian's. Danielle didn't see the Spicers' car, but the Hortons' was parked in front of the house.

Entering through the kitchen door, she found Walt sitting at the table, waiting for her. "You've been gone a long time," he greeted her.

Danielle closed the door and tossed her purse on the counter. "I stopped at the police station after I left Marie's. I wanted to see if there was any news on the safe deposit box."

"And?" Walt asked as he watched Danielle wash her hands at the sink.

"Nothing." Danielle wiped her hands dry on a kitchen towel and then went to the refrigerator and pulled out a carton of milk. "So anything exciting going on?"

"Not unless you consider reading exciting."

"I see the Spicers are gone."

"They left a couple hours ago. I heard them say something about looking for a restaurant."

"And the Hortons?" Danielle poured herself a glass of milk and then returned the carton to the refrigerator. Before joining Walt at the table, she grabbed several chocolate drop cookies from the cookie jar and set them on a napkin.

"They're upstairs in their room. Noisy couple."

"How so?" Danielle dipped one of her cookies in the glass of milk and then took a bite.

"Clomping up and down the stairs and then slamming their door." He shook his head.

Danielle took another bite of her cookie and then asked, "Where's Max? He usually greets me when I get home."

Walt shrugged. "I assume he's outside roaming around."

"I hope not. It looks like it's going to rain."

"Max isn't fond of the rain, so he's probably sleeping in some corner of the house," Walt suggested. "So tell me about your visit with Marie."

DANIELLE OPENED the door to her bedroom thirty minutes later and found Max lounging on her bed, awake, delicately grooming his front paws.

"How did you get locked in here?" Danielle said when she walked into the room. Max stood up on the bed, stretched and then sauntered in her direction.

Just as Danielle picked Max up off the mattress, a voice came from the open doorway.

"Thank goodness you're home!" Nola said in a rush as she entered the bedroom uninvited.

Holding a purring Max in her arms, Danielle turned to the woman. "What happened?"

Slightly out of breath, Nola quickly told Danielle about the experience in the library.

Danielle's eyes widened. "The books...they flew off the shelves?"

"Not all of them, but at least a dozen! They were flying around the room like something out of a Disney movie?"

"Disney?"

"Well, I prefer to think Disney as opposed to Stephen King," Nola said with a giggle. She then said, her eyes wide and excited, "I think your house really is haunted!"

"Umm...haunted?"

Max began to squirm in Danielle's arms. Leaning down, she released the cat, who promptly strolled from the room into the hallway.

"That is the only explanation!"

"You don't seem too upset about that possibility?" Danielle said in an uneasy voice.

"I will admit, it scared the bejesus out of Albert and me when those books took flight. But once we calmed down...well, I've always wanted to stay in a haunted house!"

"You have?"

"Did you know it was haunted?" Nola asked with a whisper, glancing over her shoulder as if she expected some spirit to jump out of the woodwork and shout *boo*!

"Umm...perhaps some strange things happen from time to time...but haunted?"

"My only question, whose ghost is it?" Nola asked excitedly. "Walt Marlow or the fellow who was killed in your parlor, or maybe that writer who died upstairs. What bedroom did she die in, by the way? Are we staying in it?"

———

AFTER DANIELLE LEFT NOLA, she went downstairs to look in the library. Instead of picking up the books littering the floor, she went in search of Walt. She found him in the parlor, watching television. The television turned off just as she opened the door.

"What did you do?" she asked as she entered the room, closing the door behind her.

"I would have turned the television off sooner if it had been your noisy houseguests. Trust me, I would have heard them," Walt said with a sigh. He waved his hand for a lit cigar.

"I'm not talking about the television," she said impatiently. "You know exactly what I meant!"

Walt frowned. "Are you upset with me?"

Danielle rolled her eyes and let out an impatient sigh.

"You know I hate when you roll your eyes like that. Very unlady-like," Walt admonished.

Glaring at him, she crooked her finger in his direction, beckoning him to follow her. With a shrug, he stood up and did as she wanted.

A moment later, they stood together in the library.

"Who in the hell threw my books on the floor!" Walt shouted angrily.

Startled at his outburst, Danielle looked at Walt. He seemed genuinely irate. Stomping to one book, he swiped it up off the floor and waved it angrily at Danielle. "This is a signed first edition! Do you have any idea what I paid for this?"

With wide eyes, Danielle asked, "Are you saying you didn't throw those books on the floor?"

TWENTY

Everyone was still sleeping when Lily slipped downstairs Thursday morning to put the coffee on. Alone in the kitchen, wearing her robe over her pajama bottoms and T-shirt, she stumbled sleepily around the kitchen, searching for the coffee filters. They weren't in their normal place. Just as she headed for the pantry to look there, she noticed a sheet of paper under the kitchen table.

Pausing a moment, she bent down and picked up the piece of paper and looked at it. It was a handwritten letter addressed to someone named George.

LILY TAPPED LIGHTLY on Danielle's bedroom door. A few moments later it opened, and Danielle stepped aside, letting Lily into her bedroom before closing the door again.

"I put the coffee on," Lily said, and then handed Danielle the piece of paper she had found downstairs. "This was under the kitchen table, is it yours?"

Danielle looked at it and smiled. "I must have dropped it there last night when I took the letters out of my purse."

"What letters?"

Danielle walked over to her desk and set the letter down. "When

I was at Marie's, she gave me some old letters Walt had written her father. I took them out of my purse in the kitchen. This page must have fallen under the table."

Lily walked over to the desk and picked up the page, giving it a closer look. "Walt certainly had beautiful handwriting."

"I know. It's a shame some schools don't teach cursive handwriting anymore."

Lily sat down on the foot of Danielle's unmade bed, still looking at the letter. "Unfortunately, with all the testing that's required, cursive got shoved aside, because you can't really test handwriting."

"I think it's horrible not to teach it. Imagine future generations unable to read basic historical documents that were written in cursive—or even not to be able to read old letters written by your grandparents—or their journals."

"Not only that, many believe writing cursive improves memory skills, stimulates creativity, and even helps children with dyslexia. It uses both sides of the brain. If I had children, I'd teach them cursive even if the school didn't," Lily said.

"Did your school teach it?"

"Yes. They start in third grade. But there are schools that don't teach it anymore." Lily stood up, folded the letter, and set it back on the desk.

"I just think it's a shame." Danielle grabbed the clothes she intended to wear that day from her closet and tossed them on her bed.

"So what did you do with Walt's letters?"

"I gave them to Walt; they're his. I'm not sure what he did with them." Danielle pointed to the folded page on her desk and added, "I'll have to give that back to him."

"IT HAS to be that other ghost," Lily told Danielle as she finished cooking the bacon at the stove later that morning.

"You mean the one dressed like a leprechaun?" Danielle stood at the kitchen counter, dicing up melon.

"Have you noticed any other ghosts hanging around lately?"

Picking up the small cutting board, Danielle dumped the freshly cut fruit into a serving bowl. "No. But how do we know he's really a ghost? Maybe they're growing leprechauns bigger these days." They both giggled.

"It is pretty creepy, books flying off the shelf." Lily began removing strips of bacon from the pan, arranging them on a large platter lined with paper towel.

"Strange thing, Nola was quite thrilled at the prospect of staying in a haunted house," Danielle said.

"But I thought you told me she fainted when Walt twirled the spotting scope."

Danielle shrugged. "I guess she got over it."

A knock came at the kitchen door. They both turned to see who it was. Chris was peeking through its window and gave them a wave before he opened the door and walked into the house.

"You really should keep your door locked. You never know who is going to just come walking in," Chris said with a cheeky grin.

"Morning, Chris. Did you come to mooch some breakfast?" Danielle asked as she peeled an orange to add to the fruit bowl.

"I was hoping I wasn't too late." Chris helped himself to some coffee and then turned to face Lily and Danielle. Lily was just removing the last of the bacon from the pan.

"You have a keen sense of timing," Lily teased. "Where's Hunny?"

"She's in the side yard, exploring." Chris glanced around the room. "So where is Joanne?"

"She had some doctor appointment in Portland, so I told her not to bother coming in today. We only have four guests," Danielle explained.

"So where is the old man?" Chris asked, glancing around the kitchen again.

"If you're talking about Walt, don't let him hear you calling him that," Danielle warned.

"Yeah, yeah…" Chris waved his hand dismissively. "He'll remind me I'm older than him."

Danielle shrugged. "Something like that."

"Hey, Chris, have you seen any leprechauns around lately?" Lily asked.

Chris looked at Danielle. "That guy show up again?"

———

AFTER DANIELLE TOLD Chris about the episode in the library and their speculation as to who might be responsible, breakfast was ready to be served. Chris helped Lily and Danielle carry the serving platters with food out to the dining room.

When they arrived, Albert and Nola were just sitting down. Jeannie was already sitting at the table, unfolding her napkin.

"Is Blake joining us for breakfast?" Lily asked as she set the platter of bacon on the table.

"Yes, he should be down here in a minute," Jeannie said brightly. "Nola was telling me about your ghost."

Danielle looked up from the extra plate she was setting for Chris. "Was she?"

"The haunted house angle can be a great gimmick," Jeannie said, reaching for a slice of bacon without waiting for the rest of them to be seated.

"I suspect there was some seismic activity that made those books fall off the shelves," Danielle suggested as she took a seat at the table.

"The books were flying," Nola insisted.

"I'm sure they were, dear," Jeannie said, her tone condescending. She snatched another slice of bacon. Everyone was now seated around the table except for Blake, who still had not come downstairs.

Nola flashed Jeannie a dirty look and slunk down in her chair.

After eating the slice of bacon, Jeannie dabbed her mouth with her napkin and then tossed it on the table and stood up abruptly. "Perhaps I should run upstairs and see what's taking Blake so long."

Just as Jeannie headed for the door, Walt appeared in the dining room.

"I understand the restaurant down at the pier serves a wonderful breakfast," Walt told Chris.

A FEW MINUTES LATER, Jeannie opened the door to her room. She found Blake sitting on a chair, reading a magazine.

"They're all in the dining room having breakfast, hurry," she told him.

Tossing the magazine on the floor, he stood up and headed for the door. On his way there, he grabbed a small tool off the dresser.

Jeannie rushed back to the stairs and looked down at the first floor. She could hear voices drifting out from the dining room.

Without saying a word, Blake went to Danielle's bedroom door and knelt down before its locked doorknob. Inserting the tool in the lock, he moved it ever so slightly from one direction to the next.

"Bingo," he whispered. Standing up, he opened the door and walked into Danielle's room. He was in there for about five minutes when Jeannie rushed to the open door.

"Hurry, someone is coming!"

DAVE SAT ALONE on the swing in front of Marlow House. In one hand he held a lit cigarette, and in the other was his cellphone, which he held to his ear. The line was ringing, Dave was waiting for Kissinger to answer his call.

"Did you get it?" Kissinger greeted him.

"Give me time. I just got here." Dave took a drag off the cigarette.

"What do you mean, you've been there two days. She's not going to leave it there forever."

"Slow down, red rider. I'm working on it," Dave said lazily.

"Tell me you at least found the safe," Kissinger asked.

"Yes. A rather cliché place, if you ask me. Hidden behind a painting in her bedroom. That thing will be a snap to open."

"Then why haven't you done it yet?" Kissinger asked.

"You told me Steph and I would probably be the only guests. There's another couple staying here, and they've been hanging around the place. Danielle hasn't been the issue, they have. In fact, she took off yesterday, and I was hoping I could grab it then. Unfortunately, they won't get off their fat butts and do something touristy."

"I'm sure you can think of some way to get them out of the house."

"I'm working on it. Those keystone cops come up with anything new?" Dave asked.

"Not a thing. But I think the FBI might be convinced Danielle Boatman lied about putting the gold in the safe deposit box. I overheard two of them talking, and I got the impression she's not high on their list."

"She seems okay to me. Wonder what she did to piss off those feebs?"

"Not sure, but listen to this, one of them even said something about Marlow House being haunted." Kissinger laughed. "Of course, they didn't know I was standing by the door listening when one said it."

"Haunted?" Dave sat up straighter and put his feet on the ground, stopping the swing from moving. "Did they say how?"

"How? What do you mean how haunted?"

"I meant why did they think it's haunted?"

"Hell if I know. It's not like I could ask them what they were talking about. Why?"

"You aren't going to believe this. You know that other couple staying here? The woman told a story at breakfast about the books flying off the shelf in the library here. Insists the place is haunted."

Kissinger laughed. "If it was, I wouldn't be surprised. I was reading about that place, and since Boatman moved in, two people have died there. One was murdered."

"Are you saying you believe in ghosts?" Dave asked.

"Don't be a jackass. Of course I don't believe in ghosts. But when that many people die in one house during a short time frame, some yahoo is going to insist the place is haunted."

"Well, I haven't seen any ghosts." Dave flicked his cigarette butt. It landed in a nearby bush.

"Of course, you could use this to your advantage."

"What do you mean?"

"If you really want to get that couple out of your hair, maybe convince them the place is haunted and they'll leave."

"I don't see that happening. The woman seemed rather happy over the possibility she's staying in a haunted house."

A KNOCK CAME at Alan Kissinger's office door just as he got off the phone.

Sitting behind his desk, he called out, "Yes?"

The door opened and Susan Mitchell peeked her head in the office. When she saw he wasn't on the phone or with anyone, she slipped into the room and gently closed the door behind her.

Picking a pen up off his desk, as if he were preparing to write something, he looked at Susan and said, "What do you need?"

Coughing nervously, Susan stepped closer to his desk. "We have a little problem."

"What kind of little problem? Can't you handle it?"

She stepped closer, her hands fidgeting by her sides. "It happened again."

He frowned. "What happened again?"

"A safe deposit box. Another one has been cleaned out," Susan squeaked.

The pen dropped from Alan's hand, and the color drained from his face. He stood up. "That's impossible."

"Ron Dawson is demanding to talk to you."

"Ron Dawson?"

"The man whose safe deposit box was robbed."

"I told you, no one's safe deposit box was robbed!" he fairly shouted.

"Can I please send him in here, and you can explain that?" she managed to say.

"WHAT THE HELL is going on with this bank?" the angry man shouted when he marched into Alan's office a few minutes later and was introduced as Ron Dawson.

"Please sit down," Alan said with forced calm, pointing to the chair facing the desk.

Susan, who had brought Ron into the office, quickly backed out of the room and closed the door.

"I don't want to sit down! This kind of crap never happened when Steve Klein was bank manager."

"Let's see if we can figure this out." Alan again motioned to the empty chair. Ron remained standing.

Alan picked up his desk phone and pressed one button. A moment later he said, "Please bring me the ledger for the safe deposit box vault."

Shortly after Alan hung up the phone, Susan reentered the office, handed Alan the requested item, and quickly departed. Alan opened the book and looked through the entries.

Finally, he looked up at the angry customer. "Mr. Dawson,

according to this ledger, you were the last one to open your safe deposit box. No one else has been in it since then, so perhaps you mistakenly believe you put something in it that you didn't."

"Like Danielle Boatman mistakenly put those gold coins in hers?"

Alan shifted uneasily in his chair. "I really can't discuss another bank customer's business."

"Why not? It was in the paper! Everyone in Frederickport knows Boatman is probably the richest woman in town. No way is she going to lie about those coins."

Alan studied Ron a moment and let out a weary sigh. "Perhaps you should tell me what you believe is missing?"

"It was a bracelet my grandmother left me. It was worth at least twenty thousand dollars."

"And you have something to verify this bracelet you claim is missing is worth what you say it is?"

"What are you saying?" he asked angrily.

"I hope you understand, before I proceed, I need to establish exactly what it was and its value."

Ron Dawson reached into his shirt pocket and pulled out a crumpled piece of paper. He tossed it on Alan's desk. "This is an appraisal I had done on the piece a couple years ago, from a local jeweler. Sam Hayman. His store's no longer open, but I heard he just moved back to town. He can verify he gave this estimate."

TWENTY-ONE

It didn't take Danielle long to track down Ben Smith. After her discussion with Marie the previous day, she was curious to discover if he knew anything about Sean Sullivan and what might have happened to him. After breakfast on Thursday morning, she gave him a phone call and discovered he was on docent detail at the museum.

She arrived at the museum shortly before noon on Thursday. Ben, a spry elderly man in his eighties, with kind blue gray eyes, greeted Danielle at the door. When Danielle stepped inside the museum, she glanced around. There didn't appear to be anyone in the building except for Ben and herself.

"It's not very busy today," Danielle said as she followed Ben toward the museum gift shop. Glancing down the hallway leading to the main exhibits, she wondered briefly if Eva Thorndike's spirit was somewhere in the building. Eva occasionally visited the museum, but unlike Walt, her spirit wasn't attached to any particular location. Which was why, unlike Walt, she was unable to harness any extra energy to move objects.

"We've had a few people today. But it's never that busy midweek."

"Lily tells me you had a good turnout yesterday. She had a lot of fun."

"Lily is great with the kids," Ben said. "She was a tremendous help. We couldn't have done it without her."

"I'll have to tell her that."

"I read about your July fourth open house in this morning's paper," Ben said as he and Danielle entered the room housing the museum gift shop. He took a seat on the stool behind the store's counter.

"Ahh, I haven't seen today's paper. Lily told me she was running some ads." Danielle leaned against the counter.

"I was wondering if you were going to do something this year."

Danielle turned slightly to better face Ben, resting her elbows on the glass display counter. "I confess, I considered not doing anything this year. But Lily talked me into it."

Ben chortled. "Lily can be persuasive."

"That's for sure. But we're doing it a little different from last year. We're hosting a hot dog barbecue in the backyard before the annual fireworks on the beach."

"I see you're selling tickets this year, raising money for the local schools," Ben said. "Good idea."

"It was Lily's. Last year we sent out invitations to specific groups and people in the community. This year, we're opening it to everyone. Of course, if everyone showed up, we would have a problem. Which is why we decided to sell tickets at the gate and then donate the money to a good cause. Lily chose the local schools."

"Understandable," Ben said with a nod. "So why did you want to see me?"

"I had a question for you, since your father was Aunt Brianna's attorney."

The lines around Ben's gray eyes crinkled when he smiled. "I'll see if I can answer."

"Did your father ever talk about a friend of Katherine O'Malley named Sean Sullivan?"

"Sullivan?" Ben frowned as he considered the name. Finally, he shook his head. "Sorry. That name doesn't ring a bell. Who was he?"

"He was a childhood friend of Katherine's. I know he lived in Frederickport when Katherine worked for Walt Marlow. I'm curious to find out what happened to him."

"I'm sorry. I don't recognize the name."

Danielle let out a sigh. "Drat. I was hoping you might know something."

"Why is this important?" Ben asked.

Danielle shrugged. "I suppose it's not really important, I'm just curious. I've been thinking a lot about Aunt Brianna and wondering who her father was, wondering if maybe she had siblings she never knew about."

"Are you suggesting this Sullivan was her father?"

"No. I just figured he knew the identity of the father, since he and Katherine were close friends and he was around after Aunt Brianna was born."

"I imagine this Sullivan died years ago. Not sure how he can help you now."

"Katherine's death was pretty sensational back then. It's the kind of story someone tells their kids or grandkids, considering it involved someone he had been close to."

"Sorry I can't help you, Danielle. I don't recall my father ever mentioning a Sullivan. In fact, I always got the impression Brianna was virtually alone in the world—no family or close family friends."

Danielle stepped back from the counter and repositioned her purse on her shoulder, preparing to leave.

"I'm curious, how do you know about this Sullivan?" Ben asked. "That this man ever existed?"

"Aunt Brianna mentioned him once," Danielle lied.

The next moment a bell rang; someone had just come into the museum.

Ben quickly hopped off the stool. "If you'll excuse me."

"Certainly." Danielle watched Ben scurry from around the counter and head to the entry to welcome the new arrivals.

With a sigh, Danielle turned toward the doorway, preparing to leave. Before she took a step, the space in front of her lit up brightly, as if someone had turned on a spotlight. In the midst of the bright space, what appeared to be gold glitter rained down from the ceiling, vanishing before it hit the floor.

Blinking her eyes in disbelief, Danielle silently watched as the image of Eva Thorndike appeared before her—not her entire self, just her face, which floated under the shower of glitter. Eva's likeness—so eerily similar to that of the fictional Gibson Girl of the late 1800s—looked stoically in Danielle's direction, her features devoid of expression as it weaved lazily within the now circle of light.

"Eva?" Danielle squeaked.

"Ask Angela," Eva whispered, her head still floating within the bright glitter circle.

"Ask Angela what?" Danielle asked, regaining her composure.

"Ask Angela about Sullivan."

Before Danielle had a chance to ask Eva to explain, the spirit dissolved into the surrounding air until she was no more.

"Well, that was helpful," Danielle grumbled.

TEN MINUTES later Danielle sat in her car in front of the museum, talking to Lily on the phone.

"I swear, that woman might have died a century ago, but she still has dramatic flair," Danielle told Lily.

"Are you going to talk to Angela?" Lily asked.

Leaning back in her car's seat, Danielle gazed out the windshield, holding her cellphone by her ear. "That will mean going to the cemetery. You know how I hate that place."

"You don't have to go. After all, this is just to sate your own curiosity. It's not going to make a difference to anyone if you find out the identity of Brianna's father."

"True." Danielle let out a sigh.

"Oh, my god. I forgot to tell you!" Lily said in a rush. "According to Ian, another safe deposit box was hit."

"Really?"

"He heard it when he was getting his hair cut," Lily told her. "The guy was in there at the same time, saying he was going to sue the bank."

"I'm surprised the chief hasn't called me."

"From what I understand, this all happened within the last couple hours."

"It must be some sort of inside job," Danielle said.

"That's what Ian thinks too. I don't know how it can't be."

Sitting up straight, Danielle picked up her car key and slipped it into the ignition. "I'm going to get going."

"You on your way home?" Lily asked.

Danielle turned on her ignition. "No. I think I'll stop at the cemetery and have a chat with Walt's wife."

LOUNGING ATOP THE MASSIVE HEADSTONE, Angela Marlow dangled her bare feet and wiggled her toes, teasing the top leaves of the rosebush growing at the base of her memorial. She didn't need to fear the flower's thorns, considering the state of her body—she had none.

Wearing a short, sleeveless, gold lamé dress, its hem fringed, she combed her fingers through her short blonde curls as she moved slightly, adjusting her pose.

"Good afternoon, Angela," Danielle greeted her.

Startled by Danielle's sudden appearance, Angela jumped down from the headstone, landing in the middle of the rosebush. Without missing a beat, she stepped away from the headstone and out of the foliage, toward Danielle.

"Where did you come from? Are you dead now?" Angela asked.

"Umm…no. As far as I know, I'm still alive," Danielle said, suppressing a giggle.

"I just assumed since you appeared out of nowhere, you were like me now."

Danielle shrugged. "Sorry, I got the impression you were pretty engrossed in…in whatever you were doing up there." Danielle paused and looked Angela up and down. "Gold lamé?"

"Gold lamé, what?" Angela frowned.

"Your dress. If I'm not mistaken, gold lamé wasn't a thing back in the twenties."

Angela shrugged and snapped her fingers. Her outfit changed to a more traditional flapper's dress. "I've discovered one benefit in this state, I can wear whatever I choose." Angela looked Danielle up and down, frowning at her choice of outfit: black leggings, knee-high boots, and a long pullover cotton blouse. "Death might improve your wardrobe."

"I'll try to remember that," Danielle said dryly.

"Why are you here? Is Walt finally willing to join me?"

"Umm…I don't think so. But I will be sure and ask him when I get home, in case he has changed his mind."

Angela narrowed her eyes and glared at Danielle. "Remember, he is my husband. Walt is a married man."

"Yeah, I know that. But I'm not here because of Walt. I wanted to ask you a question."

Angela hopped back up on the headstone. Sitting primly, she looked down at Danielle. "Go ahead. I suppose answering questions is better than enduring this never-ending boredom."

"Do you remember a man named Sean Sullivan?"

Angela stared at Danielle with a blank expression. "Sean Sullivan?" She shook her head. "No."

"Are you sure? He was a childhood friend of Katherine O'Malley. He used to visit her when she worked at Marlow House."

Angela frowned and considered the name again. Finally, she broke into a smile. "Sullivan, yes! I remember him now. I asked Katherine once who he was; she said they grew up together. Then I asked if he was the father of her baby, and she seemed quite horrified at the question. I don't know why, she was the one with a child out of wedlock, not me."

"Did she tell you who Brianna's father was?"

Angela laughed. "No. Like I said, she seemed rather flustered at my question."

Danielle paused a moment and then considered something she hadn't thought about before. "How about when Katherine was here with you, after her death. Did she ever tell you who the father of her child was?"

"I never asked at that point. I really didn't care. And Katherine spent most of her time fretting over what had happened to Walt Marlow and worrying about her daughter."

"Do you have any idea what happened to Sean Sullivan?"

Angela didn't answer immediately. Instead she stared at Danielle. Finally, she asked, "You mean after I died? Because before that, he was living in Frederickport. I remember seeing him just before I took off for Portland."

"So all you know is that he was still living in Frederickport when you died." *That's basically what Walt knows*, Danielle thought.

A slow smile curled at Angela's lips. "I didn't say that."

"What do you know?"

"I know Sullivan and I had something in common. Neither one of us wanted Katherine to marry my brother. Of course, I wasn't alive to voice my objection. Sullivan, unfortunately, got in my brother's way and had to be dealt with."

"Are you saying your brother killed Sullivan?"

Angela shook her head. "He didn't need to resort to that. All he had to do was use his connections to get Sullivan out of his way—legally. For Sullivan's own good, in fact." Angela laughed.

"What do you mean his own good?"

"I think the place was called Marymoor Sanatorium. You might look there." Angela yawned. "I'm bored now. If you want more information, you really need to bring Walt with you the next time." Angela vanished.

Glancing around the now empty cemetery, Danielle shook her head and muttered, "Not like that is going to happen."

TWENTY-TWO

Lily was sitting in the kitchen, eating a tuna fish sandwich when Danielle returned home. Spread out on the table before her was that morning's edition of the *Frederickport Press*, turned to the page displaying the ad they had placed for the upcoming Fourth of July Barbeque Open House.

"I see our guests' cars are gone," Danielle said as she tossed her purse on the kitchen counter.

"They asked me about recommendations for a good lunch restaurant. So I assume that's where they went." Lily took a bite of her sandwich.

"Did they go together?" Danielle grabbed some bread to make herself lunch.

"I seriously doubt it. I don't think Nola and Jeannie have hit it off. Nola and Albert left about thirty minutes ago. Jeannie and Blake just took off."

"Where's Walt?" Danielle asked.

"I haven't seen him." Lily started to giggle at her own words and then took another bite of her sandwich.

Danielle shook her head and said dryly, "Funny."

Danielle had the answer to her question a few minutes later when she sat down at the table with Lily to eat the sandwich she had just made. Walt appeared, already sitting in one of the two empty chairs at the table.

"I was going to look for you after I finished this," Danielle told Walt.

Lily glanced to the seemingly empty chair where Danielle had directed her comment. "Hey, Walt." She continued to eat her sandwich.

"I'm glad you're both here. That way I can tell you both about my morning at the same time."

Danielle then went on to tell about her visit at the museum—most of which Lily already had heard—and then went on to tell about her trip to the cemetery.

"I have to say, Walt, that Eva cracks me up." Danielle giggled and took a bite of her sandwich.

"Even as a child, before she got into the theatre, she always had a flair." Walt smiled.

"It's a shame only people like me can see her," Danielle said after she swallowed her food.

"Why do you say that?" Lily asked.

"Think about it. She would have so much more fun if she had a broader audience for her paranormal theatrics. As it is, considering the energy she's using just to travel around and to pull off what she did today, no way could she take that act to the normal, non-ghost-seeing audience."

Lily nodded. "You have a point."

"So Angela said Sullivan went to Marymoor?" Walt asked.

"Marymoor Sanatorium. Any idea where that's at?"

"It's on the south side of town," Walt told her.

"No, it's not. At least not now. There's no Marymoor Sanatorium in Frederickport," Danielle told him.

Walt shrugged. "Well, it has been a long time. I suppose that shouldn't surprise me it's gone now. But I have to wonder why Sullivan was sent there."

"I remember my mother telling me how her grandfather was sent to a sanatorium because he had tuberculosis," Lily told them.

"It wasn't that kind of sanatorium," Walt said.

Danielle glanced from Walt to Lily. "Walt said it wasn't that kind of sanatorium."

Before Lily or Danielle could ask what kind of sanatorium it was, Walt said, "It was a mental institution."

"Mental institution?" Danielle said.

"It was a mental institution?" Lily repeated.

"Considering how Sullivan believed he could see leprechauns, I suppose I understand why he got committed," Walt said.

"Walt, why would they call it a sanatorium if it was a mental institution? I always think of a sanatorium as being a place where sane but sick people are sent."

"The man who donated the land was named Marymoor. He wanted to be recognized for his donation, but he didn't like the idea of his name being attached to the word *asylum*."

Danielle repeated Walt's explanation to Lily.

Lily washed the last of her sandwich down with a drink of milk and then said, "I can understand. If it was called Marymoor Insane Asylum or Marymoor Mental Institution, future Marymoor generations would probably be tainted with the false impression one of their ancestors was locked up in the place."

"So you think Sean was sent there because he told people he could see leprechauns?" Danielle asked.

"I don't think that in itself would get him committed to Marymoor. From what I recall, the people sent there were violent, which was one reason my grandfather was initially opposed to the idea of locating it in Frederickport."

"So why did they?" Danielle asked.

Walt shrugged. "I have no idea. I just remember Grandfather reversed his position, and it was built. Of course, this was when I was just a child, so frankly, I was never aware of the details, just the bits of conversations I overheard."

"So Angela still wants Walt to join her?" Lily asked.

"I think she's bored," Danielle told her.

"Did you tell her that even if I wanted to—which I never would —that it would be impossible?" Walt asked.

"Yes, I have. But she doesn't believe me. I would think she would realize if the powers-that-be are forcing her to be confined to the cemetery as her penance for her involvement in your murder, that the powers-that-be certainly aren't going to send her you as some playmate," Danielle said.

"And I certainly have done nothing to deserve that fate." Walt cringed.

"Walt didn't do anything wrong, why should he be punished?" Lily said at practically the same time as Walt made his comment.

Danielle laughed.

Both Lily and Walt looked at her.

"Why did you laugh?" they both asked.

Danielle laughed again.

TWENTY MINUTES later the doorbell rang. When Danielle went to answer it, she found Adam and Melony standing on her doorstep.

"Why, hi, you two. What brings you to Marlow House?" Danielle opened the door wider, welcoming them inside.

"Grandma wanted me to give you this," Adam said as he handed her a checkbook. Both he and Melony now stood in the entry hall.

Danielle took the checkbook as she closed the front door. She opened the checkbook, looked inside, and then frowned. "This is mine."

"It must have fallen out of your purse when you were at Grandma's. She found it on the floor in her kitchen."

"Thanks, Adam. I didn't even know it was missing. It must have fallen out when I put those letters she gave me in my purse." She smiled at the couple. "You two have lunch yet?"

"We had lunch with Marie," Melony explained.

"Did you have dessert?" Danielle asked.

"Dessert? What do you have in mind?" Adam asked with a grin.

"I have a homemade triple-layer chocolate cake in the kitchen, fudge filling with homemade chocolate butter-cream frosting. I also have some vanilla ice cream." Danielle licked her lips.

"Sold!" Melony said.

TEN MINUTES LATER, Melony and Adam sat with Lily and Danielle at the kitchen table, each eating a generous slice of chocolate cake, with a scoop of vanilla ice cream. Walt stood nearby, leaning against the counter, watching and listening. Out of courtesy for Danielle and her guests, he refrained from smoking.

"Hey, Adam, have you ever heard of Marymoor Sanatorium?" Danielle asked as she prepared to dig the side of her fork into her slice of cake.

"You mean the insane asylum?" Melony asked.

Danielle looked to Melony. "You've heard of it?"

"Well, sure," Adam said. "It burned down when we were kids."

"Was anyone killed?" Lily asked.

"No. The asylum closed down years ago, before we were born," Melony said.

"But it was still pretty damn creepy," Adam said. "Back then, it made Presley House look cheerful."

About to take a bite of cake, Melony paused and nodded. "That's for sure. As a kid you refused to ride your bike down that street."

"Shut up," Adam grumbled, taking another bite of cake.

Melony laughed.

"So what's there now," Lily asked.

"Empty piece of property," Adam said. "It's owned by the city. They've never done anything with it. Over the years there were talks about turning it into a park, but I don't see that happening."

"Why not?" Danielle asked.

Adam shrugged. "After it burned down, it took over a year to clean it up. It wasn't that the city didn't want to haul away the debris, but it seemed whenever a crew showed up to start hauling stuff off, someone would inevitably get hurt."

"Hurt? How?" Danielle asked.

"Bill's dad for one. He was working for the city back then, and he broke his leg over there," Adam said.

"And there was that guy who almost lost his finger. His daughter was in my class; I remember her talking about it. No one got killed, but there was an inordinate number of accidents on the job site and people started talking about the property being cursed," Melony explained. "I remember my mother talking about how stupid everyone was acting. That the accidents were nothing but gross incompetence of the workers the city hired."

Adam chortled. "I can see your mom saying that. I always figured after the first couple accidents, the workers started getting jittery and ended up getting hurt because they had psyched them-selves out, mostly because the place had been an insane asylum for years. Before it burned down, people loved to talk about how the place was probably haunted."

"Is that why they haven't done anything with the property? They think it's haunted?" Danielle asked.

"Interesting," Walt murmured. "Considering its past residents, those would be some evil ghosts."

138

Adam shrugged. "Not that exactly. No one has come up with a project for the land that anyone is committed to carrying out. I suppose part of it is the stigma attached to the property."

"I find it interesting they closed it down and didn't do anything with the property all those years before it burned down," Lily murmured.

"I'm curious, ask why they closed it down," Walt asked Danielle.

"Do you have any idea why they closed it down in the first place?" Danielle asked Adam and Melony.

"My mother said something about one of the nurses there being murdered by a patient. He escaped, but they caught him before anyone else was hurt. I guess the city was up in arms about it, so they forced them to close it down and move the patients to other facilities around the state. Of course, this was even before Mom was born, so I'm not sure how accurate the story is," Melony explained.

"Interesting. I might go down to the museum and see if I can find an article about the incident in one of the back issues of the paper," Danielle said.

"If you want to learn more about Marymoor, you might ask Ben if you can look through some of those boxes Bill took over there a couple years ago," Adam suggested.

"What boxes?" Danielle asked.

"After they closed the sanatorium, they moved some of the files over to the city building for storage. A couple years ago, when they were cleaning out the basement, they came across them and decided to shuffle them over to the museum. They hired Bill to take them over there. I don't think the historical society has done anything with them yet. From what I understand, they're still sitting in the back room at the museum," Adam explained.

"Hmm...maybe they'll have something on Sean Sullivan," Danielle murmured.

"Sean Sullivan? Who's that?" Adam asked.

"Just someone Brianna mentioned once," Danielle lied. "I think he might have been committed to Marymoor."

"Sean Sullivan?" Melony said with a frown.

"Have you heard of him?" Danielle asked.

"I haven't heard of him, exactly. But there's a section at the cemetery where they used to bury residents from Marymoor, those who didn't have family to claim the bodies. We used to go through there at Halloween." Melony looked at Adam. "Remember, Adam?"

"Yeah. We did some stupid things back then." Adam picked up his napkin and wiped his mouth.

"I used to read the headstones and make up stories about the people buried there," Melony told Danielle. "I'm certain one of them was named Sean Sullivan."

TWENTY-THREE

"So what's the deal with those two?" Lily asked Danielle. They sat on the front swing, watching Adam drive away, Melony sitting in his passenger seat.

"When they got here, Mel said they had lunch with Marie."

"Interesting," Lily murmured as she leaned back in the porch swing. "I wonder if Marie is busy making wedding plans."

Danielle chuckled. "Maybe. But I can't figure out if they're just old pals or something is going on."

"They seemed pretty close when she was here for her mother's funeral."

"True."

The two young women sat back in the porch swing, the toes of their shoes gently pushing against the ground to keep the swing in motion.

"Hey, you want to go to the museum with me?" Danielle asked.

"Weren't you already there once today? You want to go through the boxes Adam mentioned, don't you?"

"I'm curious to see if we can find anything on Sullivan."

"Adam didn't mention how many boxes there were, did he? I mean, sounds like that place was open for a long time. Might take hours to find something, if it's even possible."

"I'd assume all the files for patients that were transferred after it closed were sent along to whatever facilities they were sent to,"

Danielle told her. "And if Melony is right, Sean Sullivan wasn't transferred to another facility. He died here."

"True, Dani. But that could still be a lot of files."

"Maybe we'll get lucky and the boxes are dated. We can look for anything after the time Walt died."

"You're going to make me do this, aren't you?" Lily groaned.

"It will be faster if you go with me."

"Okay, but first call Ben. I don't want to drive all the way down there if he won't let us go through the boxes."

Instead of responding to Lily, Danielle sat up for a moment and pulled her cellphone from her pocket. Sitting back on the swing, she dialed Ben's phone number.

"He said we can," Danielle told Lily when she got off the phone with Ben a few minutes later. "And we're in luck, the boxes have dates on them."

"Oh goody," Lily said dryly as she stood up from the swing.

UP AHEAD, Danielle's red Ford Flex was backing out of the driveway. It stopped, allowing Blake to pull his car in front of Marlow House and park. Just as he and Jeannie were getting out of the car, Danielle pulled up beside him and stopped. Lily was sitting in the passenger seat. They rolled their windows down.

"Where are you two off to?" Blake asked cheerfully, walking to her car.

"We're heading downtown to do some errands. Probably won't be back for a couple of hours. There's half a chocolate cake in the kitchen, help yourself," Danielle told him.

"Sounds delicious." Blake grinned.

"Did you have a nice lunch?" Lily asked.

"Burgers at the pier. It was pretty good," Blake told her.

A few minutes later, Danielle drove off and Blake joined Jeannie on the sidewalk leading up to Marlow House.

"This is our chance, baby," Blake said excitedly.

"You mean we're finally alone?" Jeannie asked with a grin.

"According to Danielle, they'll be gone for a couple of hours. And you don't see Albert and Nola's car, do you?"

"Then let's do it!"

Together they hurried toward the front door.

"While I'm getting the necklace, gather up our stuff and start wiping down the room. I don't want to leave any fingerprints behind. And make sure you wipe down the banister and all the doorknobs. And the toilet, don't forget the handle on the toilet!"

"Okay, okay," Jeannie said as she used the key Danielle had given her to unlock the front door.

WALT HAD JUST STEPPED onto the first-floor landing when he heard the door open. He was halfway down the hall when Blake and Jeannie ran through him. Pausing a moment, Walt looked down at his violated body and let out a grunt. He turned and watched the pair head up the staircase.

"What are you two up to?"

The next moment, he was at the top of the staircase, watching the couple hurrying in his direction. To avoid another run-through, Walt stepped aside and watched as the pair dashed to their bedroom.

"Well, if that's what this is all about, I'm certainly not going to stick around." In the next moment, Walt was sitting in the living room, the door open, reading the newspaper.

IN THE BEDROOM, Jeannie quickly tossed all their belongings into their suitcase and then grabbed a pillow off the bed. With several shakes, she removed the pillow from its case and began using the case as a dusting rag. In the meantime, Blake organized his tools.

"One's missing," he told her.

Jeannie paused for a moment and looked at Blake. "What do you mean?"

"The one I used to get in Danielle's bedroom earlier. It's not here."

"Where did you put it?" she asked.

"I thought I put it back with the rest of them."

"Obviously you didn't. It has to be here somewhere," she said impatiently, once again wiping down the room.

"I'll look for it. Maybe it fell under the bed or behind the dresser. You might as well go downstairs and start wiping down anything we might have touched down there. I'll finish this up after I get the necklace."

———————

WALT LOOKED up from the newspaper. Someone was coming down the stairs.

"Well, that was quick." He tossed the paper on the coffee table and stood up.

When he walked down the hallway a few minutes later, heading for the library, he was surprised to find Jeannie coming down the staircase, polishing its handrail.

"Cleaning?" Walt said with a frown.

He took a closer look. In her hand was what appeared to be a pillowcase, and she was using it to energetically wipe down the handrail.

Walt shook his head and muttered, "It takes all kinds."

Instead of going to the library, Walt decided to head to the attic. On his way up the stairs he passed Jeannie, who continued to wipe the handrail as she made her way to the first floor.

Stepping onto the second-floor landing, he watched as Blake stepped out of his bedroom, a small tool in his hand.

"Your wife is cleaning. What are you going to do, go around the house and tighten the screws?" Walt asked with a chuckle. He was about to turn toward the attic stairs when Blake stopped at Danielle's door. Kneeling, Blake inserted the tool into her lock.

"What the...?" Walt scowled.

The next moment, Walt was standing inside Danielle's room, holding onto her doorknob, making it impossible for Blake to unlock the door. Behind him he heard a meow. Still holding the doorknob, he turned to face the bed. Max sat on it, his tail swishing, as he watched Walt.

"What are you doing in here, Max?" Walt continued to hold the doorknob.

Max meowed.

"I don't know how you keep slipping in here. Do you think it's smart to allow yourself to get locked in Danielle's room?"

Max meowed again and stretched. Still watching Walt, he rolled over onto his back, pawing the air between him and Walt. Max rolled over again and then sat up. He shook his head and sneezed.

From the other side of the door, Walt heard Blake curse. He faced the closed door. "Not sure what this guy is up to, Max, but he and his wife are a little peculiar." Walt continued to secure the door. "Honestly, Max, Danielle would never survive running this bed and breakfast without me. Who would keep the nosey guests from breaking into her room and snooping around?"

"AREN'T YOU DONE YET?" Jeannie asked when she returned upstairs, wrinkled pillowslip in hand.

Blake, still kneeling before Danielle's bedroom door, looked up to Jeannie. "I can't get the damn door open."

"What?" she said incredulously. "How in the hell do you expect to get the safe open if you can't even open the bedroom door. Even I can do that!"

"Oh yeah?" Blake said angrily. He stood abruptly and shoved the tool into her hand. "You try it."

Taking the small tool, Jeannie narrowed her eyes and glared at Blake. Shoving the pillowcase in his now free hand, she marched to Danielle's door and pressed the thin tool into the lock.

Blake quietly watched as she fiddled with the lock. After a few moments, she paused and looked over her shoulder at him.

"Not so easy, is it?" he sneered.

"What is wrong with it?" she asked.

"I told you."

Jeannie asked Blake a question, but he didn't answer. Instead, he jerked his head to the right and listened.

"Damn, someone is here." Blake rushed to the staircase and looked downstairs. Coming down the hall was Nola and Albert.

Stumbling to her feet, Jeannie hurried to Blake's side and looked down to the first floor.

"Damn, now what?" Jeannie said under her breath.

"Now we have to wait."

"Then don't touch anything," Jeannie snapped.

Blake frowned. "What do you mean?"

"I'm not wiping down this damn house again!" Snatching the pillowcase from Blake's hand, Jeannie turned abruptly and headed for their bedroom door. Just as she reached it, she turned and marched back to Blake and roughly shoved the tool into his hand.

"Ouch!" Blake yelped, looking down at his right palm, now red from where Jeannie had just jabbed him. Unconcerned with his minor injury, Jeannie turned again toward their bedroom and marched inside, slamming the door behind her.

"Hello!" Nola greeted him a moment later, halfway up the staircase, Albert trailing beside her, out of breath.

Slipping the tool in his pocket, Blake forced a smile. "Afternoon, did you do anything fun?"

"We drove around. Took a walk on the beach," Nola told him. "Stopped and had something to eat at a nice little diner in town."

"Time for my nap," Albert said with a yawn.

"You can nap. I'm going to grab my book and take it downstairs," Nola said brightly. "Danielle's not here?"

"No. She and Lily went out. She said they would be gone for a couple of hours, and that was about thirty minutes ago."

Nola flashed Blake a smile and continued to her bedroom.

Blake turned and tripped over a black cat. The cat hissed and then strolled by Blake, making his way to the first floor.

Regaining his balance, Blake frowned and looked behind him again. Both Lily's and Danielle's bedroom doors were shut. "Where the hell did that cat come from?" he muttered.

TWENTY-FOUR

While Walt was busy keeping Blake from breaking in to Danielle's bedroom, Danielle had taken a detour on the way to the museum. She drove Lily to the one place she would rather avoid—the Frederickport Cemetery.

"I still don't understand why we're stopping here," Lily said. "Don't you believe Melony saw a marker with Sullivan's name on it?"

Danielle got out of the car and slammed the door shut. She waited for Lily to get out of the car before she answered her question.

"It's not that I don't believe her, but maybe it was someone with a similar name—or maybe it was another Sean Sullivan."

"Are you saying Marymoor had more than one Sean Sullivan as a patient?"

"It's possible." Danielle started for the sidewalk while Lily trailed along beside her.

"And how would we know Melony's Sullivan is the one you're looking for?"

"I suppose there's no absolute way, but I'd think the dates on the headstone would be a clue. We know he died after Walt did, and we have a general idea of when he was born."

Pausing on the sidewalk, Lily asked, "Just where is the Marymoor section?"

"I'm not sure." Danielle frowned and glanced around.

"Maybe you can ask one of your spooks for directions," Lily suggested.

"Or maybe I'll ask him," Danielle said, pointing to a groundskeeper off in the distance.

With a reluctant sigh, Lily followed Danielle toward the man.

"Hello!" Danielle called out when she got within earshot of the groundskeeper.

Glancing up from the leaves he was sweeping, the man paused and smiled. "How can I help you?"

"I'm looking for the Marymoor Sanatorium section of the cemetery," Danielle explained when she reached him.

Cocking his head, he looked at her quizzically. "The Marymoor section? No one ever visits there."

"Can you tell us where it is?" Lily asked.

"Sure." Rake in hand, he turned and pointed down the walkway. "You're going to go down that way until you reach the Marlow crypt. Then turn right, and keep on going. You'll see the sign. It's marked and surrounded by its own iron gate. The gate isn't locked. You can go on in."

"Thanks," Danielle said cheerfully. After she and Lily were about ten feet from the man, Danielle said, "I know the Marlow crypt is located in one of the oldest sections of the cemetery, so it makes sense the Marymoor section would be in that area."

"Are we going to run into Angela?" Lily asked.

"Lucky for you, you won't," Danielle said with a snort. "But I doubt even I will. She wasn't buried in the Marlow crypt, and if we keep on this trail, we won't go by her headstone. That's where she seems to hang out."

They continued to walk, the caretaker no longer in sight. June's afternoon sun shone brightly and only a smattering of white clouds dotted the sky. Glancing around, Lily couldn't see any other visitors to the cemetery.

"Is anyone here?" Lily asked in a hushed voice.

"I don't see anyone, do you?"

"No. I mean…spirits. Any ghosts hanging around?"

Danielle glanced around and then shook her head. "No. I don't see any."

When they finally reached their destination, they found the iron gate leading to the Marymoor section hanging cockeyed, one hinge missing. Danielle lifted the gate and pushed it open. She and Lily entered.

In less than five minutes, they found Sean Sullivan's headstone. Lily was the one to find it. According to the dates on the headstone, he was born several years before Katherine O'Malley and died twelve years after Walt was murdered.

"Wow, he was pretty young when he died," Lily muttered. "He wasn't much older than we are."

"To be honest, I was sort of wondering if his spirit would be hanging out here."

"Really?"

Danielle shrugged. "If it was, I could simply ask him who Brianna's father was."

"Ahh, so that's why you really wanted to stop by here first."

Danielle smiled. "I figured it would be quicker than sorting through musty old files. I know you don't really want to do that."

"If he's not here…" Lily glanced around the quiet cemetery. "If none of them are here, does that mean they've moved on?"

"Not necessarily. Marymoor residents were…well…mentally unstable. It's my personal belief—although I have no real facts to back it up—that someone who has mental issues in life has a more difficult time moving to the next level. I'm not saying they can't, but it's harder to focus on the light."

"So there really is a light?"

Daniella shrugged.

"So tell me, if that's true, where are they all?" Lily swept her hand from right to left, broadly motioning to the headstones.

"For one thing, a confused spirit—like one from a mentally ill patient—may never make it beyond the site of their death. I expect those who haven't moved on to be lingering closer to where they actually died—like at the site of the sanatorium or at a hospital. Plus, those scary old movies aren't totally off the mark."

Lily frowned "What do you mean?"

"Some spirits prefer to come out after the sun goes down. So it's entirely possible, if we visited this section this evening, there very well could be paranormal activity."

WHEN DANIELLE and Lily finally arrived at the museum, Ben

showed them to the back storage room. There were too many boxes to haul to the office, so he explained they would have to go through them in the room where they were being kept. Fortunately, there was plenty of light and chairs for them to sit down on.

"He's right, the boxes are dated," Danielle told Lily after Ben left them alone.

"Looks like about twenty…maybe thirty boxes?" Lily noted.

Hands on hips, Danielle surveyed the stack of cardboard boxes shoved against the back wall of the storage room. The room itself was filled with random boxes, some open with their contents spilling out, and tables piled with objects and memorabilia donated by locals, some of which would never be used in future exhibits.

Before they had arrived, Ben had cleared off one of the tables located near the boxes from Marymoor, making a place for Danielle and Lily to sort through the files. Instead of opening any of them, Danielle began moving aside those with dates preceding Walt's death and those dated five years after Sean Sullivan's. When Lily realized what Danielle was doing, she pitched in to speed up the task. When they were done, there were just three boxes to sort through.

Sitting down at the table, Danielle and Lily each took a box and began looking through it. They weren't at the task more than five minutes when Danielle pulled out a file and said, "Bingo. I found something on Sullivan!"

Abandoning her box, Lily shoved it aside and anxiously waited for Danielle to open the file.

"Yes, this is Sean Sullivan's," Danielle muttered as she flipped through the file. Lily silently watched as Danielle read through the pages.

"Here's something on Sullivan's admission to Marymoor," Danielle said. "He was committed just a few weeks before Katherine married Angela's brother."

Lily leaned forward, her arms resting on the table as she watched Danielle read through the papers. "Does it say why he was committed?"

"This is interesting," Danielle muttered. "It seems Sullivan was arrested, and the arresting officer recommended commitment, claiming Sullivan was a danger to himself and the public. Guess who the arresting officer was?"

"Who?"

"Hal Tucker," Danielle said.

Lily frowned. "Why is that name familiar?"

Danielle set the open file down on the tabletop and looked at Lily. "Remember, Hal Tucker was a fishing buddy of Angela's brother, Roger. He's the one who harassed Emma Jackson so she would change her story about seeing Roger coming from Frederick-port after Walt was murdered."

"Wasn't that the one who had a thing for Angela?"

Danielle picked up the file again and looked at it. "That's what Emma seemed to think. But one thing we do know about him, he was willing to help Roger get control of Walt's estate. First covering for him and now, apparently, getting Sullivan out of the way."

"Is that what you think happened, I mean with Sullivan?" Lily asked.

"I'm starting to. Maybe Sullivan knew what Roger was up to and tried to get his friend to see she was being seduced by a con man. Maybe Roger had his old buddy get Sullivan out of the way in the same way he helped with Emma."

"Fortunately, he didn't commit Emma."

"True. But he threatened to have her deported from Oregon, and considering the times, he had all the power."

"I'm assuming he died at Marymoor, since he's buried in their section," Lily suggested.

Danielle quickly flipped through the pages in the file until she found what she was looking for. "Looks like that poor guy spent the rest of his life there, twelve years. According to this, he died of influenza."

"Why did they keep him so long? I would think eventually he'd be released. Walt never said he was violent, did he?" Lily asked.

"No. I'm looking for any doctor's notes. Hold on…" Sorting through the file, Danielle found what she was looking for. Removing the pages, she set the file back down on the table and leaned back in the chair as she proceeded to read.

After a few minutes, Danielle murmured, "This is interesting."

"What?" Lily asked anxiously.

"The doctor's notes. Apparently Sullivan talked a great deal about this leprechaun he reportedly saw."

"Just like Walt said."

"Not just any leprechaun. One named Paddy Fitzpatrick. Apparently, Paddy loved to torment poor Sean. At least, that's what

Sullivan conveyed to the doctor. But what is particularly interesting…" Danielle paused and looked up from the papers to Lily. "Sullivan described his leprechaun to the doctor—who then included that description in his notes."

"And?"

"Green derby hat, red jacket…leather apron."

"Are you saying the leprechaun, or whatever he is, that has been hanging around Marlow House is this Paddy Fitzpatrick?" Lily asked.

"That would be my guess."

"Don't tell me there really are leprechauns!"

Danielle shook her head and set the doctor's notes down on the file. "The notes also reference other sightings Sullivan claimed to have seen."

"Like what?"

"He claimed his grandmother visited him when he was a child —after she died. And that after one of the Marymoor residents was killed in an accident, Sullivan claimed to have seen him wandering the grounds."

"What are you saying?" Lily asked.

"I suspect Sean Sullivan had something in common with me and Chris and Heather…and Evan."

"He could see spirits?"

"Sounds like it."

"Danielle, just because you aren't crazy and can see spirits, it doesn't mean this Sean Sullivan wasn't nuts, nor does it mean he could see spirits any more than I can. What makes you so sure he wasn't simply a nutcase. Maybe he did belong at Marymoor."

"For one thing, both Sean Sullivan and I have seen the same spirit. Our friend who likes to masquerade as a leprechaun."

"Are you convinced he wasn't a leprechaun?"

Danielle frowned. "Seriously? Leprechauns? You aren't really suggesting they exist."

Lily sighed. "I suppose not."

Danielle tossed the doctor's notes back in the file. "Well, I did learn one thing today."

"What's that?"

"I won't be able to find out who Brianna's father was. At least, not from Sullivan."

"Why do you say that?"

"He obviously never got married. Never had children. Being locked up at Marymoor, he might never have known what happened to Katherine, so no one to share the sensational tale with. I'll read through the rest of the file, see if he ever mentioned Katherine, but I seriously doubt it. My guess, whatever he knew about Brianna's father probably died with him."

"What about his spirit?" Lily suggested.

"We didn't see him at the cemetery. According to the notes on his death, he died at the sanatorium. So, if his spirit didn't move on, I suppose it would most likely be at the sanatorium site."

"Then what are we waiting for?" Lily asked brightly. "Finish reading through the file, and then let's head over to check out what's left of Marymoor."

TWENTY-FIVE

"I don't think I've ever been down this road before," Lily said as Danielle turned on the street leading to where Marymoor Sanatorium once stood.

"Same here." Hands firmly on the steering wheel, Danielle continue to drive down the quiet residential street.

Located on the edge of town, Danielle suspected the area had not been developed back when the buildings of Marymoor stood, considering the age of the houses lining both sides of the street. She guessed they had all been built within her lifetime.

The Marymoor site was located on the end of the road, sectioned off by chain-link fence sporting a large *No Trespassing* sign. Danielle pulled up along the piece of property and parked her car. Together she and Lily sat in the vehicle and silently studied the site.

"It looks like a big piece of property," Lily noted. "No wonder there was talk of turning it into a park."

"I don't know what the zoning is, but it would be a good site for a condominium complex," Danielle said.

Lily turned to look at the nearby houses. "I imagine the home-owners on this street wouldn't appreciate that."

"Probably not. But it's large enough to cut out at least six home sites, maybe more."

"Did Adam say the city owned the property?"

"I think so. You want to get out and have a closer look?" Danielle asked.

Leaning forward in her seat, Lily surveyed the fenced area. "Do you see anything?"

"Do you mean like ghosts?"

"Umm, yeah…"

Danielle smiled. "No. I don't see any ghosts."

Danielle pulled her keys from the ignition and opened her car door while Lily exited her side of the vehicle. Together the two women approached the locked gate.

There was no sign of the buildings that had once stood on the property. Danielle knew they were originally destroyed by a fire approximately twenty-five years earlier, and since that time the property had been cleared of any debris, replaced by weeds and wildflowers.

It wasn't until Danielle was about two feet from the fence that she felt it—a tingling of apprehension moving down her spine. She stopped abruptly.

Noticing Danielle's hesitation, Lily paused and looked at her friend. "What is it? Do you see something?"

"No…" Danielle said with unease, her eyes fixed on what lay beyond the chain-link fence. "But I feel something."

"What?" Lily asked anxiously.

It was then Danielle saw it. A woman dressed in a nurse's uniform stood just inside the gate, her image transparent yet gradually darkening and coming into full view.

"It's a nurse," Danielle whispered, taking a step toward the fence. She and the ghost locked gazes.

"You can see me," the nurse said, taking a step toward Danielle.

"What's your name?"

"Molly. What's yours?"

"I'm Danielle, Molly. You used to work at Marymoor, didn't you?" Danielle asked.

Molly smiled and cocked her head slightly, studying Danielle through the fence. "I'm not alone," she told her. "They are hiding now. But they will come out tonight."

"The other spirits?" Danielle asked.

Again the woman smiled, taking a step closer. She grabbed hold of the fence, her fingers wrapping around the chain link as she stared at Danielle. Nearby Lily stood speechless, her eyes focused on Danielle, wondering what she was seeing—who she was talking to.

"Are there many?" Danielle asked.

"I take care of them. That's why I've stayed. They need someone to take care of them."

Danielle's gaze shifted to Molly's right shoulder. Blood soaked her white uniform, as if she had been stabbed. Danielle wondered if this was the nurse Melony had told her about, the one who had been killed by a patient, the reason Marymoor had been closed.

"Do you know who Sean Sullivan is?" Danielle asked.

Molly cocked her head in the other direction, her mouth firmly closed but still smiling. After a moment she spoke. "Sean doesn't like it here. He moved on."

"Then you knew him?"

"He could see people like us, you know. I never believed him. But now I know."

"Do you remember him talking about a leprechaun?" Danielle asked.

Molly's smile broadened, now showing her teeth, stained and crooked, with a wide gap between her two front bottom teeth. "Sean always talked about his leprechaun. Paddy Fitzpatrick. A troublesome character, that one."

"Are you saying you met Paddy Fitzpatrick?"

Molly shrugged. "I suppose we all did after we moved on."

"You mean when you died?" Danielle asked.

Molly frowned and took an abrupt step back away from the fence. "What do you mean?" she asked angrily, no longer smiling. "I'm not dead! How dare you say that!"

Abrupt wind replaced the calm, sending dust in all directions, and when it stopped, Molly was no longer there.

"What happened?" Lily asked, looking around curiously.

"I think it was the nurse who was murdered. At first, I thought she understood she was dead, but I don't think so…I mean, she's still confused."

"Are you going to help her so she can move on?" Lily asked.

A chill moved up Danielle's spine. Wrapping her arms protectively around her body, she shook her head and stepped away from the fence. "I think we should go. Something about this place… really…we need to go."

"That freaked me out," Lily said after she was back in the car and putting her seatbelt on.

Danielle turned on the ignition. "I don't like the energy here." She pulled her car back into the street and started for home.

"Did you learn anything?" Lily asked.

"Sounds like Sullivan wasn't the only one to see Paddy Fitzpatrick. But from what Molly said, my guess, she and the others saw him after they died."

"Molly?" Lily frowned.

Danielle then began to recount her exchange with Molly's spirit. Engrossed with the retelling, she failed to see the man step in front of her car until it was too late. She slammed on the brakes and screamed. He was no longer standing in front of her vehicle, but in the middle of her car's hood.

"What the…?" Lily could feel her heart race as she held onto the handle of the car door. "Why did you stop?"

Staring at the man looking at her through the windshield—a man wearing a green derby hat, red jacket, leather apron—Danielle stammered, "Uhh…I guess you don't see him."

"Who? What do you see?" Lily asked, her heartbeat still racing.

"I suspect we were right, our leprechaun is probably a ghost, since I see him and you don't." Danielle's gaze remained fixed on the apparition.

"You see him?" Lily looked out the windshield and noticed nothing out of the ordinary.

"Ohhhh…yeah…" Danielle swallowed nervously and took a breath. "I really hate when they do that." She turned off her ignition.

"Do what? And why are you stopping the car in the middle of the street?" Lily glanced behind her. They were still on a residential street, and no cars were in sight.

Slowly, Danielle opened her car door and stepped out of the vehicle.

"Have you been following me?" the leprechaun asked angrily. "I saw you talking to Molly. Are you looking for me?"

"Molly? So you know her?" Danielle asked, now standing by her car, her car door wide open.

"What's it to you? If you think you're going to catch me and demand three wishes, you'll see I'm much faster than you!"

"Are you a leprechaun?" Danielle asked.

"Do I look like a leprechaun?"

Danielle looked him up and down. He remained standing in the center of her car's hood. "Hard to tell with you standing in the middle of my car. Move over there." She pointed to the street in front of her.

"Is this some trick?" he asked suspiciously.

Danielle shrugged. "You say you're quicker than me, so why not let me have a better look? This car door is between us. If I start to chase you, you'll get away before I can get around it."

He considered her suggestion and smiled. "True." He stepped into the street, giving her a full view of his unusual clothing.

After looking him up and down for a few minutes, she shook her head. "Nope. You are definitely not a leprechaun."

He frowned. "What are you talking about?"

"For one thing, you're taller than me. I know I'm not exactly tall, but I sure as heck am taller than a leprechaun. Nope. You're just some guy dressed up like one."

He shook his head. "You have no idea what you're talking about."

"You don't even have much of an Irish accent. Just a hint. No. You're no leprechaun."

He studied her through narrowed eyes. "If I wasn't a leprechaun, I wouldn't have my gold back."

"What gold?" Danielle asked.

"The gold you tried to steal."

"Are you saying you took the gold coins out of the bank?"

He laughed. "You can't trick me. I know all the tricks."

"What are you doing here? What do you want?" Danielle asked.

"I told you. I came to get my gold back. The gold you stole."

"If you're talking about the gold coins I put in the bank—if that's the gold you took—it wasn't your gold. It belonged to Walt Marlow and Jack Winters."

He frowned. "Walt Marlow?"

"Yes. That gold belonged to him. Did you have something to do with taking the gold coins out of the bank? Was it you who left the shamrock?" She studied him. "It was, wasn't it?"

He smiled. "It's my gold now."

"Are you Paddy Fitzpatrick?"

All traces of his smile vanished. "What did you just say?"

"Are you Paddy Fitzpatrick? You are, aren't you? You were

haunting Sean Sullivan, making everyone think he was crazy, but it was you, wasn't it?"

Visibly angry, he seemed incapable of uttering a word. He opened his mouth to speak, but no sound came out. His breathing became labored, his complexion a deeper red, and when he opened his mouth again as if to speak, he instead vanished, leaving Danielle standing alone on the street.

"Danielle, Danielle!" Lily called out.

Shaking her head to clear out the cobwebs, Danielle glanced to Lily, who was now pointing up the street. There, facing her, was a police car attempting to drive down the same street her vehicle was currently blocking.

To her relief, the officer who stepped out of the now parked police car was Chief MacDonald.

"Danielle?" he called out, walking toward her. "Are you okay?"

Danielle let out a breath she didn't know she had been holding. "Oh, Chief, it's you!"

"Are you okay? Are you having car trouble?" he asked when he reached her.

"No…more like ghost trouble."

"Ghost?" He glanced down the street. "Were you down at the Marymoor site?"

Danielle nodded.

"So is it true, is that place haunted?"

"Well, it has at least one Marymoor ghost, yet I suspect there may be more. But that's not why I'm standing in the middle of the street."

"Why are you standing in the middle of the street?"

"I think I just met the party responsible for removing the gold coins from the bank."

"Please tell me. That entire case has become a major pain."

"I'm not sure what I'm about to tell you will help you much."

"It's a ghost? Right?" the chief asked.

"His name is Paddy Fitzpatrick, and for some reason he believes he's a leprechaun. And, well, you know…leprechauns have this thing for gold."

TWENTY-SIX

B efore Danielle could tell the chief what she knew about Paddy Fitzpatrick, another car drove down the street, stopping behind the police car. MacDonald quickly returned to his vehicle, and Danielle returned to hers. After they each drove their respective car to the side of the road, they parked again.

"This is better," the chief said when Danielle and Lily met him by the front of his car, each standing on the sidewalk. "So tell me about this Paddy Fitzpatrick."

Danielle didn't have much to tell, but she told him all that she knew.

"Did he say anything about a bracelet?" the chief questioned.

"Bracelet?" Danielle asked.

"Another safe deposit holder claimed something was missing from his box. This time, an expensive heirloom bracelet."

"Ian told me about that," Lily said. "He ran into the guy at the barber shop. I guess he was pretty upset. Claimed he planned to sue the bank."

"I suspect it's all over town by now," he said with a weary sigh. "I'm not sure what I'm supposed to do with the information on Fitzpatrick. I can't very well tell Wilson and Thomas about him. And what is he exactly? A ghost? An oversized leprechaun?"

"My guess, a ghost," Danielle said. "But you're right. This information just makes solving the robbery more frustrating."

"Fitzpatrick, you say?" the chief asked.

"Yes, Paddy Fitzpatrick," Danielle said.

"Agatha Pine was a Fitzpatrick, if I'm not mistaken," the chief said.

"Who's Agatha Pine?" Lily asked.

"She's Joyce Pruitt's mother," the chief explained. "Some people call her Gran."

"Ahh, the one who comes across as if she's some sort of duchess?" Danielle asked with a chuckle.

MacDonald smiled. "That's the one. Joyce moved to Frederickport after her divorce, with her mother and four kids. I remember Agatha telling me once she was originally from Frederickport, but moved from town after she was married. I asked her if she still had family here, and she said they were all gone. Never asked if that meant they had all died or moved."

"You think this ghost could be related to Agatha Pine?" Lily asked.

The chief shrugged. "It's possible, I suppose. Same name. I wonder why he's sticking around Frederickport." He looked at Danielle. "You've never seen him before?"

"Like I told you, Heather was one of the first to see him. But a week ago, I didn't even know the guy existed."

"If he is responsible for tampering with the safe deposit boxes, I'd like to recover the gold and bracelet and send him on his way," the chief said.

"Well, first, we need to figure out why he's hanging around," Danielle said. "Unless we figure that out, it's practically impossible to get him to move on, much less tell us what he did with the items he took."

"I'm more interested in why he's dressed up like a leprechaun," Lily said.

WHEN DANIELLE and Lily returned to Marlow House, they found Nola in the library, reading a book. Stretched out on the sofa, her stockinged feet crossed at the ankle on the couch cushion, she looked up from the book.

"Albert is taking a nap," Nola told them. "And the Spicers left about twenty minutes ago. They said something about doing a little antiquing. I told them about a cute little antique shop Albert and I found downtown."

"I don't know about antiquing," Walt said when he appeared in the library the next moment. "But the Spicers are a little odd. I think the word you use today is kinky."

Danielle arched her brows at Walt, yet said nothing.

Fifteen minutes later Danielle and Lily excused themselves from Nola. Lily went across the street to see Ian, while Danielle went into the parlor with Walt.

"Do you know what *kinky* means?" Danielle asked Walt as she closed the parlor door.

"I do read, Danielle." He sounded offended.

"I mean how we use the term today. I believe it was used differently back in your day. I just want to make sure we're talking about the same thing."

"I'm not talking about the tightness of Mr. or Mrs. Spicer's hair, if that's what you're asking." Walt took a puff off his cigar and then released several smoke rings. He watched as they drifted to the ceiling and then disappeared.

"You said you read about the word? You understand today's meaning?"

Walt rolled his eyes. "Yes."

"Just what have you been reading?" she asked with a laugh.

Walt looked at her and wiggled his eyebrows. Smiling, he said, "Wouldn't you like to know?"

"I have one question." Danielle took a seat on the sofa.

"What's that?"

"Actually, I have two," she clarified.

"Ask away." Walt took a puff off the cigar and then blew another smoke ring.

"Were you able to wiggle your eyebrows like that when you were alive?"

Walt shrugged. "I honestly don't know. Can't recall looking in the mirror when I ever did it. And now…well, as you know, my looking-in-mirror days are over." He flicked an ash off his cigar. It fell to the floor and disappeared. "What was your other question?"

"Why did you call the Spicers kinky? You haven't gone into their room…have you?"

"Please, Danielle, that question is insulting."

"Sorry," Danielle said sheepishly.

"When they arrived home after you left and realized they were alone in the house, they ran up the stairs like two naughty teenagers and locked themselves in their bedroom."

"Well…that is actually kind of sweet. What's wrong with a married couple getting a little romantic…and feisty?"

"Feisty maybe, but I don't think Mr. Spicer has much endurance. Not considering the short time they spent in their room."

"I still don't understand why you called them kinky."

"For one thing, after their brief interlude—and I mean brief—Mrs. Spicer decided to run around cleaning your woodwork. I would expect enjoying a cigarette would be a more normal response."

"Brother," Danielle said under her breath. She decided not to mention that she would never have a cigarette—not even after. Yet she preferred to avoid turning their conversation in *that* direction.

"And then Mr. Spicer tried to break in to your room. I imagine to poke through your lingerie drawer."

"I don't have a lingerie drawer…wait, you said he tried to break in to my room?"

"Isn't that what I just said?"

"Why would he try to break in to my room?" Danielle frowned.

"Didn't I just tell you? To poke through your—"

"I don't have a lingerie drawer!"

"Well, he doesn't know that. I told you the man is kinky."

"Walt, please stop saying the word *kinky*. It sounds weird coming out of your mouth. And I seriously doubt that's what he intended to do."

"You're too naïve, Danielle. I really do shudder to think about you and Lily here alone while strange men wander around the halls at night while you're alone in your rooms."

"That's why I have you, Walt." She smiled sweetly.

He let out a sigh and sat down on the chair facing her. "So if it wasn't for prurient reasons, then why was he trying to get in your room?"

Danielle considered the question a moment. "I do have the Missing Thorndike locked in the wall safe. Maybe we have a jewel thief under our roof?"

"Is he aware you have a safe? Have you mentioned where it's

located? Has he or his wife ever gone into your bedroom? Do they even know you have the necklace here?"

"Umm…I think I can safely answer no to all those questions. Yet I suppose it is possible for them to assume I might have the necklace here, considering all that's gone on."

"Another thing, while we're on the subject of your locked bedroom. You might want to check under your bed before you lock your door."

"Why? Will I find a bogeyman under my bed?" Danielle giggled.

"No. But you might find Max there. He was locked in your room again today. I let him out."

"Oh, that stinker. Thanks. Okay, I'll try to remember to check from now on. As for Mr. Spicer, can you just keep an eye on him for me? They're leaving Sunday."

"Certainly." Walt flicked aside his cigar butt; it vanished in the air.

"Hey, Walt, remember our leprechaun?"

"Yes, what about him?"

"Well, I saw him again today." Danielle then went on to tell Walt about her outing with Lily.

"Fitzpatrick?" Walt murmured after Danielle finished recounting the day's events. "No. I don't recall a Paddy Fitzpatrick. Although, I do recall a widow who lived in Frederickport with her son—her last name was Fitzpatrick. She took in laundry. I don't remember the son's name. But I don't think it was Paddy."

"No, the son would be too young. If the spirit who I saw today was Paddy Fitzpatrick, I suspect he was about your age when he died. And if he was haunting Sean Sullivan, then he would have died at least before the time Sean started talking about him."

"I have no idea how long Sean had been seeing his leprechaun."

"If my suspicions are right, this leprechaun wannabee has taken off with your gold."

"Your gold," Walt corrected.

"It appears he grabbed someone's bracelet too. I'd like to figure out where he's hidden it, and then see if I can help him move on."

"How do you intend to do that?"

Danielle stood up and removed her phone from her pocket. "Well, according to the chief, Agatha Pine's maiden name was Fitzpatrick." She sat back down on the sofa and began looking through her list of contacts.

"Agatha Pine?"

"You probably don't remember her. The only time she has ever been here was during our open house last year. She came with her daughter, Joyce, and her four grandchildren. They spent a good deal of their time outside, if I remember correctly."

Walt shook his head. "The name is not familiar. But there were a lot of people here that day."

"Ahh, here it is. I have Joyce's phone number." Danielle looked up at Walt and smiled.

"Just what do you have in mind?"

"The next time I encounter Fitzpatrick—and I'm fairly certain that's who I'm dealing with—I'd like to know more about him. That way, maybe I can convince him to return the items he took, and perhaps convince him he would be better off if he moved on."

"So you're thinking this Agatha Pine has a leprechaun in her family tree?" Walt teased.

"Ha-ha." Danielle looked back at her cellphone and proceeded to place a call to Joyce Pruitt.

TWENTY-SEVEN

Danielle decided this had to be her most hectic day in recent memory. Once again, she was backing her red Ford Flex out of the driveway. This time she was en route to Joyce Pruitt's house to talk to Joyce's mother, Agatha Pine. Danielle had decided to either wait until tomorrow to talk to Agatha, or call before it got too late in the afternoon. She didn't want to intrude on their dinner hour. As it turned out, she was able to get ahold of Joyce and arrange a meeting today.

On her drive over, she had Lily on speakerphone, who had stayed behind at Ian's house.

Her eyes on the road ahead, and her hands firmly on the steering wheel, Danielle said, "I have to say, Joyce acted a little strange when I called."

"What do you mean strange?" Lily asked.

"Hard to explain. When she answered her phone, she sounded fine. But when she realized who was calling, she started stammering. It was weird. But when I told her why I was calling, that I wanted to talk to her mother about some Frederickport history, her tone changed completely."

"Joyce has always seemed a little high-strung to me," Lily said.

"I suppose."

"Ian and I are driving over to Astoria for dinner. Do you and Chris want to join us?" Lily asked.

"Thanks. But I think I'll pass. Walt tells me the Spicers are acting a little odd, and I would rather stick around the house tonight."

"You want Ian and me to come over? We don't have to go to Astoria."

"No, that's okay. I'll be fine with Walt there. But instead of leaving Sadie home alone, why don't you leave her at our house? I'm sure Walt would love to visit with her, and she can help him keep an eye on the guests while I'm out."

———

JOYCE PRUITT'S home was located in one of the less desirable neighborhoods in Frederickport. Most of the houses on her street had been built in the 1950s, and none seemed to have the cozy cottage feel or personality as many of the other homes in Frederickport.

Danielle had never been to Joyce's house before, yet she knew it was the gray one on the corner, with the sparsely landscaped front yard. Parking in front of the Pruitt house, she noticed its clapboard siding was in desperate need of a fresh coat of paint. Danielle turned off her engine, removed the key from the ignition, grabbed her purse off the passenger seat, and opened her car door.

When she arrived at the front porch, there was no reason to knock or ring the bell. Joyce was already opening the door to greet her.

"Your call was a surprise." Joyce's tone was less than cheerful and somewhat guarded.

"I hope I didn't catch you at a bad time," Danielle asked, standing on the front porch, looking into the house.

"No." Joyce shook her head. "I had just gotten home from work when you called. Here, come in." Joyce opened the door wider and stepped aside for Danielle to enter. "Mother is in the living room. I told her you were coming."

Danielle followed Joyce into the living room, where she found Agatha Pine sitting on a leather recliner, her feet propped up on the footrest, and a knitted shawl wrapped around her frail shoulders. The elderly woman gazed at Danielle through shrewd eyes.

"My daughter tells me you want to ask me some questions about local history," Agatha greeted her.

"Yes. I appreciate you seeing me."

"No reason not to. What else have I to do while I sit here waiting to die?" Turning her attention to her daughter, she snapped, "Bring us some lemonade!"

Danielle didn't have the opportunity to decline the offer of a beverage—which wasn't exactly an offer. Joyce hurriedly scurried from the room to do as her mother ordered before Danielle could utter a word.

Agatha pointed to the sofa facing her chair. "Sit."

Danielle smiled and took a seat on the sofa, setting her purse on the floor by her feet.

"I saw your ad in the paper," Agatha said. "I enjoyed your party last year. It's too bad your cousin had to ruin everything."

"The celebration will be a little different this year." Danielle chose not to engage in a discussion about her cousin, Cheryl, who last year had left the open house celebration with the Missing Thorndike and ended up murdered.

"I notice you plan to charge admission this year. And just serving hot dogs?"

"We're donating the money to the local schools."

Agatha let out a snort. "I can't imagine you would raise that much money. I'm surprised you don't just donate it yourself and give away free hot dogs."

Joyce reentered the room, carrying a tray with three glasses of lemonade.

"You've got to be pretty rich now. I understand they let you keep those gold coins Jolene found at the Hemming house."

At hearing her mother's words, Joyce flinched, causing the tray to slip in her hands, almost dropping it. She managed to regain hold of it without spilling the glasses, but the lemonade sloshed from side to side.

"Be careful!" Agatha snapped.

"Actually, the gold has been stolen." Danielle glanced over to Joyce and noticed the woman's hand trembled as she removed each glass from the tray to be served.

"Yes, I heard. Won't your insurance reimburse you?" Agatha asked.

Danielle accepted the beverage Joyce offered, the woman's hand still trembled. "No. I didn't have the coins insured, and the bank isn't responsible for insuring the contents of a safe deposit box."

"Then I suppose you should have been more careful," Agatha said as she snatched the glass Joyce now offered her.

"I understand you wanted to ask mother about local history," Joyce said as she took a seat on the sofa with Danielle.

"Yes." Danielle looked at Agatha. "I was at the museum earlier, going through some old documents, and I came across the name Paddy Fitzpatrick, who I believe used to live in Frederickport sometime in the early 1900s, maybe even in the late 1800s. I understand your maiden name was Fitzpatrick and that you're from Frederickport, so I was wondering if perhaps he was a relative."

Agatha took a sip of her drink and then set the glass on the end table. "My grandfather was named Patrick Fitzpatrick, but everyone called him Paddy. But he wouldn't be the man you're asking about."

"Why do you say that?" Danielle asked.

"My grandfather never lived here. My grandmother moved to Frederickport with my father after her husband died. So he couldn't be the same man."

"Do you know if there were any other Fitzpatricks in town back then?" Danielle suspected Agatha's grandmother was the Fitzpatrick Walt had mentioned.

Agatha shook her head. "Not that I ever heard about."

Danielle took a sip of her drink and then set it on a coaster on the coffee table. *Perhaps,* she thought, *the spirit of Agatha's grandfather followed his widow and son to Frederickport.*

"Can you tell me anything about your grandfather?" Danielle asked.

"Why? I told you he never lived in Frederickport."

"I just find family history fascinating." Danielle smiled sweetly.

Agatha frowned. "Other people's family history?"

"I don't really have any family of my own—not anymore. So I suppose I do enjoy listening to other people tell their stories. There is no one left in my family to tell me about my ancestors."

"If you're really interested." Agatha settled back in the recliner and readjusted her shawl. "According to my father, Grandpa Paddy enjoyed his whisky—a little too much, as most men seem to do. And he was a practical joker. Some found it amusing, others didn't."

"Practical joker?" Danielle asked.

"Yes, he was always playing jokes on people. Unfortunately, he didn't know when enough was enough. Father claimed his mother adored her husband—in spite of his penchant for pushing a joke beyond the limits—and she was constantly making excuses for him. In turn, he was quite in love with her. At least, that was my father's perception. I suspect his opinion was tainted by personal bias."

"Why do you think that?" Danielle asked.

"I would think if a man truly loved his wife and son, he would be working to support his family, coming home at night, not getting drunk night after night, stumbling home drunk." Agatha frowned in disgust.

"So he was an alcoholic?"

"I think back then they just said he enjoyed his drink. In the end, his foolish ways left behind a widow forced to support herself and her son. She moved to Frederickport, lived in a little shanty on the end of town and took in laundry to support herself and my father. Had I been my grandmother, I would have kicked him out before he killed himself."

"He killed himself?" Danielle asked.

"It's not like he put a gun to his head and pulled the trigger. But he might as well have."

"He was drunk and fell off a horse," Joyce quietly explained.

"It was not that he was just drunk," Agatha scoffed. "It was Saint Patrick's Day, and he decided to dress up like a leprechaun. Made a fool of himself before he got himself killed, wearing a ridiculous green derby hat, red jacket and a leather apron—"

"Red jacket?" Danielle interrupted.

"Yes. Leprechauns used to wear red, or so my father told me," Agatha explained.

"Umm…and a leather apron?"

"It was a blacksmith apron, but it was supposed to be a cobbler's apron," Agatha told her.

"According to legend, leprechauns repair shoes," Joyce explained.

"Apparently my grandfather left his wife and son at home so he could go drink with his buddies. After he got drunk, he went around town, trying to convince everyone he was a real leprechaun and daring them to catch him. Because, according to legend, if you catch a leprechaun, he'll grant you three wishes. Someone took him up on the offer, a chase on horseback ensued, and the foolish man ended up falling from the horse and breaking his useless neck."

"Oh my, that's horrible." Danielle gasped.

"My grandmother was devastated. She loved the old fool.

However, I suspect one reason she moved after his death, people were rather cruel."

"Cruel?" Danielle frowned.

"From what my grandfather told mother," Joyce explained, "the townspeople seemed to find the circumstances of his death more amusing than the tragedy it was to his family. He was portrayed as a drunken fool. I don't think my great-grandmother wanted her son exposed to that."

"This is my story! I can tell it!" Agatha snapped. Joyce immediately retreated into silence.

"It must have been difficult for your grandmother."

Agatha scoffed. "What woman could really love a man like that? I imagine she was seduced by his good looks. Unfortunately, the handsome ones are typically not worth a lick,"

"Handsome? Does this mean you have a picture of him?" Danielle perked up.

"Certainly, in our family album. Would you like to see it?" Agatha asked.

"I would love to!" *This has got to be our leprechaun. His picture will confirm it!*

Agatha turned to face Joyce. "Go get the family album and find the photograph for Danielle."

Submissively, Joyce stood and scurried to the nearby bookshelf to retrieve the album.

Anxious to have her suspicion confirmed, Danielle waited for Joyce to bring the album to her.

Before returning to the sofa, Joyce opened the leather-bound photo album and turned to a specific page and then showed her mother. "This is him, isn't it?"

"Yes." Agatha nodded, pushing the album away.

Danielle remained sitting on the sofa when Joyce sat down beside her, sitting much closer than she had been a moment earlier. She placed the open album on Danielle's lap and pointed to the black-and-white photograph of her great-grandfather.

Staring at the photograph, Danielle frowned and leaned closer, her eyes now squinting. After a moment of silently studying the picture, she looked up at Agatha and blurted, "This isn't him."

TWENTY-EIGHT

I nstead of going straight home after leaving Joyce Pruitt's house, Danielle took a detour and drove to the south side of town, to Chris's new business offices, previously known as the Gusarov Estate. It had taken Chris's real estate agent, Adam Nichols, a little finagling to get the prime beachfront property rezoned to allow the Glandon Foundation to use the mansion for their new headquarters. The building itself already had more an industrial, as opposed to residential feel, with its extensive use of glass and steel construction. There was no signage on the massive building or on the wrought iron fence surrounding it. This wasn't because the city wouldn't allow it, but because Chris did not want it.

If she didn't already know Chris normally parked his vehicle on the long driveway, beyond the security of the fence and out of sight from the street, she would assume no one was at the Glandon Head-quarters, since there were no cars parked nearby.

Driving up to the building, she pulled along the sidewalk and parked her car. The front gate did not appear to be locked, so she saw no reason to call Chris and ask him to let her in.

When Danielle reached the front door, she didn't bother knock-ing, but instead turned the doorknob to see if it was locked. It wasn't. The moment she opened the door, Hunny greeted her. The excited puppy barked; her plump sausage body wiggled and tail wagged.

Stepping into the entry hall, Danielle dropped to her knees, letting her purse fall to the floor. She scooped the puppy up in her arms, accepting the wet kisses now covering her face. "You are never going to make it as a guard dog!" Danielle laughed.

She heard a woman's voice say, "Danielle?"

Looking up from Hunny, Danielle turned to face the doorway leading into what had once been the living room, and found her neighbor Heather Donovan looking down at her.

Heather wore a calf-length purple knit dress and black leggings. Her dark hair was pulled into two pigtails and twisted into buns. It might have given her a Princess Leia look if not for the spiky way the ends of her pigtails randomly stuck out from each bun. Her straight bangs had recently been trimmed, revealing delicately arching brows.

"What are you doing here?" Danielle asked in surprise as she stood up, leaving Hunny on the floor, begging for more attention.

"I'm working here now!" Heather cheerfully boasted.

Before Danielle had a chance to ask more questions, Chris appeared from down the hallway, a broad smile on his face. "Hey, what a surprise! Did you meet my first official staff member?"

"Yes, I did." Danielle glanced from Chris to Heather, who brimmed with excitement.

"I'm just answering the phones right now and—" a phone ringing in the waiting area—previously the living room of the Gusarov Estate—interrupted Heather. Flashing Danielle and Chris a smile, she abruptly turned from the pair and rushed to answer the phone.

When Danielle was alone with Chris, she turned to him and whispered, "Heather?"

Chris reached down and picked up Hunny, who was now vying for his attention. Holding the squirming pup in his arms, he looked at Danielle and shrugged. "She really needed the job."

Danielle glanced toward the waiting area and back to Chris. In a low voice she said, "I know, but Heather? She drives you nuts."

With another shrug, he said, "I know. But she's really been struggling, and we both know her heart is in the right place."

Danielle grinned. "I think it's sweet of you."

"Considering everything that's happened the last few months, I felt it would be wise to surround myself with people I feel I can trust. Heather has certainly been known for going out of her way to right a wrong, even when she couldn't afford it financially." Leaning down, Chris released Hunny, who ran into the waiting area.

"I'm glad you did."

"So, to what do I owe this unexpected visit? Did you just miss me?"

"Actually, I wanted to talk about leprechauns." Danielle glanced to the doorway leading to the waiting area and back to Chris. "And since Heather is here, we might as well include her in this conversation."

———

HEATHER AND CHRIS sat in silence as they digested what Danielle had just told them.

"But that doesn't make any sense," Heather finally said.

"Tell me about it," Danielle agreed. "If Agatha's grandfather hadn't been wearing that leprechaun outfit when he died—one identical to the one worn by the spirit who has been hanging around our neighborhood—I would assume the name was simply a coincidence and the Paddy Fitzpatrick mentioned in the doctor's notes had nothing to do with Agatha's grandfather."

"Are you sure it wasn't the same person?" Heather asked. "I've had pictures taken of me that later I thought didn't look anything like me."

Danielle shook her head. "No. Without a doubt these are not the same men. The one we saw had strawberry blond hair. Agatha's Paddy had coal black hair." She paused a moment and looked at Heather. "Like yours."

"I assume it was a black-and-white photograph. How can you be sure his hair wasn't red?" Chris asked.

Danielle shook her head again. "No. It was black and our leprechaun is more blond than red. Plus, the man in the picture looked nothing like the guy we saw. Different shaped face, different nose. The man in the picture was handsome, but our guy is rather plain, even a little homely."

"Is it possible for a ghost to take on a different look? Maybe he changed his appearance?" Heather suggested.

Danielle looked to Chris for input. Unlike Heather, who was a relative novice when dealing with spirits, both Chris and Danielle had been encountering spirits since they were children.

"I've never experienced that. The only thing, a spirit doesn't necessarily show himself as he looked at death. He might show a younger—or even older—version of himself. But never as another person. I suppose it's possible. But I've never seen it," Chris explained.

"I would be happy to ignore this spirit if I wasn't fairly certain he's the one who somehow moved that gold from the bank. And apparently, another safe deposit box was hit. With him hanging around our houses, it's like having a burglar primed to hit at any moment, yet we can't even call the cops or lock our doors to keep him out."

"I have a new blend of oils I've been wanting to try," Heather suggested. "I could get them."

"To do what exactly?" Chris asked.

"At least we could keep him from entering our houses. He's already been in Danielle's bedroom. I could start by setting up a diffuser at Marlow House."

Danielle smiled. "Umm…if the oils really work at driving away spirits, what about Walt?"

Heather started to say something but paused. With a frown, she reconsidered her suggestion.

Chris grinned. "Maybe Heather is right. Let's get that diffuser running at Marlow House."

"Oh, funny," Danielle said dryly. She stood up.

"Where are you going?" Chris asked.

"I need to get back to Marlow House. I've been gone all day, and we do have people staying there, and a couple of them have been acting a little strange. It's a good thing I have Walt keeping an eye on things."

"So this is a no on the diffuser?" Chris asked with a faux pout.

———

THE MAN DANIELLE knew as Blake Spicer sat alone on the porch swing of Marlow House, smoking a cigarette and holding his cellphone to his ear as he waited for Alan Kissinger to answer his call.

"Have you got it yet?" Alan answered a moment later.

"No. The Hortons—who, by the way, not only sound like something out of a Dr. Seuss book, but I'm beginning to think they belong in one—don't know what a freaking vacation is supposed to be. They're both just hanging around the house and won't get off their butts and go somewhere and do something."

"Where is Boatman? And that other woman who lives there?"

"Danielle has been coming and going all day long. The other one, Lily, she took off with her boyfriend earlier. I think she said something about going to Astoria. This should be freaking easy!"

"Maybe you need to do something with the Hortons?"

"Do something, what?"

"I don't know, you have your gun with you, don't you?"

"Whoa!…I am not killing them."

"Don't be stupid," Alan snapped. "I didn't mean for you to kill them. But you could take them by gunpoint, tie them up, and then take the necklace and get the hell out of there. You're in disguise and Boatman's going to know who took it anyway once you take off early and she realizes the necklace is missing."

"Now who is being stupid?"

"What do you mean?" Kissinger asked.

"Our plan only works if we have time to get far away from Marlow House before Danielle knows the necklace is missing and realizes we took it. Time to dump the rental car and get out of these disguises. But what happens if someone shows up at the house three minutes after we leave, and finds the Hortons tied up? And don't even suggest we take them with us, because I don't do kidnapping."

"Okay, okay. You have a point. But your window of opportunity is narrowing."

"Tomorrow is Friday, and the Hortons are checking out then. According to Danielle, the next guests arrive Saturday afternoon. So I figure once the Hortons leave, all we have to worry about is getting rid of Danielle and Lily for a couple hours. Lily seems to take off a lot with her boyfriend, anyway. So I don't think she'll be a problem."

"Isn't there a housekeeper?"

"Yeah, but she doesn't seem to stick around much."

Five minutes later, the woman Danielle knew as Jeannie joined Dave on the swing. He had just gotten off the phone.

"Who were you talking to?" she asked.

"Alan. He keeps asking me why this is taking us so long."

"Yeah, we always take the risks and he nags." Jeannie leaned back in the swing. "So did you tell him about our problem getting into the room?"

"You mean being unable to get the doorknob to unlock?"

Jeannie nodded. "I don't know what the problem was. I watched Danielle unlock that door with her key. It's not like it was broken or anything. I've never had a problem picking a lock."

"How do you think I felt?" He patted her knee.

"I'm sorry I was such a bitch up there about it," she apologized. "I acted like the whole thing was your fault."

"I understand." He patted her knee again.

"It might be easier if we got ahold of Danielle's bedroom key," she suggested.

"I wonder what Alan would say if he knew we couldn't even get the stupid door unlocked."

"You know what I think?" she asked.

"What, babe?"

"I think this time, after we get the necklace, we tell Alan to stick it and keep his share."

Dave laughed. "I would agree with you, babe, but think of all the good leads we'd miss out on."

TWENTY-NINE

Danielle made one final stop before heading back to Marlow House. She went by the Chinese restaurant and ordered take-out. Lily and Ian were in Astoria and weren't returning until after dinner. Danielle wasn't responsible for feeding her guests, and since she had heard them discussing where they intended to go for dinner, she didn't see the need to buy extra. When Chris had walked her out to her car earlier, he had invited her to dinner, an offer she declined. She explained she was exhausted and would have to take a rain check.

While her intention was to buy Chinese for one, she couldn't decide what she wanted to eat, so she ended up purchasing enough food for several extra people. As she carried the purchase out to her car, she thought it a shame Walt no longer ate food.

When Danielle arrived back at Marlow House, Sadie greeted her as she walked through the back door into the kitchen. By the way the golden retriever persistently nosed her leggings, she suspected she was smelling Hunny.

The Hortons' car was not parked by the house, and Danielle assumed they had already left for dinner. The Spicers took off minutes after she arrived home, leaving her alone with Walt, Sadie and Max. Where Max was exactly, she wasn't sure. He hadn't greeted her, but she suspected he was tucked in some corner, napping.

"That is an odd couple," Walt told Danielle as he watched her sort through her sacks of takeout she had set on the kitchen counter.

"How so?" Danielle pulled a wonton from a sack and took a bite.

"They couldn't wait for the Hortons to get out of here. I was fairly certain the moment they did, the Spicers would be making another run for the bedroom and the Mrs. would be whipping out her dust rag."

Danielle laughed and popped the rest of the wonton in her mouth.

"But the minute you showed up, it was like they changed course and were out of here."

"Maybe they just like privacy. Wanted the place all to themselves. But now that I'm home, they decided to head down to the beach and find a secluded hideaway." She looked at Walt and attempted to wiggle her brows, which made her look more like she had something in her eyes.

Ignoring Danielle's unsuccessful brow wiggle, Walt waved his hand for a cigar. "Perhaps. It was just rather abrupt." He looked down at the sacks of food. "Is Chris coming for dinner?"

Danielle shook her head. "No. He asked me if I wanted to go out, but I told him I just wanted to come home and crash."

"Then who's coming? I thought Lily and Ian went to Astoria for dinner?"

"No one's coming, why?"

Walt glanced again at the sacks of food. "I see you worked up an appetite today."

Danielle opened her mouth to object and then changed her mind. Looking again at the sacks of takeout, she shrugged. "Yeah, I guess I did overdo it."

"Are you just going to stand there and eat the food straight out of the boxes? Or are you going to sit down at the kitchen table?" Walt took a puff off his cigar.

"Actually, I was considering taking this food upstairs, having a shower, and then eating in bed."

THIRTY MINUTES LATER, Danielle, now freshly showered and wearing plaid flannel pajama bottoms and a T-shirt, sat cross-legged on her bed, the sacks of food sitting around her on the mattress while she held a bowl of chow mein in one hand and a pair of chopsticks in the other. Sitting next to her on the bed was Walt, who stretched out on the mattress as he leaned against the headboard. Napping on the floor between the bed and door were Sadie and Max.

"I'm just trying to figure out who he is," Danielle told Walt. She had just recounted the events of the day, including the mystery of Paddy Fitzpatrick.

"Let me try it," Walt suggested.

"Try what?" Danielle un-daintily slurped up a mouthful of chow mein while wielding a pair of throwaway chopsticks.

"See if I can make myself look like someone else."

"Who?" Danielle set the chopsticks in the bowl for a moment and grabbed a napkin. She wiped her mouth.

"You tell me," Walt said.

Setting the napkin on her lap and still holding the bowl, she watched Walt. "Okay, do it."

Walt closed his eyes and concentrated. His face transformed. When he opened his eyes, he found Danielle staring at him. "Well? What do I look like?"

"Like a ten-year-old Walt. Gosh, you were a cute kid. But you're still you. I'd recognize you anywhere."

Walt frowned. "I was going for Evan."

Danielle shook her head and took hold of her chopsticks again. She speared another helping of chow mein. "Nope. You don't look a thing like Evan."

"Let me try again," Walt insisted.

"Okay, go for it." Danielle watched as Walt transformed again. Danielle laughed.

"What is it? Who do I look like?"

"A much—*much*—older Walt. I wish I could take a picture so you would know what you would have looked like had you been able to grow old. But, still you."

"I was trying for Brian."

Danielle laughed again. "I think Brian might be insulted. Not how you look per se, but that you imagine he is *that* old. Of course, he isn't aware you exist, so moot point."

When Danielle looked back at Walt after taking another bite of food, she noticed he was back to his normal self—neither a younger or older version of the man she knew. With a sigh, she proceeded to eat her dinner.

Still by Danielle's side and leaning against the headboard, Walt silently considered the recent events. His gaze wandered for a moment and then froze—someone was looking in the window.

"Don't move," Danielle whispered.

"Do you see him?" Walt whispered back, not moving.

"It's him. It's the leprechaun."

Walt continued to stare at the window while the object of his attention was unaware he was being watched. Finally, Walt said, "No, Danielle, it is not the leprechaun."

"Yes, it is," she hissed. "It's the one who I talked to on the street. The one I saw looking in my bedroom before." Diverting her eyes, Danielle took another bite of food so the man looking in the window wouldn't know he had been detected.

"No, Danielle. It is not a leprechaun."

"Okay, we agree there. It's a ghost. And all evidence points to it being Paddy Fitzpatrick's ghost, except for that stupid picture says otherwise."

"No, Danielle, it's not Paddy Fitzpatrick either."

"Then who is staring in my window?"

"That, Danielle, is the ghost of Sean Sullivan."

On the floor Max was just waking up. With a yawn he lifted his head and gave it a little shake. He heard Walt and Danielle talking. They were still lounging on the bed. While he didn't understand their words exactly, if Walt focused some of his energy on him, he would be able to pick up the gist of the conversation. Being the curious cat he was, Max stood up and stretched and then leapt onto the bed, accidentally knocking over a container of sesame chicken. For a moment Max was distracted by the sweet-smelling chicken, yet motion at the window made his head jerk upward. He let out a piercing cry at the sight at the window. Sadie woke abruptly and leapt up, charging to the window to have a better look. When she got there, the man was gone.

"Crud," Danielle grumbled. Setting the bowl down on her blanket, she reached for the chicken that had fallen from the container. No longer interested in what was at the window, Max turned his attention back to the chicken and tried to grab a piece, only to be shoved away by Danielle.

Walt looked at the window. "He's gone."

"Darn animals scared him away. I wanted to talk to him." Danielle climbed off the bed and started to pick up the opened containers. Still curious, Max attempted to poke his head into various cartons, only to be pushed away again. He was persistent, nosing the containers, causing them to fall, sniffing the escaping food now on Danielle's once clean blanket. She groaned.

"Max!" Walt snapped, now out of the bed.

Danielle froze and watched as Max floated up over the bed, a confused expression on his feline face as he looked down at Sadie, who now sat by the bed, curiously watching the cat float overhead to the nearby sofa, only to be dropped unceremoniously onto the couch cushion.

Max let out a tortured meow as he made contact with the sofa, and then he flew off the couch, taking refuge under the bed. Meanwhile, the cartons of food drifted up into the air and then floated effortlessly to the nearby desk, where they settled without more food spilled. The food that had been spilled also floated upward, its final destination, Danielle's food bowl.

Picking up the bowl, her chow mein now littered with random food Max had nosed, she looked up at Walt and frowned. "Thanks...I think."

"I intended to put that in your trash can, but changed my mind. I was afraid it would stain the wicker."

"Thanks, Walt. You're always thoughtful," Danielle said dryly. Turning to the desk, she set the bowl down. After getting a damp washcloth from her bathroom, she proceeded to mop any sauce or grease from her blanket. "I guess bringing all that food on my bed wasn't the smartest idea."

"I think we would have been fine if we hadn't had an unexpected visitor." Walt sat back down on the bed.

Danielle took a seat at her desk. Picking up one of the boxes, she began eating its contents with her fingers. "So why is Sean Sullivan dressed up as a leprechaun?"

"And why is he here? From what you told me, he's been dead for almost eighty years."

"I'd like to talk to him, but before I do, I need to know why he thinks he's a leprechaun."

"Danielle, how do you expect to do that? Find out why he thinks he's a leprechaun? Are you sure he actually thinks that?"

Taking another bite, Danielle chewed her food carefully and

considered the question. "Yes, I do. I got the impression he really believes he's a leprechaun."

Crossing his legs at his ankles, Walt turned in the bed to get a better look at Danielle, who remained sitting at the desk, now grazing through the various cartons of Chinese takeout.

"What do we know about Sean?" Danielle asked.

"I know he was a little unstable, always talking about some leprechaun tormenting him."

Danielle stopped eating. She looked up at Walt. "According to those notes by Sullivan's doctor, he claimed not to just see a leprechaun, but his grandmother after she died…and someone else. Someone who died at Marymoor."

Walt arched his brow. "So?"

Setting the half-empty carton of food on the desk, Danielle stood up and started pacing the room. "And then what Agatha said about her grandfather—he was a prankster. Never knew when to quit, always pushing it too far. And how he was killed wearing that leprechaun outfit."

"And your point?"

"You said Sean Sullivan was odd—even thinking he might be crazy, which was why you talked to Katherine O'Malley about him."

"I still don't get your point."

"Sean Sullivan wasn't crazy—at least not when you knew him. He was like me and Chris. As a child he could see spirits—but he didn't understand. They thought I was crazy too."

"Okay, but why is he masquerading as a leprechaun now, in death?"

"I suspect after Paddy Fitzpatrick died, he followed his wife and daughter here to be close to them. It's not uncommon for a spirit to be dressed in whatever they wore when they were alive. Only after a spirit becomes aware of his or her true circumstance are they able to —well—change clothes. And in Paddy's case, maybe he didn't want to."

"Why wouldn't he want to?"

"A person's personality doesn't alter after they die. Oh, maybe like Cheryl they become more self-aware and regret the mistakes they made when alive. But according to Agatha, her grandfather was a great jokester. He was killed after being thrown from a horse while trying to get people to chase him—while insisting he was a leprechaun."

"You think he tried to do that after he died?" Walt asked.

"Either he was in that confused state, and he actually believed he was a leprechaun, confusing those last memories of life with his new reality. Or perhaps he was bored. While waiting for his wife—who he reportedly loved—to join him in the hereafter, maybe he latched onto Sean, someone who could actually see him, and decided to play jokes on him."

"But then what happened?" Walt asked.

Danielle stopped pacing and faced Walt. "I don't know. Maybe Paddy's antics pushed Sean over the edge. Maybe in the end he had truly gone mad. We know he spent his last years at Marymoor. Living in a place like that could in itself make one go mad. Maybe Paddy moved on when his wife finally passed, leaving behind a confused Sean Sullivan, who for some reason actually came to believe he was a leprechaun."

THIRTY

A fter breakfast on Friday morning, Nola and Albert excused
themselves to go pack. They planned to check out later that
afternoon. As the pair went upstairs, Blake and Jeannie headed for
the front door, announcing they were going to take a walk on the
beach. Joanne had come into work that morning and was currently
busy cleaning up after breakfast, while Lily went with Danielle to
the parlor. Once in the parlor and the door closed, Danielle updated
Lily on all that had happened the day before.

"So what now?" Lily asked.

Danielle walked to her desk and sat down. She turned on her
laptop. "I'm going to see if I can find anything about Agatha's
grandmother and when she died. I wish I had thought to ask that
question when I was there yesterday. They'd think I was crazy if I
called them now and asked."

"If she died before the forties, you aren't going to find anything
online from the local paper." Lily was referring to the fire that had
destroyed the offices of the *Frederickport Press* in the 1940s, along with
its collection of past papers. Now, the only editions of the paper
prior to the fire were those donated to the museum from past
subscribers or their families.

"I know that. But there are other ways to find death information
online."

Lily sat down on one arm of the sofa and watched Danielle. "What do you hope to accomplish by finding out when Agatha's grandmother died?"

"I want to see if it backs up one of my hunches."

"What hunch?"

"That Paddy Fitzpatrick stuck around until his wife died."

Lily shrugged. "I'm not sure what that will prove."

Ignoring Lily's point, Danielle focused her attention on the computer. Ten minutes later, she had her answer.

"Well, according to this information," Danielle began, her eyes still focused on her monitor, "Paddy's wife died about a year after Sean. Which would mean, if his spirit was sticking around, waiting for his wife to pass on, he could have feasibly hung out with Paddy in the spirit realm for that year. I mean, why not? He was obviously hovering around Sean while he was alive, making a nuisance of himself."

"That's what you assume. But what would it matter if they were together in death?"

Danielle shut her computer and turned to face Lily. "When Heather and I saw Sean's spirit, he was alone. Neither of us noticed a second spirit. Makes me think he's traveling solo these days. But when I asked Sean if he was Paddy Fitzpatrick, he got this strange look and just vanished."

"So?"

Danielle stood up. "So I think we have one really confused ghost on our hands. One who believes he's a leprechaun. The only thing that makes sense to me, Paddy's last practical joke before he moved on was to convince a newly departed soul—one who was already troubled in life—that he was a leprechaun."

"Okay, say you're right. Tell me, why now? If this guy died like eighty years ago, why is he being a problem now? You've been here for a year and Chris for six months, why didn't one of you see him before?"

Danielle shook her head. "I don't know, Lily. I honestly don't know."

WHEN POLICE CHIEF MacDonald asked him to stop by his office because there was someone he needed to talk to, Special Agent

Wilson expected that someone to be Danielle Boatman. It had been almost a week since she had reported her gold coins missing. Since his initial interview with her after he had taken over the investigation, she hadn't once contacted him, requesting an update. Wilson found her lack of apparent interest in the missing coins peculiar—especially for an uninsured innocent victim.

Upon entering the chief's office, Wilson found a woman sitting in one of the two chairs facing the desk. But the woman was not Danielle Boatman. It was someone he had never seen before. Whomever she was, it was obvious she was nervous, considering the way her eyes darted anxiously about. She gnawed on the nail of her left index finger; it twisted and scratched against her teeth. By her lack of makeup and the fact her shoulder-length muddy blond hair looked as if she had barely combed it, Wilson wondered if she had simply been in a hurry that morning or if she was always so casual in her appearance. Dressed in a T-shirt, faded jeans, and flip-flops, she fidgeted anxiously.

"Special Agent Wilson, thank you for coming in," the chief greeted him. "I'd like you to meet Abby Dawson. She has something I think you need to hear."

"Dawson?" Wilson frowned. "Are you related to Ron Dawson?"

Still sitting, she nodded. "He's my husband."

The chief motioned to the empty chair. Wilson sat down, his eyes on Abby. He hadn't noticed before, but there was a small box sitting on her lap.

Removing the finger from her mouth, she picked up the box and handed it to Wilson. "I think you need to see this."

Wilson accepted the box and opened it. Inside was a diamond bracelet. Still holding it, he looked to the woman for an explanation.

"It's the bracelet Ron claimed was in the safe deposit box," she explained after first clearing her throat.

"You had it all along?" Wilson asked.

She shook her head. "No. He did. And he's going to kill me when he finds out what I've done." Abby looked to the chief. "You promised, when I'm finished here, a couple of your men will escort me home so I can get my things."

The chief nodded in reply.

With a frown, Wilson set the lid back on the box. "Are you saying your husband lied when he claimed the bracelet was stolen?"

"Ex-husband. Well, soon-to-be ex. I'm not going to live like this anymore, and I'm certainly not going to be involved in some felony."

"Abby, go ahead and tell Special Agent Wilson what you told me earlier, everything," the chief gently urged.

She took a deep breath and sat back in her chair. "We've been having money problems. Things have been rough this past year, and I told myself I was going to stick it out. After all, I made a commitment to this marriage. But it has been one thing after another, and now this. This is just too much."

"What exactly?" Wilson asked.

"My husband's grandmother left him this bracelet. It's supposed to be worth something like twenty thousand bucks. He kept it in the safe deposit box. When things started going in the toilet, he tried selling it. He took it out of the bank a couple months ago, but he hasn't been able to find a buyer. Not someone who is willing to pay what he believes it's worth."

"So he lied about it being in the safe deposit box?" Wilson asked.

She nodded. "The bracelet is insured. We had it appraised back when he inherited it. When he couldn't sell it, he knew if he reported it stolen and tried to collect the insurance, someone would look into our current finances and the insurance company might investigate him for insurance fraud. But when he heard Danielle Boatman's coins were stolen from a safe deposit box at the bank, he figured this was his chance. I mean, if someone took her gold, who's to say they didn't take the bracelet? We already had a safe deposit box there."

———

"THAT'S COLD." Thomas grimaced after Wilson recounted the interview with Abby Dawson. "She threw her husband under the bus." The two agents sat at a booth in Lucy's Diner, drinking coffee.

"I suspect that marriage had more than just money problems." Wilson dumped sugar in his coffee.

"But still, that's pretty harsh."

Wilson stirred his coffee with a knife. "Oh, come on. Are you telling me if your wife was committing insurance fraud, you would just sit back and do nothing?"

"I'd hope I would be able to talk her out of it. And if not, give her an ultimatum, let her know I wasn't going to be party to something like that." Thomas picked up his coffee cup.

"According to Dawson, she had no clue what her husband was up to. He came home, told her someone had stolen the bracelet, and when she questioned him—because she knew it wasn't at the bank—he insisted he had put it back without her knowledge and that it had been stolen."

"That sounds like he knew she wasn't going to go along with it." Thomas sipped his coffee.

"Unfortunately for him, she found where he had stashed it."

"In that case, I don't blame her. It was too late to reason with him. She could have gotten hurt."

"She was obviously worried about that, considering she requested a police escort to get her things."

Thomas shook his head. "Okay, not cold. She was in survival mode."

"Which brings me to another matter," Wilson announced.

"What's that?"

"Danielle Boatman. I was always skeptical of Ron Dawson's claim. But now we know he was lying. I'm more and more convinced Danielle Boatman never put those coins in her safe deposit box."

"You don't think the coins were stolen?" Thomas asked.

"No. There is nothing on any of those surveillance cameras we reviewed, aside from that one lens moving. And that could have occurred because of some seismic shift. Or maybe it's just an old building, or a wobbly camera and draft from the heating vent. One thing we do know, none of those cameras caught someone taking the coins from the building."

"So what is Boatman's motive?" Thomas asked.

"Money, of course."

"But they weren't insured," Thomas reminded him. "Even if Boatman intends to shake down the bank, why not insure the coins before pulling something like this off?"

"What, and have the insurance company take a closer look? They aren't going to simply pay off a claim like this—not just because a bank employee claims the box was heavier before."

"Then why?"

"A million-dollar tax write-off. Pretty sweet deduction, and she gets to keep her coins. And not having insurance makes her look all the more innocent." Wilson picked up his coffee cup. Before taking a drink, he added, "I think we need to keep a closer eye on Ms. Boatman. Maybe she'll lead us to her coins."

THIRTY-ONE

Later Friday morning, Danielle reluctantly returned to the Marymoor site. This time, she went alone. Parked near the section of chain-link fence boasting the no-trespassing sign, she sat in her car, hands still on the steering wheel, ignition turned off, staring out the window. She didn't see any spirits, but she knew they were there—she could feel them.

Danielle wanted to find Sean Sullivan. She would try his grave site when she was done here, but since this was the street where she had last seen him, this was where she decided to begin. Taking a deep breath and steeling her courage, she exited the car. Just as she slammed her car door shut, an apparition appeared behind the fence—it was the nurse she had talked to the last time she had been here.

"You again," Molly said.

"Hello, Molly, I was wondering if I could ask you a question."

Molly stared at Danielle a moment and then nodded. "What did you want to ask?"

"What did you mean when you said Sean Sullivan had moved on?"

Molly stepped closer to the fence. "He didn't like it here, so he left. But sometimes he comes back. He came back yesterday after you were here."

"Molly, do you believe Sean is a leprechaun?"

Molly shrugged. "Sean believes it."

"Is it because Paddy told him he was?"

Molly smiled. "How did you know that?"

"I heard Paddy was a jokester. He liked to tell people he was a leprechaun."

"Paddy left to be with his wife. He told Sean it was now his responsibility to take over the duties of a leprechaun. That he had to stand guard over their gold."

"Gold? What gold?" Danielle asked.

"I don't know. You'll need to ask Sean." Molly disappeared.

"Molly!" Danielle shouted, looking around for any signs of the spirit.

"Drat," Danielle muttered as she abruptly turned from the fence to her car—and almost ran into the spirit of Sean Sullivan. Startled, Danielle let out a gasp, but quickly regained her composure.

"What are you doing here?" Sean asked angrily.

"I'm looking for you."

He narrowed his eyes and took one step back. "You want three wishes, don't you?"

"No, Sean, I don't want three wishes. I just want to talk to you."

He took another step back. "You're trying to trick me!"

"Sean, can I please show you a picture?"

He frowned. "What picture?"

"It's in my shirt pocket." Moving slowly so as not to startle the confused spirit, Danielle slipped a photograph from her pocket. It was a picture of Katherine O'Malley, one she had found in the box Melony had brought her. Holding the picture up, she showed it to Sean.

"Who is that?" Sean asked.

"Take a closer look."

Hesitantly, Sean stepped closer to Danielle and looked at the photograph.

"It's Katherine O'Malley. Do you remember Katherine? You were close once. You knew each other as children."

Sean leaned toward the photograph. When his eyes widened and he let out a gasp, Danielle knew he recognized the woman in the picture.

"Katherine," he said in a hushed whisper, his gaze still focused on the photograph. The picture floated from Danielle's hand to

Sean's as he continued to stare at it. He whispered, "You never visited me. I thought you would come. But you never did."

"She couldn't, Sean. She couldn't come to see you while you were at Marymoor," Danielle said in a soft voice.

He looked up to Danielle and frowned. "What do you mean?"

"She died, Sean. I'm sorry to have to tell you that. But Katherine died not long after you went into Marymoor."

Sean looked at the photograph again and shook his head. "He told me she wasn't real. But there she is. I knew it."

"Who told you Katherine wasn't real?"

"Paddy. I waited for her. Each day I waited. Paddy told me I'd made her up, that Katherine was a figment of my imagination…but here she is."

"Was Paddy with you at Marymoor?" Danielle asked.

He nodded. "Yes. He told me that someday he would get me out. And he did."

"You got sick first, didn't you, Sean?"

Looking up from the photograph again, Sean frowned. "How did you know?"

"You got sick at Marymoor, so sick, and then you weren't sick anymore, and you left with Paddy."

"He said leprechauns had to stay together."

"He told you, you were a leprechaun, didn't he?"

The photograph, now hanging in midair in front of Sean, suddenly dropped, falling to the ground. Rubbing his temple, Sean shook his head in denial. "You're confusing me."

"Sean, I want you to listen very carefully to me. Listen, and deep down you'll recognize the words as the truth. Your name is Sean Sullivan, and from the time you were a small child, you saw things other people couldn't. You saw your grandmother after she died."

Rubbing his temple harder, he frantically shook his head. "No…no…"

"You weren't crazy. You and I are the same. I can see spirits too. Paddy Fitzpatrick was not a leprechaun. He was a spirit of a man who followed his family to this town. He liked to play jokes on people, and since you could see him, he attached himself to you."

"No…no…" Sean turned away from Danielle, his back now to her.

"I'm pretty sure Paddy has finally moved on. I imagine he

moved on a long time ago, after his wife died. But he left you here, confused."

It could have been her words, or perhaps it was the photograph of Katherine O'Malley, or maybe it was the combination of the two, but Sean Sullivan's perception was beginning to shift, and just as with Walt and the other spirits Danielle had helped along the way, reality was coming into focus, and he was able to see what had been hidden to him for almost eighty years.

———

DANIELLE SAT with Sean at his grave site in the Marymoor section of the Frederickport Cemetery. It was almost noon, and the sun was shining brightly overhead. Danielle was glad she had said her final goodbyes to the Hortons before leaving that morning. Otherwise, she would be feeling guilty about staying away so long. But she couldn't leave Sean yet.

He was no longer dressed as a leprechaun. His choice of clothes reminded her of what a laborer might have worn in the twenties. In his hand he fiddled with what looked like a vintage newsboy's hat. The beard he had worn when she had first seen him had also disappeared.

"I had gone over to talk to Katherine," Sean explained, looking down at the hat in his hands. "She just couldn't see Roger for what he really was. He showed up, we argued, and I slugged him right in the chin. He went down. Katherine was screaming at me, and I left."

"Then what happened?"

"Roger's buddy Hal Tucker showed up, arrested me. Next thing I know, I'm committed to Marymoor. I suppose it didn't help that I admitted to seeing Paddy."

"You never saw Katherine after the day you hit Roger?"

He shook his head. "No. But I figured she had to know what had happened to me. We'd been friends since we were kids. I couldn't imagine she would abandon me. I thought for sure she would come to see me, at least." Sean looked up at Danielle. "What happened to her?"

"She married Roger not long after you were committed. But before they left on their honeymoon, something happened. She shot and killed Roger, and she fell down the stairs. She died several days later."

"Why did she shoot him?"

Danielle shook her head. "I have no idea. I can only speculate. I suppose she may have realized her mistake."

"What happened to little Bri?"

"The court appointed an attorney to oversee her estate. She was sent to a private boarding school, and when she came of age, she came into her inheritance—the money and property her mother had inherited from Walt Marlow."

"I recognized Walt Marlow; I knew him, but I didn't know from where—or exactly who he was. He's like me; he's a ghost now, isn't he?"

Danielle nodded. "Yes. But unlike you, he's trapped in Marlow House. At least, until he decides to move on."

"Move on?"

"Something you'll be able to do now. But I hope you'll wait until I ask you a few more questions."

"Can I ask you a question first?"

Danielle smiled. "Yes."

"Why are you at Marlow House?"

"When Brianna grew up, she married my grandfather's brother. They traveled all over the world. They didn't have kids, but I believe she was happy. When she died, she left me her estate."

Sean smiled. "I'm glad it worked out for Brianna. But I'm so sorry I wasn't able to save Katherine."

"Sean, you never came here before, have you?"

"The cemetery? No. I told you this was the first time I'd seen my grave."

"Had you come here, you might have seen Katherine's spirit. She refused to move on until Brianna could go with her. Her spirit lingered here at the cemetery. But she moved on not long after Aunt Brianna passed."

"You mean I missed her?"

"You'll see her again, and soon, if you choose to go. But like I said, I'd like you to answer a few questions for me first."

Sean flipped the hat up, tossing it atop his mop of strawberry blond hair. Grabbing its bill, he tilted it to and fro, fitting it to his head. "I owe you a debt of gratitude for helping me see clearly again. What do you want to ask me?"

"First, I would like to know who Brianna's father was. Walt told me he thought you knew."

"Yes, I knew. She worked for his family; he was a married man. Very influential, very wealthy. He seduced her. But she refused to go to him and demand he help take care of Brianna. She made me promise to never tell him the baby was his."

"He didn't know?"

Sean shook his head. "No. She left his employment after she realized she was pregnant. And she made me promise that if he ever found out she had had a child, she didn't want him to know it was his."

"Did he find out she had a baby?"

"I'd be surprised if he didn't know. But they ran in different circles, and if he did find out, he never showed any interest in Brianna or finding out if he was the father."

"I assumed he knew about the baby. Walt overheard you and Katherine arguing once about the father. You were angry that he wouldn't take responsibility."

Sean sighed. "Katherine and I argued a lot about it. But Walt Marlow misunderstood. I wanted her to go to him, demand he help her. The fact was, Katherine always said he didn't know, but I wasn't certain that was true."

"What was the man's name?"

When Sean gave the man's name, Danielle's eyes widened. "Are you certain?"

"Yes, why? Do you know who that is?"

"Well, I know who he was. Holy crap."

"What else did you want to ask me?"

"First, I need to find some way to process what you just told me." She looked at Sean. "Are you certain?"

"Yes. He was the father. What else did you want to know?"

After a moment, Danielle said, "About the gold. Why did you think it was yours? Do you know where it is?"

Sean smiled. "It's interesting how everything is so crystal clear now. Had you asked me that question yesterday, the answer would be all muddled in my brain."

"Then tell me, please, what you know about the gold."

"After I died—funny how I remember that now, being so sick in my bed at Marymoor and then waking up and no longer feeling pain. Paddy was waiting for me; he said we had to leave. But I just wanted to find Katherine."

"You hadn't bought into being a leprechaun yet, had you?"

He shook his head. "No. Paddy followed me to Marlow House; I wanted to find Katherine. I went through all the rooms, and it was like no one lived there anymore."

"Walt was dead by then. No one was living at the house."

Sean nodded. "I saw Walt when I was there. I knew he was dead. But I didn't understand that I was dead. So I left quickly so he wouldn't see me. Paddy was waiting for me outside and convinced me to go into the Hemming house and look around. No one was living there either."

"That was after George Hemming and his family moved out. I remember Marie saying it was difficult for her father to stay in the house, since he was the one who had found Walt hanging in the attic."

"Paddy and I stayed at the Hemming house. We found the gold coins hidden there. It convinced me Paddy was right, we were leprechauns, and I had to protect my gold. Paddy eventually left. Over time new people moved in. It was never a problem until the man with the dog moved in. The dog could see me."

"Ian and Sadie," Danielle said.

"I left, returned to Marymoor. I would come and go and occasionally returned to the Hemming house to check on the gold."

"Do you know where the gold is now?"

Sean smiled up at Danielle. "Yes. Would you like me to take you to it?"

THIRTY-TWO

From the passenger seat of the parked black sedan, Special Agent Thomas peered through the binoculars.

"What is she doing?" Wilson asked from the driver's seat.

"She's just sitting there next to the grave. It looks like she's talking."

"I wonder whose grave it is. Not unusual for people to visit a grave site and talk to whoever is buried there."

"It looks like the older section of the cemetery," Thomas explained, still looking through the binoculars.

"The more I think about it, the more I'm convinced Boatman has that gold."

Thomas lowered the binoculars and turned to his partner. "Maybe. But the chances of her actually leading us to the gold today are slim to none."

Determined, Wilson shook his head. "I just have this gut feeling we need to stick with her today."

"You and your gut feelings." Thomas lifted the binoculars back to his eyes. "Hey, she's getting up. Looks like she's on the move."

"WILL the bracelet be with the gold?" Danielle asked.

"Bracelet? What bracelet?" Sean asked Danielle as he followed her back to the parking lot where she had left her car.

"Didn't you also take a bracelet from the bank?" Danielle asked.

Sean frowned. "No." Sean then laughed and said, "I remember now!"

Danielle stopped walking for a moment and looked at Sean, who also stopped. "You remember what, that you took the bracelet?"

He laughed and started walking again, along with Danielle. "No. I don't know anything about a bracelet. I only moved the gold. But now I know where I saw that necklace before."

"What necklace?" Danielle asked.

"The one in your safe. I was planning to take it." He laughed again.

"The Missing Thorndike?"

"Yes! I saw you remove it from your safe, and I knew it looked familiar. I just couldn't place it. I'd seen pictures of the necklace before. How did you get it? I remember reading how it went missing after Eva Thorndike died."

"It's a long story. Walt Marlow had it all along, and since the Thorndikes left it to him in their will, I ended up with it."

"Very interesting," Sean murmured.

A moment later he asked, "Where is this next level exactly? Is it heaven?"

"I don't know. I just know there's something beyond this, and when you're ready to move on, you'll be able to." Danielle smiled and then added, "Well, that's not entirely accurate."

Sean glanced over at Danielle. "What do you mean?"

"What do you remember about Walt Marlow's death?" Danielle asked.

"I remember he killed himself…oh…I understand…is that why Walt Marlow is stuck at Marlow House?"

Danielle shook her head. "No. Walt was actually murdered by his brother-in-law, Roger."

"I knew there was something wrong with Roger!"

"Walt's wife, Angela, was involved in the plot, but she was killed before her brother carried through with it."

"I knew Marlow's wife had been hit by a car," Sean said "I had no idea Walt Marlow had been murdered. I certainly didn't know his wife was involved in her husband's death."

"So now, as her penance, she's confined to the graveyard."

"Why is Marlow trapped at Marlow House?"

"He's not trapped exactly. Oh, at first he was, because he was confused after the murder—just like you were confused. That confusion makes it impossible to move on. I believe a person must first accept his death before taking the next step."

"Marlow still hasn't accepted his death?"

"Yes, he has. Which is why he can move on if he chooses."

"But why did you say we can't always move on if we choose to?"

"I was thinking of Walt's wife, Angela," Danielle explained. "Had we taken another route to your grave site, you could have met her. Like I mentioned, for her crimes against Walt, her spirit is confined to the cemetery."

"So there is no hell? No fire and brimstone?"

Danielle shrugged. "I suppose hell can mean different things to different people. And just because Angela is doing penance here, I have no idea what waits for her on the other side when she is finally allowed to move over—if she ever is."

"I'll admit I'm getting curious to find out," Sean said. They had just reached Danielle's car in the parking lot.

"Please take me to the gold first," Danielle asked as she climbed into her driver's seat.

"What are you going to do with the gold, take it back to the bank?" Sean asked as Danielle slipped her key into the ignition.

Instead of turning on her engine, she dropped her hand from the key and sat back in the seat. "That's a good question. What am I going to do with it?"

"Don't you want to take it back to the bank?"

"I can't really do that. They'll wonder why I have it." Narrowing her eyes, she silently considered her various options. "I suppose I'll have to call the chief. Explain what's going on, and let him send someone to find it. He can say he received an anonymous tip."

"I hope it's still there."

Danielle looked to Sean. "You mean it might not be?"

He shrugged. "I can't say for certain. It's possible someone moved it."

"Then we better make sure it's there, and then I can call the chief and have him send someone to pick it up." Danielle reached for the key and then turned on the ignition. She pulled out into the street.

"Keep going down this way," Sean told her. "And then turn left. I'll show you where it was."

Danielle didn't notice the black sedan following her car, several car lengths behind her. When she did glance up into her rearview mirror, it was to see a white Jeep pull into the street, between her car and the one following her. She didn't for a moment imagine she was being followed.

The summer meant more traffic on the streets of Frederickport, and since it was a Friday, it was busier than midweek. Danielle followed Sean's directions and found herself parking in a residential area adjacent to the beach. She had been here before.

"It's here?" Danielle asked after she turned off her ignition, not making a move to get out of her car. A couple sporting swimwear and carrying beach towels walked by the front of her car and gave her a wave as they headed down to the beach.

"We have to go down that path," Sean explained as he pointed in the direction where the couple had just gone. "There are some shacks down there. The gold's in one of them."

"I know what's down there. That's where I found my cousin, Cheryl, last year."

Sean turned to Danielle and frowned. "What do you mean you found your cousin there?"

"Last year, around this same time, my cousin disappeared after a party. I found her body in one of those huts. She had been murdered."

"Is her spirit still down there?" he asked.

"No. She's moved on. But going to those huts…" Danielle cringed.

As she discussed the beach huts with Sean, she failed to notice the dark sedan drive by her parked car, traveling down the road and turning left onto another street. It parked around the corner. Had she thought to look in that direction, she would not have seen it because of the other cars parked along the street.

"The beach hut where the gold is, is it locked?" Danielle asked.

"Yes. But locks aren't a problem," Sean boasted. "Moving a tumbler is a snap."

Danielle looked over at Sean and considered the energy he had been able to harness. It was obvious to her he could move small objects—like gold coins and tumblers inside a lock—yet she had seen no indication he had any of the powers Walt had mastered, which didn't surprise her considering Sean obviously utilized most of his energy to allow him to move from one location to the next, something Walt couldn't do.

"Okay. Let's go down there. I want to see if the gold coins are where you say they are, and then I'll call the chief."

NO HOUSES LINED the west side of the street where Danielle had parked her car. The sidewalk there butted up to the sandy ground leading to the beach. While there were no houses along this ocean-side section of the road, a short distance down, both north and south, there were beachfront houses, yet any possible ocean view was obscured by an uncooperative elevation and excessive foliage.

Wild grass grew randomly along the sandy trail leading down to the beach. Ahead, Danielle spied a worn wooden bench situated along the side of the trail. She remembered waiting there for the police with Bill Jones after finding her cousin's body. Beyond that, the row of six beach shacks, each painted with a different red number, one through six, came clearly into view.

The couple who had passed by her car and waved when she had parked were nowhere in sight. There were some people on the beach, but they were a considerable distance from her and she couldn't see their faces, nor could she imagine they could identify her.

When she reached the beach shacks, she was grateful there was no one milling around. She knew the huts were used to store items like beach chairs and surfboards for some of the rental houses in Adam Nichols's rental program. When she remembered that, she couldn't help but grin. *Adam would absolutely flip if he knew the gold was in one of his beach huts!*

Sean pointed to hut six, where the gold was being kept. For a brief moment Danielle considered returning to her car and simply calling the chief and telling him to send someone down to find the gold. However, if the gold had been moved, she didn't want to send the chief off on some wild-goose chase. First, she would make sure the gold was still there, and then she would call him.

Glancing around the beach, checking to make sure no one was close by, Danielle stepped closer to hut six and patiently waited for Sean to open the lock. With relative ease, the lock clicked open.

After a final look around the general vicinity to make sure she was alone, Danielle slipped into the shack, not quite closing the door all the way shut behind her. Light coming in through a window illuminated the small space.

"It's in there," Sean said, pointing to a red ice chest.

Hastily kneeling down on the floor by the container, Danielle used her elbow to knock its lid onto the floor, unwilling to leave behind her fingerprints.

She stared at the gold coins a few moments and then whispered, "It's still here,"

"Yes, it is," came a voice from behind.

With a jerk, Danielle turned to the now open doorway. Standing there were Special Agents Wilson and Thomas.

THIRTY-THREE

"What has she gotten herself into now?" Officer Brian Henderson asked as he stood in the small office adjacent to the interrogation room, looking through the two-way mirror at Danielle, who sat alone at the table, absently tapping her fingers against the desktop. The chief was out in the hallway, talking to Wilson, while Joe Morelli was in the room with Brian.

"They seem to think the bank robbery was a hoax," Joe told Brian as they watched Danielle.

In the other room, Danielle turned to the mirror and smiled. The next moment she waved.

"She knows we're watching her," Brian said with a chuckle.

"There is no way Danielle lied about putting those coins in there," Joe insisted.

"Even Susan claims the box was heavy when it was put back into the vault," Brian added.

"Wilson seems to think Susan is in on it. Thomas went to get her and bring her in for questioning. I think they're going to try to get her to flip on Danielle," Joe said.

"What is Danielle saying about finding the coins?" Brian asked.

"She said she only went down to the beach huts because she was thinking about Cheryl."

"Ahh, that's right. It's been almost a year."

"Next week," Joe said.

Brian let out a sigh. "Back then, I really thought Danielle was responsible for her cousin's death. I've rather gotten used to her."

"I'm not sure what Wilson and Thomas can do if Susan sticks to her story," Joe said. "It will be difficult to prove a motive. Wilson thinks Danielle intended to claim the missing coins on her taxes, but since she obviously hasn't filed her taxes yet, it's just a theory."

"Not to mention, Danielle hasn't really earned the reputation of being greedy, considering she keeps giving her money away."

"True. But Wilson and Thomas think she's guilty," Joe said.

"I get it. I've been there, done that. Wanted to send that girl to jail."

"I better call Lily. Wilson took Danielle's phone away, and I don't think he's let her make a call yet."

DAVE STERLING WAS SITTING in the living room at Marlow House, reading, when his cellphone rang. Tossing the magazine aside, he looked at his phone to see who was calling: Alan Kissinger.

"Hey, Alan, what's up?" Dave asked when he answered the phone.

"This might be your chance to get the necklace and get out of there. Have those other guests left yet?"

Dave glanced at the open doorway leading to the hallway. "Yeah, they took off about thirty minutes ago. I don't know where Danielle is. She left after breakfast and hasn't been back. Lily flew out of here about ten minutes ago."

"Boatman is down at the police station, and I bet money her friend Lily is on her way there. Those two are going to be gone all afternoon. Now's the chance to get the necklace and get out of there."

"The housekeeper is still here. She's up cleaning the room the Hortons were staying in. What's Boatman doing down at the police station?"

"The FBI found her with the missing gold. She's down there being interrogated. They just left the bank with one of my employees, who I think they believe was in on it with her."

"The one you were telling me about, Susan Mitchell?"

"That's the one," Alan said.

"Okay. As soon as the housekeeper leaves, we'll take care of business."

BRIAN HENDERSON DROVE DIRECTLY to Frederickport Vacation Properties without calling first. When questioning witnesses or suspects, he preferred not to give them advance notice he would be arriving. He found Adam Nichols in his office.

"Hey, Brian, what brings you over this way?" Adam asked as he tossed his pen on his desk and leaned back in his office chair.

"I need to ask you a few questions about those beach huts you own, the ones where we found Cheryl's body."

Adam arched his brows and leaned back even farther in his chair. "Yeah, what about them?"

"Do you keep them locked?"

"Yeah, what's this about?"

"Who has keys to number six?"

"Bill has a set; we keep a set here. Each hut is assigned to a different rental in that neighborhood. Use of the huts are included with the rentals, so we keep the keys in the houses. But the house assigned to hut six isn't currently rented. We had a broken pipe in there a couple weeks ago, and it did some serious damage. Had to replace the floors and some cabinets. So what is this about?"

"Is the key to hut six still in the house?"

Adam shrugged. "It should be."

"I assume you've had a lot of workers coming and going in that house because of the repairs?"

"Sure. Probably a dozen or more, why?"

"Would any of those workers have access to the key where you keep it in the house?"

"Are you serious?" Adam laughed. "Just an oversized surfboard keychain with the words Beach Hut Six painted in red on it, hanging in the kitchen. Sure. Anyone could grab it. But it's not like we keep anything of value in those buildings. Now will you tell me, what is this about?"

"The missing gold coins, they were found this afternoon in an ice chest in hut six."

Adam let out a low whistle and sat up in the chair. "No kidding? Who found them?"

"Danielle Boatman."

Adam frowned. "Danielle? What do you mean?"

Brian then went on to tell Adam about Danielle finding the coins and the FBI agents finding Danielle.

"Where is she now?" Adam asked.

"She's down at the station, being interrogated by Special Agent Wilson. He seems to think Danielle was behind the missing coins—that she never put them in the bank."

Adam narrowed his eyes and glared at Brian. "That's BS."

Brian nodded. "I know."

Adam's expression softened. "You don't think she's behind it?"

Brian shook his head. "I don't know how or why Danielle gets herself in these predicaments, but no. I don't believe she'd do it."

After Brian left Adam's office a few minutes later, Adam immediately picked up his phone and placed a call.

"Hello?" a female voice answered the call.

"Mel, this is Adam. You need to get down to the police station. I think Danielle might need a lawyer."

WHEN BRIAN HENDERSON returned to the police station, he learned Danielle was with the chief in his office with Lily, while Susan Mitchell was in the interrogation room with Special Agent Thomas. Instead of barging into the chief's office, he went directly to the lunchroom to get a cup of coffee. He was alone in the room, pouring himself a cup, when Wilson entered.

"Did you speak to Nichols?" Wilson asked.

"Yes. He said they keep the huts locked. But there were probably a dozen or more people who had access to that beach hut."

"Boatman didn't have a key on her," Wilson explained.

"Then she has to be telling the truth. She went down there because she was thinking of her cousin, found a hut unlocked, and went inside. It's a coincidence."

"All it proves is she didn't have a key," Wilson argued.

"Come on, you think Boatman put that gold in the hut and then didn't lock it?" Brian asked.

"My guess, the last person in the hut—prior to us finding Boatman there—was the person who put the coins in the ice chest.

That person obviously didn't lock the hut. That person could be Boatman."

"I don't buy it," Brian muttered.

"What about Nichols? He's a friend of Boatman's. He very well could be part of this."

Coffee cup in hand, Brian turned to face Wilson. The oldest member of the Frederickport Police Department, Brian was also the most cynical. His cynicism had spilled over onto his feelings for Danielle until he came to realize—he had been wrong. Being wrong tended to annoy Brian, but he dealt with it. Which also meant he didn't have a problem pointing out when someone else was in the wrong.

"No way." Brian took a swig of coffee.

"Nichols is a friend of yours?" Wilson asked.

Brian shrugged. "I've known him for years. Hauled him in a few times when he was a teenager for minor stuff. You know, underage drinking. Wasn't a bad kid. He doesn't always use the best judgment, but, no way. For one thing, I don't believe Danielle would get involved with something like this. Hell, she keeps giving her money away, why try some tax scam?"

"Maybe she figured she could give even more money away. Maybe she has some sort of Robin Hood complex."

Brian laughed and took a seat at the table. "That's an interesting theory." He took a sip of his coffee.

Wilson sat down across from Brian. "Don't you think there is something a little...different about Danielle Boatman?"

Slowly lifting his cup to his mouth again, Brian took a sip, his eyes never leaving Wilson. He then lowered the cup just as slowly and asked, "Different, how?"

Wilson shrugged. "There is just something a little...off about her. Not normal."

With a grunt Brian said, "You're telling me."

Wilson perked up. "So you see it too?"

"Maybe Danielle just takes a little getting used to. Even her house is different."

"Her house? What do you know about her house?" Wilson asked excitedly.

"Never mind, hard to explain," Brian muttered.

"No, I want to know. What exactly have you noticed?"

Brian studied Wilson for a moment and then smiled. "Something happened to you when you were there, didn't it?"

"What do you mean?" Wilson asked defensively.

Brian set the cup on the tabletop. "Well, let's see, once when I was there, I could swear someone slugged me. But there was no one there."

"What do you mean slugged you?"

"I think you know what I mean. It's like the place is…haunted."

Wilson stood up. "Now you're just being ridiculous."

"Hey, you're the one who brought it up."

Special Agent Thomas walked into the lunchroom, interrupting their conversation. "I had to let Mitchell go." Thomas eyed Brian's coffee. "Hey, do you mind if I pour myself a cup of that?"

"Sure, no problem, help yourself." Coffee cup in hand, Brian motioned to the coffee pot sitting on the counter.

"I'm assuming she stuck to her story?" Wilson asked.

"Didn't budge. I was getting nowhere with her quick. Unless we can find something to tie her to Boatman, like a transfer of funds, or if someone else comes forward with some additional information, I don't see her folding. She was tougher than I thought she'd be."

"She probably knows we really don't have anything on Boatman unless we get her to flip. And if she flips, it might keep us from filing charges against her, but she'll still lose her job. I say it's too soon in the game for her to fold," Wilson suggested.

"Of course, there could be another possibility," Brian suggested.

Both Thomas and Wilson looked at him.

"What's that?" Thomas asked.

"Danielle and Susan are innocent. I don't believe they're involved in some scam. Those gold coins were in that safe deposit box just like they said, and you two are looking in the wrong direction. Someone moved it, but it wasn't them."

"And just who was it? A ghost?" Wilson sneered.

Brian smiled. "Maybe."

THIRTY-FOUR

W alt anxiously paced the attic floor, stopping periodically to pause by the window to look outside. He kept hoping to see either Lily or Danielle drive up. Lily had barged into the attic earlier, looking for him. She had said something about Joe calling. She then rambled on about Danielle finding the gold and something about the FBI. None of it made sense. Since it was impossible for Lily to see or hear him, there was no way for him to ask her any questions. The only reason Lily knew he was in the attic when she burst in was because she asked him if he was there, and he responded by tilting the spotting scope up and down.

Now standing by the window, Walt looked across the street at Ian's house. Lily had also mentioned something about Ian being in Portland. He assumed Sadie had gone with him, as he normally left the dog at Marlow House instead of leaving him across the street alone.

Walt spied Joanne's car parked in front of the house. The last time he was downstairs, she was putting clean sheets on the bed the Hortons had used. New guests would be arriving tomorrow afternoon. He then noticed Max, who was sitting inside the gate, looking out at the street, his tail swishing back and forth.

With a sigh, Walt resumed his pacing.

"I'M TAKING OFF NOW," Joanne called out from the doorway leading into the living room. She stood in the hallway. The guests she knew as Blake and Jeannie Spicer sat together on the living room sofa.

Blake looked up toward the doorway and smiled at Joanne. "Have a nice afternoon."

"Thank you, you too." Joanne paused a moment and glanced down the hallway, noting the sunshine pouring through the front window. She looked back into the living room. "You two should get outside, get some sunshine. It's a beautiful day today."

Blake yawned and stretched before saying, "We will. But I'm just a little tired. I think I'll go upstairs and take a nap."

Joanne smiled. "Well, it's your vacation. Enjoy. If you get hungry, there's a coconut cake under the cake pan in the kitchen. I don't know where Lily ran off to, she left in a hurry, so I have no idea when she or Danielle will be back."

Jeannie made a show of stretching out her arms before letting one rest behind Blake's shoulders. "We'll be fine. Have a nice day."

Joanne flashed one parting smile and then hurried down the hallway. Blake and Jeannie silently looked at each other, listening. After they heard the front door close, Blake got up from the sofa and peered out the living room window.

He watched as Joanne drove away. Still looking out the window, he said, "I thought she'd never leave!"

"What are you going to do about the bedroom door if you still can't open it?" Jeannie stood up from the sofa.

"If I have to, I'll break the door down," Dave said.

"Just as long as you can get into the safe."

"I don't know what happened with the door earlier, but I'll get in there. You just do what you need to."

"I already packed and wiped down our room, so I'll finish down here and wipe down anything we might have touched, while you take care of the safe."

Blake gave her a nod and headed for the doorway. Jeannie remained standing in the middle of the room, hands on hips, surveying the area. After a moment of consideration, she made her way to the doorway and then to the downstairs bathroom, where she grabbed a hand towel. After dampening the towel with water, she wiped her prints off the bathroom faucet.

WALT MOVED EFFORTLESSLY from the attic to the first floor, bypassing the second floor. Once there, he found Jeannie Spicer rushing up and down the entry hallway, wiping down the switch plates and doorknobs.

"We're doing this again," he said with a snigger. Walt turned to make his way to the library but then paused. He looked back to Jeannie and frowned and then glanced upstairs. "If you're down here, what is he doing?" Walt murmured.

A moment later Walt was on the second floor. There he found Blake sitting by Danielle's bedroom door. Blake wore a pair of leather gloves, and in his hands he held a small tool.

"That again?" Walt moved to Blake's side "Okay, this time I'm going to let you in there so I can see what you're up to." Walt watched as Blake poked a thin tool into the lock on Danielle's bedroom door and moved it to and fro.

After a moment, Blake let out a celebratory shout and quickly stood up. He opened Danielle's bedroom door and looked around. Instead of going into the room, Blake rushed to the stairwell and looked down. "Steph, I'm in!"

Walt heard Jeannie...or was it Steph?...let out a shout from downstairs. He then heard her racing up the stairs, still holding the hand towel.

"I wonder why we couldn't open it before?" Jeannie asked when she reached the second floor.

"Because I was holding it, you thief," Walt grumbled.

"I'll go back downstairs and finish up. Let me know when you get it," Jeannie said excitedly before turning abruptly and dashing downstairs.

Walt eyed Blake. "Before you get what? Hmm...I think I know."

Walt followed Blake into Danielle's room. Leaning back against the loveseat, arms folded across his chest, he watched as Blake removed the painting from the wall and set it on the bed. Blake then dashed from the room, and when he returned, he carried a small case. Setting the case on the bed next to the painting, he opened it, revealing a set of delicate tools.

"A safe cracker? Is that what we have here?" Walt smirked. "I'm curious to see just how good you are. I think I'll give you enough rope to hang yourself." Walt cringed, his hand going to his own throat, remembering the rope that had killed him. Glancing up at the ceiling toward the attic, he mumbled, "Poor idiom choice." Turning his attention back to Blake, he watched.

Narrowing his eyes, Walt smiled. "I think I have an idea."

Leaving Blake with the safe, Walt moved downstairs. He found Jeannie going into the downstairs bathroom. He watched as she set the towel on the sink and then shut the bathroom door. Walt assumed to use the facilities.

"This is convenient," Walt murmured. "I don't have to shove you in there to keep you out of the way. You made my job easier." Focusing his energy on the door's lock, he forced the mechanism inside to shift slightly from right to left until it jammed, which would make it impossible for Jeannie to open the door when she wanted to come out again. Smiling, Walt turned from the bathroom and headed back upstairs.

When Walt returned to Danielle's bedroom, Blake was just swinging the wall safe door open. Letting out an excited shout, the would-be jewel thief removed the velvet pouch. His hands trembled as he pulled out the antique necklace. Impulsively, he used his teeth to jerk off one of his gloves, letting it fall to the floor. Shifting the necklace from one hand to another, he dropped the pouch to the floor with the glove and then removed the second glove.

Reverently, Blake fondled the diamonds and emeralds, holding the piece up over his head to allow the gems to capture the sunlight coming through the window.

"You might as well enjoy it now; you won't be enjoying it for long." Walt spied a folded bath towel sitting on the sofa. "That might work," Walt muttered.

While Blake's attention was focused on the necklace in his hands, he failed to notice the bath towel rise slowly off the sofa and float across the room. He was taken by surprise when it wrapped around his face and head, seemingly held tight from behind by an attacker.

Blake screamed. He dropped the necklace and his hands went to the towel, desperately trying to wrench it from his face. From Blake's perspective he was being attacked from behind, and whoever it was took him to the floor and jerked his arms behind his back, forcing his face, still wrapped in the towel, into the hard floor.

"Get off me!" Blake shouted again and again.

His muffled cries went unanswered. Someone was wrapping

heavy tape around his wrists and then his ankles. What he hadn't seen was the tape floating down from the attic as his head was being wrapped in the towel.

For good measure, Walt located rope and used it to further secure Blake's arms and legs. Walt had remembered Danielle telling him once how if a person knew what he or she was doing, it was possible to break out of duct tape. Walt didn't want to give Blake that opportunity.

Walt stood over his prisoner and watched him squirm on the floor, unable to see who or what had attacked him. With calm, Walt went over to Danielle's desk and removed a blank sheet of paper from the drawer, along with a pen.

The woman locked in the bathroom downstairs goes by the name Jeannie Spicer, but I believe her first name might actually be Stephanie. This man goes by the name Blake Spicer, but I suspect that is not his real name.

He broke in to Danielle's safe in an attempt to steal the Missing Thorndike. Please take them to jail.

WALT STOOD up and walked to Blake, setting the note next to his squirming body. Picking up the Missing Thorndike, he set it atop the note.

Walt then returned to the desk and removed a second blank sheet of paper from the drawer. Sitting down again, he picked up the pen.

The woman locked in this bathroom attempted to steal the Missing Thorndike. You will find her accomplice, along with the proof of their crime, upstairs in Danielle's bedroom.

Picking up the paper, Walt stood up, stepped over Blake, grabbed the roll of tape, and headed downstairs.

"Dave? Dave! The door is stuck! Help me! I can't get it open! Dave!"

Standing in front of the powder room door, Walt smiled. Calmly, he taped the note on the outside of the door and then headed for the parlor.

In the parlor, Walt looked at the phone. "This better work, or I'm going to have to figure out some way to get Max to come back into the house, and see if he can convince Heather to get down here."

Sitting down at the parlor desk, Walt dialed 911. Setting the receiver on the desk, he waited.

"911, what is your emergency?"

BRIAN BARGED into the chief's office. MacDonald was there alone with Lily, while Danielle was in the interrogation room with Special Agent Thomas, Melony by her side.

MacDonald looked up to Brian. "What is it?"

"We just got a 911 call in. Whoever is on the line, they won't say anything."

The chief frowned. "You know what to do."

"Chief," Brian glanced to Lily and back to the chief, "the call is coming from Marlow House."

Lily jumped from her chair and immediately pulled out her cell-phone and dialed a number. "Joanne, where are you? Are you okay?" Lily asked when the housekeeper answered the call. They spoke a few more words before Lily got off the phone. She looked from the chief to Brian.

"Joanne isn't at the house. The only ones there are two of our guests, Blake and Jeannie Spicer. Something must be wrong."

Brian gave Lily a nod and then dashed from the office.

The chief turned to Lily. They looked at each other. "And Walt," the chief said.

"Yeah. I know." Narrowing her eyes, Lily looked to the door where Brian had just dashed from.

THIRTY-FIVE

"We've already gone over this," Melony reminded him calmly. Sean Sullivan, who had been silently watching the exchange from the corner of the interrogation room, studied Melony, who wore slacks and a blouse, her blond hair secured atop her head in a bun.

Danielle's gaze darted over at Sean for a moment and then looked back at Melony, who was addressing Agent Thomas.

"I'm just trying to understand how your client happened to come across those gold coins if she didn't put them there."

"She already explained that—numerous times. And since they belong to her, I don't see what the problem is."

"Considering she reported them missing and—"

"I assume you have checked the coins for fingerprints? The container they were found in?" Melony asked.

"Yes. There were other fingerprints found—as to be expected considering the number of people who've had access to those coins over the years. But your client's fingerprints were also found on the coins."

"As you said, Agent Thomas, that is to be expected. My client is the victim here. And what exactly would be her motive? The coins were not insured, and the bank is not responsible."

"But she could have written them off on her taxes," he reminded her.

"Do you have copies of her current tax return? Has she attempted to write them off as a loss?"

"You know I don't—"

"Exactly," Melony snapped. "I believe your time would be better spent looking for whoever compromised the security of the bank's safe deposit box, before another safe deposit holder is victimized."

THERE WAS no way Lily was going to stay at the police station. Plus, she had a key to Marlow House and it seemed a little ridiculous to allow the local police to break the door down when answering a 911 call at her home. However, she did agree to wait in her car until they told her it was okay to go in.

Special Agent Wilson insisted on accompanying Joe and Brian on the call while Danielle—who was unaware of the 911 call—remained with Melony and Special Agent Thomas in the interrogation room. Also in the interrogation room was Sean Sullivan, yet that was something only Danielle knew, and Lily and the chief suspected.

Wilson believed the 911 call might in some way be connected to Danielle and the coins. He felt it too much a coincidence considering the recent turn of events, and Wilson was not a big believer of coincidences.

Lily drove her own car back to Marlow House. She parked behind the police car, which had arrived a few seconds before her. She had already given Joe the keys to the house. With the passenger window down, Lily anxiously waited. She watched as the three officers—Joe, Brian, and Wilson—stealthily made their way to the front door.

So focused on watching the three make their way to the front door of Marlow House, she failed to notice the shady black figure approach her car. When it leapt unexpectedly through her open window from the sidewalk, she managed to stifle her scream, in spite of her now racing heart.

"Max!" Lily scolded, a war drum now beating in her chest. The purring cat strolled across the empty passenger seat to Lily. "You scared the crap out of me!" Picking up Max, who was now nuzzling his head into her chest, she held him tightly while refocusing her attention on Marlow House.

"I suppose it's a good sign that you're out here purring," Lily muttered as she scratched under Max's chin, her eyes focused on the front of Marlow House.

JOE SLIPPED the key Lily had given him into the doorknob while Brian and Wilson stood behind him, waiting. The three men remained quiet as Joe gently pushed the door open. The moment he did, they heard a woman's muffled shouting from down the hallway.

"Dave, dammit, this isn't funny! Help me get out of here!"

Now standing at the closed door leading to the bathroom, Joe and Wilson exchanged glances as Brian peeled a sheet of paper off the door. Together, the three silently read the note.

"So they sent you three," Walt said to deaf ears when he reached the hallway. "I would have preferred the chief."

Stepping away from the door, Joe and Brian readied their guns while Wilson reached for the door handle.

"I think you're going to need my help here," Walt muttered, focusing his energy on the lock mechanism he had jammed.

As Wilson slowly turned the doorknob and began to push the door in, the woman's voice shouted, "It's about time, Dave!"

Wilson stepped back and grabbed his gun when the door was jerked from his grasp and swung inward.

In the next moment the three came face-to-face with a woman, who, upon seeing them, exploded into a shrill scream as she leapt backwards, grabbing her chest in surprise. Eyes wide, she stared at the two uniformed officers and the conservatively dressed man in the dark suit. Stunned, she blinked her eyes in confusion as her mind raced to make sense of the unexpected turn of events—and then she quickly shifted into survival mode.

"Oh, thank goodness," the woman said with a wide smile as she dramatically released the breath she had been holding. "I was hoping someone would help get this door unstuck, but I never imagined I would have three such handsome rescuers."

"Oh, brother," Walt groaned, rolling his eyes. He glanced over to the three officers and was relieved to see none of them appeared to be falling for her damsel-in-distress routine.

"Ma'am, would you please step into the hall," Joe said curtly.

Wide eyed, she smiled up at Joe. "Why certainly, Officer. I'm not certain what is going on or why you're all here—although I'm glad to see you, considering I've been stuck in this bathroom for what seems like forever. I'm Jeannie Spicer. I'm a guest of Marlow House. You can ask Danielle Boatman." Flashing another smile, she stepped into the hallway.

Joe looked at Wilson and said, "Why don't you stay down here with her, and we'll check upstairs."

Less than five minutes later, Joe returned to the first floor without Brian. He looked at Wilson and said, "I think you better come up here. Bring her with you."

The smile vanished from Jeannie's face.

DAVE, aka Blake, had been rolling around on the floor prior to the officers' arrival. Walt had been keeping an eye on him, pushing him away from any furniture, such as when it looked as if he might topple the desk or tip over its chair. Walt didn't imagine Danielle would be thrilled if she returned to a bedroom that looked as if a wrecking ball had been let loose.

Breathing heavily, but lying still, it was obvious Dave was attempting to figure out who was in the bedroom with him. Was it the person who had attacked him from behind, blindfolded him, and tied him up?

When Steph, aka Jeannie, stepped into the room, Wilson closely by her side, she let out a little gasp upon seeing her husband bound and blindfolded on the floor, but she said nothing.

"Steph? Steph?" Dave called out.

"I thought you said your name was Jeannie," Brian said as he leaned down and grabbed Dave by the forearm, jerking him to his feet. Still tightly bound, Dave wobbled unsteadily, trying desperately to keep erect.

Instead of removing the bindings securing Dave's feet or hands, Brian removed the towel wrapped around his head, held in place with duct tape.

Now able to see his surroundings, Dave blinked several times, his eyes adjusting to the light as he looked around frantically trying to figure out what was going on.

"Oh, Blake, who did this to you?" Stephanie called out dramatically. "I was in the bathroom and someone locked me in. Are you okay?"

"Yes…yes…someone must have broken in to Marlow House." Dave looked from Joe to Brian and then said in a rush, "I'm so happy to see you officers!"

"I bet you are," Joe muttered. "Maybe I need to get Lily now."

"Oh yes, Lily! She'll tell you who we are," Stephanie urged.

Wilson instructed Stephanie to stand quietly next to the wall. Without comment, she immediately complied, but looked nervously at her husband.

After Brian released Dave from his restraints, he ordered him to stand next to the woman. Like Stephanie had done, he did as he was told, yet said, "We really are guests here. Honest. Lily will tell you."

"Stay there and be quiet," Brian gruffly demanded. "You'll get your chance to tell your side in a minute." He then pointed to the note still on the floor, the Missing Thorndike on top. Neither Brian nor Wilson knew the reason the man on the floor hadn't rolled over the note was due to the fact Walt had kept him away from it.

Kneeling down beside the letter, Wilson cocked his head slightly so he could read the handwritten message. When he was done, he glanced up to the wall safe, its door still wide open.

"Who do you think foiled their burglary?" Wilson asked Brian.

"Apparently, whoever wrote that note," Brian answered.

When Lily arrived upstairs with Joe and looked into Danielle's bedroom, she knew exactly what had happened.

Brian pointed to the couple huddled nervously by the wall. "They say they're guest here. They claim to be Blake and Jeannie Spicer, but according to the notes we found with them, that might not be their real names. According to one of the notes, she also goes by Stephanie, and when we found him, he was calling out to someone named Steph, and when we were downstairs, she was calling out to someone name Dave."

"I have a brother name Dave!" the woman blurted out. "I was locked in the bathroom and panicked. I meant to say Blake!" She looked frantically at Lily. "Tell them, Lily, that we're guests here."

"Yeah, you're guests here," Lily said dryly. "But it doesn't mean you aren't also jewel thieves."

MORE OFFICERS ARRIVED to process the crime scene as Marlow House's two remaining guests were put into the back of a police car to be taken to the station for further questioning. According to their identification, they were Blake and Jeannie Spicer, yet until their fingerprints were processed, Brian wasn't certain who they actually were.

Lily sat on the sofa in the living room, a napping Max by her side. She detected a heavy scent of sweet cigar smoke in the room.

"Hey, Walt," Lily said. While it appeared she was alone in the room with Max, she knew she wasn't. "Good job up there."

"Who are you talking to?" Wilson asked when he entered the room the next moment.

Lily looked up at Wilson and smiled. "Max, of course."

Brian followed Wilson into the room. He pointed to the sleeping feline next to Lily. "The cat."

Wilson and Brian each sat down, sitting in the chairs facing Lily.

"So what did Blake say when you questioned him? What did he say happened?" Lily asked.

"According to Mr. Spicer, he and his wife were alone in Marlow House when he heard someone walking around in Danielle's bedroom. Knowing there was not supposed to be anyone in there, he went in to investigate, and someone attacked him from behind."

"Someone? Like who?"

"He said he didn't see them. Next thing he knew, he was tied up and on the floor, blindfolded. Claims he had nothing to do with opening the safe or removing the Missing Thorndike."

Lily arched her brows. "Do you believe him?"

"Not sure why someone would leave behind the necklace if they went to all that trouble to steal it. We also found a pair of gloves on the floor and the tools used to open the safe. They'll be finger-printed, as well as the Missing Thorndike," Brian explained.

Lily flashed Brian a smile and leaned back on the sofa. "Glad to see you have it under control."

Wilson stood up and handed Lily a yellowed sheet of paper. "Have you ever seen this before? We found it on Danielle's desk."

Taking the paper from Wilson, Lily looked at it and smiled. "Sure. This is a letter Walt Marlow wrote George Hemming."

"Walt Marlow?" Wilson frowned.

Brian glanced up to the ceiling and shifted nervously in his seat.

"His grandfather built this house. He's the one who left the Marlow Estate to Danielle's aunt."

Wilson snatched the letter back from Lily and turned the page from side to side. "How do you know Marlow wrote this? I don't see a signature."

"Obviously it's only the first page of the letter. Marie Nichols—George Hemming's daughter—gave Danielle some old letters Walt had written to her father. She figured Danielle would be interested in them since she now owns Marlow House. Danielle dropped that page in the kitchen when she was going through the letters. I found it on the floor and took it up to her room. So what is the big deal about this letter?"

"The handwriting in the letter is remarkably similar to the handwriting on the note left by whoever locked Jeannie Spicer in the bathroom and tied up her husband," Wilson explained.

Pulling her bare feet up on the sofa, Lily tucked them under her as she made herself more comfortable. Leaning back again against the back cushion, she smiled up at Wilson. "About that…how exactly did Jeannie get locked in the bathroom downstairs? She claims the door was stuck, she couldn't open it, but didn't I hear you opened it up? Was it hard to open? I don't recall ever having a problem with that door before."

Walt shook his head and took a puff off his cigar. "Lily, Lily, you probably should have said the door was known for sticking. But you couldn't resist, could you?" Walt sniggered. Lily couldn't hear a word he said.

"Don't change the subject." Wilson shook the letter at Lily. "Who really wrote this?"

With a cringe, Lily inched away from Wilson, scooting back on the sofa. "I told you, Walt Marlow. If you don't believe me, ask Marie Nichols. She's the one who gave it to Danielle."

"No. It could not have been Walt Marlow. Whoever wrote those notes this morning and called 911 is the same person who wrote this letter."

Narrowing her eyes, Lily looked up at Wilson and smiled. "You might want to read the date on the letter you're brandishing. And if you don't believe the date or Marie Nichols, then I'd suggest you have your lab run some sort of test on the age of the ink used in that letter. The FBI does that sorta stuff, doesn't it?"

"Are you trying to tell me Walt Marlow wrote those notes this morning?" Wilson snapped.

"Is that what you're saying?" Walt asked deaf ears.

Unfolding her legs, Lily stood up from the sofa and faced Wilson. "No. What I'm saying, either someone with remarkably similar handwriting to Walt Marlow wrote those notes, or else Walt Marlow's ghost wrote them. You decide."

From his chair where he had been sitting quietly, listening to the exchange, Brian groaned.

THIRTY-SIX

"You expect Marie Nichols to contradict Lily's story?" Brian Henderson asked. He drove in the car with Special Agent Wilson. Joe stayed behind at Marlow House with Lily while his team finished processing the crime scene.

"Lily insists Marie Nichols will back up her story. We might as well call her bluff and get that out of the way."

Brian gazed out the side window of the sedan. Without turning in Wilson's direction, he asked, "You think Lily was lying?"

"You actually believe Walt Marlow wrote those other letters?" Wilson snapped back.

Brian looked over at Wilson. "I don't know what to think anymore. But there's one good thing."

Both hands on the steering wheel, Wilson continued to keep his eyes on the road ahead as he asked, "What's that?"

"At least some invisible hand didn't give me a push or try to punch me when we were in the house. How about you? Did Walt give you a shove?" Brian sniggered.

"You don't believe that place is really haunted."

With a shrug, Brian leaned back in the seat and let out a sigh. "Like I said, I don't know what to believe anymore."

"I don't know how Danielle Boatman gets all of you under her spell, but she's up to something. More I think about it, I'd say it's a publicity stunt. Isn't her Anniversary Open House next week?"

"It's on the fourth. So, you're saying all of this is some publicity stunt? The missing coins, the jewel heist?"

"I can't really call it a jewel heist, since nothing was taken."

"What was the Spicers' role in all this?"

"Either they're working with Boatman, or she hired someone to attack her guests and set this thing up."

"That's a pretty big leap. I don't see Danielle doing something to endanger her guests, not to promote Marlow House."

"Then they're working with her."

"I guess we'll know more about them when we get back to the station."

Ten minutes later, Special Agent Wilson and Officer Brian Henderson stood on the front porch of Marie Nichols's house. She didn't ask them inside.

Holding the letter just handed her, Marie looked from it to Wilson. "Yes, I recognize this. Why do you have it?"

"Do you know who wrote it?"

Marie frowned. "Certainly. Walt Marlow. What is this about, and why do you have this? I thought I gave this to Danielle. Is Danielle alright?"

"Danielle is fine," Brian assured her. "It's just that we're trying to identify whoever wrote this letter, because it looks exactly like the penmanship of two notes we found at Marlow House."

Marie scoffed and said, "Then I'd say Walt Marlow wrote those other notes you found. I gave Danielle a stack of letters; maybe they're from those."

––––––––––

"THEY'RE IN LOCKUP," the chief told Brian and Wilson when they returned to the police station. "The driver's licenses they gave you are fake. Their real names are David and Stephanie Sterling. They're from Clackamas, where they own a safe shop. Our Mr. Sterling is a professional locksmith. The car they were driving is a rental. Sterling rented the car under his alias, Blake Spicer; that was also the name on the credit card they were using. They don't have any prior, but his fingerprints are all over the Thorndike diamonds, and I suspect we'll find his DNA on the gloves you found.

Now sitting in one of the chairs facing the chief's desk, Wilson glanced over to Brian, who was sitting next to him, and then looked back to the chief. "If this David Sterling is the one who opened Boatman's safe, do you have any idea who stopped him?"

"I have no idea," the chief lied. "But right now, I'd rather focus on the Sterlings."

"Obviously, someone wants us to think Walt Marlow wrote those letters," Wilson snapped. "Whoever it was went to a lot of trouble imitating Marlow's handwriting."

Brian glanced to Wilson and smiled. "So you now believe Lily was telling the truth, that Marlow wrote the letter we found on the desk?"

"It has to be some sort of publicity stunt," Wilson grumbled.

"Or perhaps whoever wrote those notes today does not wish to be identified for some reason, so rather than penning them in his own hand, he tried to imitate an old letter he found sitting on the desk. You did say that's where you found Marlow's letter? And I would assume whoever wrote those notes probably sat at Danielle's desk when he wrote them. I was told our people found blank paper matching the ones our mystery man used today in Danielle's bedroom desk," the chief said.

"Why would this person wish to remain anonymous?" Wilson asked.

Brian considered the question and smiled. "I can think of one person. Chris Johnson lives down the street from Danielle, they're close, and I bet he has a key to her house. We know Chris likes to fly under the radar. I don't see him wanting the publicity something like this would bring him."

"Then let's bring him in!" Wilson said.

The chief smiled and leaned forward, his elbows resting against the tabletop. "With all due respect, this one is our case. I suggest you might want to focus on yours. From what I understand, your partner is about finished with Danielle, and her attorney is asking that she be allowed to go home."

Without a word, Wilson stood and turned to the door.

As he marched from the room and disappeared down the hall, Brian studied MacDonald. Finally, he asked, "Hey, Chief, you don't think Chris wrote those letters, do you?"

MacDonald smiled softly and then stood up. "Lily told me earlier, Chris went to Portland with Ian this morning. I talked to them on the phone a few minutes ago. They're still in Portland; they haven't left yet."

Before Brian had a chance to respond, the chief's desk phone rang. After MacDonald answered the call, Brian stood up, preparing to quietly slip from the office so his boss could have his conversation in private. But when he started to turn away from the desk, the chief motioned for him to sit back down while he continued talking on the phone.

"Well, that was interesting," the chief said when he hung up the telephone and looked at Brian.

Sitting back down in the chair, Brian asked, "What?"

"You know that cellphone you found on Sterling?"

Brian nodded.

"They've finished going through his calls. Over the last week, beginning on the day Danielle discovered her gold was missing, our Mr. Sterling has had frequent phone conversations with an employee from our local bank."

"Are you suggesting Sterling is connected with the bank job?"

"I don't know. But the person he has been talking to all week happens to be the new manager of the bank."

Brian let out a low whistle and leaned forward. "Are you saying Alan Kissinger is somehow connected to David Sterling?"

"It looks that way. You might want to go get Wilson and Thomas. I need to let them know. Which means..." MacDonald let out a sigh. "This may not just be our case."

———

DANIELLE STOOD by the front desk of the Frederickport Police Station and gave Melony a hug.

"I really appreciate you coming down here. That was really sweet of Adam to think of it."

"Hey, I'm more than happy to be of help." Melony grinned. "How could I not after Adam said you were a rich client who was always getting herself in trouble, so I could make a bundle."

Danielle laughed. "Did he really say that?"

"Actually, he was sincerely worried about you. But yeah, he added that after I told him I would come."

Danielle laughed again.

Melony grabbed her right hand and gave it a reassuring squeeze as she said, "And remember, if those FBI agents want to talk to you again, you call me first. I don't want you talking to them without me there. You aren't out of the woods."

Danielle nodded. "I understand."

"You going home now?" Melony asked as she reached for the door.

"No. I want to talk to the chief first."

Pausing at the doorway, Melony glanced down the hallway leading to the chief's office. "I saw him going in there with those two agents."

"I know. I'll wait out here."

After Melony left, Danielle took a seat in the front waiting area of the police station. Earlier, when her cellphone had been returned, she was told about the 911 call at Marlow House. After the chief had told her all he could—considering they had an audience—she phoned Lily, who confirmed most of what the chief had said.

Danielle waited patiently for her turn to talk to the chief in private and was surprised when Brian walked into the office with Alan Kissinger, who seemed clearly annoyed and unhappy to be there. She would have expected him to be boasting a smug smile, assuming he had been told about the gold being found—with her. But he wasn't smiling, and when he walked past her, he didn't notice her sitting there.

"I DON'T UNDERSTAND why you had to drag me down here; I already know you found the gold coins and that I was right—Danielle Boatman never put them in her safe deposit box. I'm going to advise the bank to sue Ms. Boatman for damaging the bank's reputation with her false claims."

"Please sit down." Agent Thomas motioned to the table in the center of the interrogation room. In the next room, looking through the two-way mirror, was Agent Wilson, Brian and the chief.

Annoyed, Alan slammed down in the seat and glared up at Thomas.

Calmly, Thomas removed photographs from a file he carried. He sat them on the desk. "Do you know these people?"

Alan looked at the photographs and shook his head. He was telling the truth. They looked faintly familiar, but...

"No. I don't."

"How about these two." Thomas removed two more photographs from the file and set them on the tabletop.

Alan stared at the pictures. Saying nothing, he swallowed nervously.

"Well? Do you?"

"Umm…yes…that's David and Stephanie Sterling."

Thomas sat down across the table from Alan. "So tell me, how do you know them exactly?"

"David is my cousin," Alan explained.

"Really?" Thomas reached over and pushed the first two pictures closer to Alan. "You might want to take a second look at the first pair. Same people. Your cousin and his wife seem rather adept with changing their identity."

Alan shrugged. "Stephanie used to be a makeup artist in Hollywood. Sometimes she likes to dress up." He looked up from the photographs. "What is this about?"

"I see you and your cousin have been talking a lot on the phone."

Again, Alan shrugged, shifting uncomfortably in his chair. "Like I said, he's my cousin."

"I assume your cousin came to town to visit you?"

Alan shook his head. "I didn't know they were in town."

"Really? Yet you talked to him every day—sometimes two or three times a day."

"I really don't know why I'm here. Would you please just tell me so I can leave."

"Your cousin and his wife are in lockup right now, waiting for their attorney to arrive."

Alan's eyes widened. He said nothing.

"But you might want to talk before they do, or they might just blame this all on you."

"I don't know what you're talking about. My cousin is under arrest? Why?"

"For trying to steal the Missing Thorndike, of course. After their attorney gets here, they might decide to throw you under the bus for a lighter sentence. Of course, that's only if they make the deal first."

"This is ridiculous. Am I under arrest? Because if I am, I demand to see my attorney. If I'm not, I demand to be released."

"We know you worked with your cousin to take the gold out of Danielle Boatman's safe deposit box. We don't know how you did it exactly, but it's only a matter of time before your cousin tells us. After all, his fingerprints are all over Boatman's necklace. It's not going to take long for your cousin or his wife to realize telling us how you did it is preferable to going to jail for a botched jewelry heist."

Alan stood abruptly. "Am I under arrest?"

Thomas eyed Alan. "Not yet."

"Then I am free to go?" Alan asked curtly.

"Yes, I suppose you are."

Without another word, Alan Kissinger turned abruptly from Thomas and headed for the door.

THIRTY-SEVEN

G uilt had prevented Joyce Pruitt from getting a good night's rest. Since Danielle's visit to see Gran, she couldn't stop thinking about what Danielle had told her about the coins not being insured. It was one thing to keep the coins, knowing Danielle would be reimbursed. After all, it wasn't like they were treasured heirlooms; Danielle had intended to sell them anyway. Joyce figured this way, both her and Danielle could profit from the treasure. After all, insurance companies were rich; it would mean nothing to them.

Knowing Danielle hadn't insured the coins changed everything. Joyce liked Danielle; how could she steal from her? But then Joyce remembered that Danielle was a wealthy woman. Would she really miss the coins? A couple months ago, Danielle hadn't even known they existed.

Joyce kept going back and forth—keep them—give them back. Whatever she intended to do, she couldn't leave them at their current hiding place indefinitely. Once Adam was finished with the repairs of number six beach cottage, it would be rented for the summer, and the new tenants would be using its beach hut.

While wrestling with her dilemma, Joyce ran errands. The first stop was the pharmacy to pick up Gran's prescription, and then she had to stop at Frederickport Vacation Properties to pick up her paycheck. She pulled into the pharmacy parking lot. Just as she was about to get out of her car, another vehicle drove in and parked next to her. Joyce waited for the driver of the other car to turn off his engine before she exited her vehicle.

She was closing her door when the driver from the other car—who had just got out of his vehicle—said, "Joyce?"

Joyce turned to the driver and for a moment was speechless. It was Samuel Hayman.

"Sam?" Joyce said hesitantly, walking toward him as he walked toward her.

"Hello, Joyce. How have you been?" he said, sounding as hesitant as she had a moment before.

"Umm…I'm fine. When did you get back?"

Sam smiled sadly. "I just got back in town last week."

Joyce thought he looked much thinner than the last time she had seen him. She imagined prison did that to a man. His clothes were baggy and she suspected they were probably something he had worn before his arrest last year—when he was heavier. Still clean shaven, his curly brown hair was shorter than he had normally worn it. Despite the dark circles shadowing his eyes, he was still a pleasant-looking man. She remembered he had straight white teeth, but he wasn't smiling in the same way he normally did, so she couldn't see them.

"You look good." She didn't sound convincing.

Samuel smiled, showing off those straight white teeth she remembered. "No, I don't, but it is sweet of you to say so. I might as well acknowledge the elephant in the room. I am out of prison. I decided to come home. I didn't know how much I would miss this place until I was locked up for the last year. And you will never imagine how much I regret what I did."

"We all make mistakes, Sam. And I'm glad you came home." Impulsively, Joyce reached out and gave him a hug.

When the hug ended, his smile broadened. "Thank you, Joyce, you have no idea how much I needed that."

"Well, I am glad you came home," she insisted.

"How is your mother?"

Joyce shrugged. "The same. Never changes. Still demanding."

Samuel laughed and then asked, "And your kids?"

"Good. They all still live in town."

Samuel let out a sigh. "You're lucky, Joyce."

His comment caught her by surprise. "I am?"

"Yes. You have a family and home. I have a lot of regrets these days. On the top of the list, not having a family by now. But the choices I made, well, I understand I've made it much more difficult for myself to have the future I once envisioned."

"Don't be so hard on yourself, Sam. You paid your time. Look at this as a new beginning."

"You're sweet, Joyce. Just promise me, if you ever stumble across a million-dollar necklace and think it would be just so easy to take—no one would find out or get hurt—step away."

JOYCE COULDN'T GET Samuel's words out of her head as she drove to the offices of Frederickport Vacation Properties. She was still thinking about them when she stepped into the office a few minutes later and found Leslie sitting at the front desk.

"Hi, Joyce. You here to pick up your check?" Leslie asked brightly.

"Yes, I am." Joyce looked nervously to the back of the office and the hall that led to Adam's office.

Just as Leslie was handing Joyce the envelope with her check, she said, "Oh, I just remembered! Adam wants to see you."

"He does?"

"Yeah. You can just go on back."

When Joyce came to the open doorway leading into Adam's office a few minutes later, she found him sitting behind his desk. Standing by the open door, she knocked on the door jamb, waiting for his permission to enter. He looked up and waved her in.

"Leslie said you wanted to see me?" She approached his desk.

"I was wondering if you've seen the hut key for number six beach house?"

Joyce frowned. "The hut key?"

"I went over there earlier today and it wasn't hanging where it normally is in the kitchen. I know we've been having workers going in and out of there for weeks. I was just wondering if you might have seen it when you were over there cleaning, or maybe moved it somewhere?"

Joyce shook her head. "Umm...no...you want me to go over there and have a look?"

"Nah, that's okay. I have a copy; I just wondered where it went."

After Joyce was finished talking to Adam, she stopped by Leslie's desk again and whispered, "Do you know why Adam is looking for the hut key for house six?"

Leslie glanced back in the direction of Adam's office, then leaned toward Joyce and whispered, "Just between you and me, someone broke in to hut six."

"Broke in? What was taken?"

"That's just it. Nothing was taken exactly." Again, Leslie's eyes darted toward the hallway leading to Adam's office as she leaned closer to Joyce. "You know that gold that was taken from the bank?"

Wide eyed, Joyce nodded. "What about it?"

"It was found in that hut! But here's the kicker—Danielle Boatman found it!"

Joyce frowned. "Danielle?"

"She's been arrested by the FBI. I overheard Adam talking about it. He sent his friend Melony Jacobs over to the police station to help her; she's an attorney."

"I don't understand. Why would Danielle be arrested? The gold belongs to her."

"Because they believe she faked the bank robbery and then stashed the coins in the hut. I think that's why Adam is looking for the key. He's trying to find who took it, hoping it will prove someone else hid the coins in the hut. But Danielle could have easily gotten a key when she visited Adam. He keeps them in his desk."

"Danielle arrested?"

Leslie nodded. "That's what it sounded like. But please, don't say anything."

JOYCE HAD BEEN SITTING in her parked car in front of the Frederickport Police Department for thirty minutes, debating with herself on how to proceed. She didn't want to go to jail, but she couldn't live with herself if Danielle did.

Why didn't I run into Sam last week, before I found those stupid coins? Joyce asked herself, thinking of Samuel's words on poor choices made.

Joyce sat there another ten minutes until she finally worked up the courage to do the only thing she could do. With a sigh, she grabbed her purse off the passenger seat, removed her cellphone, and dialed the number.

"Frederickport Police Department," came a woman's voice.

"I need to speak to Chief MacDonald," Joyce said into the phone.

"He's with someone right now. Can I help you, or would you like to leave a message?"

"Please tell him it's urgent. Tell him Joyce Pruitt is calling, and she has personal knowledge about who put Danielle Boatman's gold coins in hut six. And it wasn't Danielle Boatman."

THEY BROUGHT her to the interrogation room. The chief explained she needed to speak to Special Agent Wilson, as he was in charge of the bank investigation. Joyce was not happy. While Leslie had mentioned the FBI involvement, she had hoped to discuss the matter in private with the chief first—she knew and trusted him and hoped he might be willing to help her. However, he did promise to be with her when she spoke to Agent Wilson.

Sitting at the table in the center of the interrogation room, her hands folded atop the table, Joyce's heart hammered in her chest. She watched as the chief and Agent Wilson sat down at the table with her. Brief introductions had already been made, but the loud noise in her head made it difficult to focus on anything beyond what she needed to say.

"Chief MacDonald told me you have personal knowledge on who put the gold coins in the hut. Who do you believe put it there, and how did you come across the information?" Wilson began.

"I put them there," Joyce blurted out.

Wilson stared at her. "You put it there? How did you get the coins?"

By the tone of Wilson's words, Joyce knew immediately he didn't believe her. *He thinks I'm one of those nuts who confesses to crimes.*

"Maybe you should start at the beginning," MacDonald said gently, ignoring Wilson's question.

Joyce took a deep breath and smiled up at the chief. "My mother and I have a safe deposit box at the bank. After we read in the paper about the missing coins, Mother insisted I go to the bank and clean out our box. When I opened our safe deposit box, it was filled with the gold coins."

"They were in your safe deposit box?" Wilson asked incredulously.

Joyce nodded. "Yes. On top of our things. When we rented a box, Mother insisted we rent the largest one, even though it wasn't necessary."

"Do you remember the number of your safe deposit box?" MacDonald asked.

Joyce nodded and gave him the number.

He looked at Wilson and said, "I think that's near Danielle's box, or very close to it."

"So you just took the coins?" Wilson asked.

"I know I was wrong. But they were there in my safe deposit box…and…and…well, I wasn't thinking straight." She looked up at Wilson and said in a rush, "But I didn't take any of them. What Danielle found in the hut was all of them, honest."

"How did you know about Danielle finding the gold coins?" Wilson asked.

"I clean houses for Frederickport Vacation Properties. After I found the coins, I took them with me. I wanted to hide them until I could decide what I should do. I remembered no one was at beach house six. I didn't want to leave the gold in the house, not with the workers coming and going, but I knew no one would be going to the beach hut, so I took the key and hid the coins there."

"How did you know about Danielle finding the gold coins?" Wilson repeated the question.

"When I picked up my paycheck at the office today, Leslie, who works in Adam's office, told me about Danielle finding the gold and how she had been arrested. I knew what I had to do. I couldn't let Danielle go through this, especially when she had done nothing wrong. I was the one who did something wrong. I'm here to face my consequences."

JOYCE WAS ALLOWED to go home, but she was told not to leave town. Wilson joined MacDonald in his office and waited quietly until the chief got off the phone.

"Susan Mitchell verifies Joyce's story," MacDonald said after he hung up the phone. "Joyce got into her safe deposit box after the coins went missing. Susan remembers it was heavy. She made a comment to Joyce about it at the time. But she never saw what was in Joyce's safe deposit box."

"The question now, how did the gold coins get from one box to another?" Wilson murmured. "And why?"

The chief had his own ideas, but he wasn't going to express them.

"This convinces me of one thing," Wilson said as he stood up.

"What's that?"

"It was an inside job. And I have a good idea who was involved."

"Who?" McDonald asked.

"Kissinger, of course."

THIRTY-EIGHT

David Sterling sat with his attorney at the table in the interrogation room with Special Agent Wilson. His attorney, Mr. Burls, had just arrived from Portland.

"As I mentioned before," Mr. Burls said, "I demand you release my client's wife immediately. You admitted yourself she was found locked in the downstairs bathroom at Marlow House when you found her husband upstairs. Obviously, whoever set up my client locked his wife in the bathroom to keep her out of the way."

"We'll get to your client's wife in a minute. But we are prepared to offer your client a deal." Wilson took a seat across from Sterling and Burls. He dropped the folder he had been carrying on the tabletop.

"A deal? What kind of deal?" Burls asked.

"I have no doubt we will win a conviction against your client. He and his wife checked into Marlow House under aliases. Because of his close relationship to the bank manager and the fact they have been in constant communication this past week—which we can show by his cellphone records—it will be easy to prove he was fully aware of the fact the Missing Thorndike had been moved from the bank to a safe at Marlow House.

"Your client's fingerprints were all over the necklace. The tools used to open the safe were found in Ms. Boatman's bedroom, and they also had your client's fingerprints all over them. I have no

THE GHOST AND THE LEPRECHAUN

doubt we'll find Mr. Sterling's DNA on the gloves our jewel thief wore to open the safe, especially considering the teeth marks we found. With Mr. Sterling's line of work, I don't believe a jury will have a difficult time convicting him on all charges."

"You mentioned a deal?" Burls asked.

Dave sat quietly at the table, not saying a word.

"We believe your client was responsible for breaking into a safe deposit box at the bank his cousin manages. They moved some valuable coins from one box to another. I believe your client's cousin knew the owners of the coins intended to remove them from his bank, and he wanted to move them somewhere until he could take them out of the bank—before she did. Our only problem, we don't know how they did it."

Dave began to laugh. "You think I broke into that safe deposit box?"

"David, please, let's hear what Agent Wilson wants to say," Burls urged.

Dave let out a snort, but settled back in his chair, refraining from comment.

"What do you want from my client?"

"If he tells us how he did it, how they managed to get into that vault without the cameras detecting him, we will see that all the charges be dropped in exchange for state's evidence."

Unable to contain himself, Dave said, "That would be great if I did it."

"May I speak to my client alone, please?" Burls asked.

———————

LATE FRIDAY AFTERNOON Wilson sat with MacDonald in the break room, drinking a cup of stale coffee.

"He's not going to flip?" MacDonald asked. He already knew what the answer was. The chief was fairly certain Sterling and Kissinger had nothing to do with the coins being moved from one box to another. Why exactly Sean Sullivan did it, he didn't know. When he was finally able to speak to Danielle alone, he was hoping to get the answer.

Wilson shook his head. "No. He's sticking to the story that someone broke in to Marlow House while he and his wife were there. He insists he walked in on the burglar and was attacked from behind and tied up. Claims the reason they didn't take the necklace was that it was all a publicity stunt for Marlow House's upcoming anniversary."

"So why leave the necklace?" the chief asked.

"According to Sterling, he thinks that was all part of the publicity stunt, to make it look more mysterious—all at his expense," Wilson said. "To be honest, that does not sound so farfetched to me."

"Did he explain using a false name or using a credit card with a false name?"

"Sterling claimed it was no more than role-playing he and his wife enjoy when they go on vacation—pretending they are someone else. As for the credit card, while it was in an alias, he kept it paid up, so he hasn't really defrauded anyone."

"And his fingerprints?"

"Whoever tied him up forced him to touch the necklace, of course," Wilson grumbled.

"What now?" the chief asked.

"I think it's in your court. If we can't prove that he was involved with breaking in to the safe deposit box, I see this as clearly your case, not ours. I think you can handle it from here. I don't see Sterling changing his mind on this. Sterling knows we have nothing to tie Kissinger to what happened at the bank—only him. But he also knows whatever Kissinger might have on him. Which means, if Kissinger does the final flip, Sterling might find himself spending even more time behind bars than what he might get for taking the entire hit for the botched jewel heist."

NIGHT HAD FALLEN and with it the outside temperature. To protect herself from the chilly June evening, Danielle wrapped herself in a vintage parka, purchased from the same shop where she had found the dress she had worn with the Missing Thorndike for last year's open house July fourth party.

"Why didn't you tell me Joyce moved the coins from the bank?" Danielle asked Sean. Together they sat outside of Marlow House in the front swing.

"You didn't ask me."

"You know…you're right. I didn't. I just assumed you had

THE GHOST AND THE LEPRECHAUN

removed them from the bank. Although, I couldn't figure out how you did it. I thought the only way was at night, when there was no one around to see gold coins floating down to the beach. So tell me, if your intention was to reclaim the gold—believing it was yours, why did you put it in Joyce's safe deposit box?"

"I didn't put it in her safe deposit box."

Pushing the toes of her shoes on the ground, Danielle brought the swing to a complete stop. Turning, she looked at Sean. "If you didn't take the gold out of my safe deposit box, who did?"

"I never said I didn't take the gold out of your safe deposit box."

Danielle lifted her feet from the ground, allowing the swing to gently move to and fro. "I don't understand. Who moved the gold out of my safe deposit box? And who moved it to Joyce's?"

"I suppose I technically moved them to Joyce's safe deposit box."

Clutching the parka closer around her, she frowned over at Sean. "You aren't making any sense."

"When I think of it all now—with a clear head—it seems silly. Strangely, I remember what I was thinking back then, but back then, I didn't realize how my thoughts were so…so…fractured."

"Please explain what happened at the bank."

"After the gold went missing from the Hemming house, I started looking for it—and at the same time, I started looking for better hiding places. I ended up in the bank and eventually the vault room and all those safe deposit boxes."

"So you basically stumbled on the gold again?"

"Yes. I followed one of the safe deposit holders into the vault and listened to the questions she asked the bank employee about the security. They discussed the cameras monitoring the room. At the time, I didn't even consider the possibility of the cameras capturing my image. Now I know it's impossible since I'm a spirit, but then, I didn't even know what I was."

"But you later decided to move the camera?"

"Just the one aimed at your safe deposit box. I didn't care if they saw me, I just didn't want them to see where I had moved the gold. In my mind, I wasn't moving them from your safe deposit box to Joyce's. To me, her safe deposit box was simply my new hiding place."

"Why did you leave the shamrock?"

Sean smiled. "When going through the bank, I stumbled across that in a storage room. When taking the gold coins, I decided to leave the shamrock as a warning—not to mess with what belongs to a leprechaun." He laughed at his own foolishness.

"You know what I do wonder, when you moved that shamrock from the storage room to the vault room, one of those cameras must have picked it up."

Sean shrugged.

Danielle silently considered the possibility of Special Agent Wilson poring over the security videos and finally noticing the small green shamrock floating from one end of the bank to the other. She smiled at the thought.

"I think I'm ready to move on now," Sean announced.

Danielle looked over at Sean and smiled. "I thought you might be ready."

"I'm anxious to see Katherine again. Is there anything you want me to tell her?"

"Perhaps…thank her for leading me here. For bringing me to Walt and Marlow House."

"I thought Brianna was the one who left you the estate."

"Oh, she was." Danielle leaned back and gave the ground a little push with her toe to set the swing back in motion. "But only because her mother wanted me to help Walt."

"I imagine he would still be stumbling around in the dark, confused, like I was. Thank you for helping me, Danielle. While reality seems ridiculously clear to me now, just days ago I was shrouded in a suffocating haze. Thank you."

"I'm glad I could help."

"Before I go, I'm curious. Why did you want to know who Brianna's father is? It's not like she was a blood relative, and all the parties have long since died."

Danielle shrugged. "I just was. I tend to enjoy a good mystery—and I also enjoy unraveling the secrets hidden in family trees. This one was a particular surprise—and frankly, difficult to believe."

"It's true. I wish there were some way I could prove it, but I suppose you'll just have to take my word for it."

"Actually," Danielle smiled. "I think I know a way to scientifically prove—or disprove—your claim."

Sean frowned. "You do?"

"Sure. You'd be surprised at the advances of DNA since you died."

"DNA? What's that?"

THIRTY-NINE

The vacuum's shrieking hum made it impossible for Danielle to hear Lily, who had just asked her a question from the open doorway. Too preoccupied with pushing the vacuum around the hardwood floor of her bedroom, she failed to see Lily standing there.

"Are you sure you're supposed to be doing that?" Lily shouted for the second time, louder than before.

Stopping what she was doing, Danielle looked to the open doorway and turned off the vacuum. "What did you say?"

"I asked if you were supposed to do that. Isn't this room still a crime scene?"

"I talked to the chief on the phone, and he said I could clean the room. They're done processing it." Danielle unplugged the vacuum and then stepped on a lever at its base, recoiling its cord.

"Why didn't you just let Joanne do that when she comes tomorrow morning?"

"Because it grossed me out thinking of Blake—or Dave—whatever he calls himself—crawling around in my room."

Lily stepped inside the doorway. "Well, I don't think he was *crawling* in here, exactly."

"Maybe not. But he was rolling around on my floor…ugg…I know this probably sounds silly, but I feel violated."

"Hey, I get it." Lily walked over to the desk and sat down. "Is the FBI done questioning you?"

Danielle pushed the vacuum out the doorway, into the hall and left it there. She walked back into the bedroom and sat down on the foot of her bed. "At least in regards to the gold coins. Now that Joyce admitted to taking the coins out of the bank, they know I put them in my safe deposit box. Of course, figuring out how they got from my box to hers is going to drive Wilson and Thomas insane."

"Are they looking into Kissinger?"

Danielle shrugged. "I have no idea. But I would expect them to, especially considering Kissinger's connection to the Spicers—or whoever they are. Of course, you and I both know neither Kissinger or his cousin had anything to do with what happened in that bank vault."

"What about Joyce, is she going to be charged with anything?"

"When I talked to the chief on the phone, I told him I didn't want to press charges against Joyce. What she did was wrong, but in some way very human. Heck, I've forgiven Adam after he broke in to Marlow House to treasure hunt. And she did the right thing in the end. Lots of people would have kept quiet."

"I wonder what she would have done had you not found the coins, yet had been arrested. Would she have sacrificed a fortune to keep you out of jail?"

"Good question. I would like to think she would have. But we will never know the answer to that. And I suspect, if asked the question, Joyce may not know what she would have done."

Lily stood up. "Okay, now that we have *that* behind us, I think we should work on the open house."

"Okay. I promise, this weekend I'll sit down and help you plan it. But tonight, I have one more thing I need to do."

"What's that?"

"I want to find out if Sean Sullivan was right about something."

"Right about what?"

"He told me who Brianna's father was."

Lily's eyes widened. "You didn't tell me that."

"Things have been a little bit crazy around here."

Lily smiled. "No kidding. So who was he? Not that I will actually recognize his name."

"Oh, I think you'll recognize his name."

"I will?"

Danielle nodded.

"Okay, who is it then?"

Danielle told Lily the name of Brianna's father.

Lily frowned. "Who?"

Danielle repeated the name.

Lily shook her head. "No. I don't believe that. I mean…no… that's impossible."

"Why? What's so impossible about it?"

"For one thing, they were from two different worlds. How did they even get together?"

"According to Sean, she was working for him. He seduced her, they had an affair, and she got pregnant."

"Was she in love with him? How could she have been in love with a man like that?"

"Think about it, Lily. Katherine O'Malley was not known for having good judgment when it came to men. Marrying Roger Calvert cost her her life and left her daughter orphaned."

"You have a point. So how do you intend to find out if Sean was right about the identity of Brianna's father?"

"I asked Melony if she and Adam could stop over here before we all meet them at Pearl Cove for dinner." Danielle glanced at the clock on her nightstand. "I need to get in the shower and get ready for dinner before she gets here."

"Melony? How is she going to help you prove it?"

––––––––

DANIELLE DIDN'T BELIEVE she needed an audience when discussing Brianna's parentage with Melony. She feared it might make Melony uncomfortable, and that was the last thing she wanted to do, considering the circumstances.

Before Adam arrived with Melony, Lily walked over to Ian's house. Ian had already agreed to pick up the chief on the way to Pearl Cove. When it was time for Adam and Melony to take off for the restaurant, Danielle would go with them, and they would pick Chris up at his house, along the way.

"I'm happy it all worked out for you!" Melony told Danielle when she arrived at Marlow House with Adam.

"I hope you know what you're doing," Walt cautioned from the sidelines, a thin cigar in one hand.

245

Danielle glanced quickly to Walt and then back to Melony. "I really appreciated you coming down to the police station." Danielle looked at Adam and gave him a sisterly sock on his arm. "And I appreciate you thinking of sending her."

"Hey, I told Mel how much money she could make off you, considering how often you get arrested." Adam grinned as he followed Danielle and Melony to the parlor.

Walt moved effortlessly from the entry hall to the parlor, arriving before the three stepped into the room.

Danielle laughed. "Yeah, Melony told me that."

"As it turned out, you didn't need me after all."

"Trust me, those guys from the FBI can be intimidating," Danielle told her. "It helped having you there with me so I didn't have to talk to them alone."

"Anytime," Melony promised.

"I think Adam is rather smitten with Melony. He can't seem to take his eyes off her," Walt observed. "Not sure I'm getting the same from her. That expression she's giving him looks more sisterly."

"Don't forget to get her retainer signed, with a nice hefty payment," Adam teased.

Melony playfully elbowed Adam to be quiet.

"See, did you see that?" Walt asked Danielle. "Reminds me of what a sister might do to her kid brother."

If I could elbow you to be quiet right now, I would too, Danielle thought. *And my feelings toward you aren't exactly sisterly. If they were, my life would be a heck of a lot less complicated.*

Directing her attention back on Melony and Adam, Danielle attempted to block out Walt, who was too distracting.

Melony turned her attention to Danielle. "So what is it you want to talk to me about? You said to bring the user name and password to my mother's Ancestry.com account with me."

"Did you bring it?" Danielle asked.

"Sure. But why did you want it?"

"Remember that DNA test your mother took?"

"Yeah, what about it?"

"When you log into your mother's account and look at the test results, do you know if she checked the box to give permission to allow her results to link to other family tree results? It's under settings."

Melony shrugged. "I really don't know. Like I told you before, I haven't had time to really go over the tests."

"Would you mind looking? And if she didn't, maybe check that option?"

Narrowing her eyes, Melony studied Danielle. "Now you have me curious. What's this about?"

"I think maybe your mother was related to my aunt Brianna."

"How?"

"Since you gave me that box with my aunt's belongings, I've learned Renton was the one responsible for having her DNA tested. I have to assume he got someone at the facility she was staying at to collect her saliva. Her results are linked to a family tree he created for her, under the Ancestry account he opened. I know it's his account because it's under his name. When I logged into it, the annual membership hadn't been paid, which was no surprise since he was arrested almost a year ago. I went ahead and paid it, because I figured I wouldn't be able to use all the search features without it. If my hunch is correct, and my aunt was related to your mother, your mom didn't click the option to share information, because she didn't show up on Brianna's tree."

"What makes you think they could be related?" Adam asked.

"It's hard to explain. Just a series of events, things I have read. But the only way to know for sure one way or the other is to see if Jolene linked to other family trees—and if she didn't—to do it now."

Pulling a slip of paper out of her purse, Melony handed it to Danielle. "I have to say, I'm curious. Go for it."

"I didn't expect Melony to go along so easily with your request. In my day, people tended to conceal information regarding illegitimate children or philandering ancestors in their bloodline." Walt absently rolled the end of the cigar between several of his fingers and waited to hear what Danielle found on the computer.

Melony and Adam stood behind Danielle, who now sat at the desk in front of her laptop computer. With minimal clicks Danielle was on the Ancestry.com website. Entering the username and password Melony had jotted down on the slip of paper, Jolene's Ancestry.com account opened on the computer. After another click, the screen moved to the DNA section, and after another click, to settings.

"No. Your mom didn't opt in to link to other family trees," Danielle announced after reviewing the page.

Melony snickered. "Honestly, that sounds like Mother. She goes to all the trouble to have her DNA tested, but she doesn't want to share the information."

"That's what I was talking about," Walt murmured. "Family secrets stayed in the family."

Danielle glanced over her shoulder at Melony. "Is it okay if I opt in for you?"

"Sure. I would have done it anyway when I got around to checking out the results. I don't really see the point of having the DNA test done if you aren't going to utilize all the search options."

After opting into linking with other family tree results, Danielle closed the page and moved to another. She studied the results now on the screen, as did Melony and Adam, who continued to look over her shoulder.

"Brianna was your mother's aunt?" Adam said in surprise.

"Holy crud," Melony murmured as she leaned closer to the screen, staring at the evidence before her. "Mom's grandfather, Ralph Templeton, fathered Brianna O'Malley? So, he wasn't just a mass murderer, he was an adulterer."

"Apparently, she worked for him, they had an affair, and she got pregnant." Danielle turned in her office chair and faced the pair.

"How did you know?" Melony asked.

"Like I said, just bits and pieces I fit together," Danielle lied.

"Ahh, it was Renton, wasn't it?" Melony suggested, nodding her head at the idea.

"What about Renton?" Adam asked.

Yes, what about him? Danielle wondered.

"I understand now why Renton had the test run in the first place. He must have somehow known about my mother being Brianna's biological niece. Maybe he intended to use that information somehow to overturn the will in favor of Mom and get a portion of her share. After all, they were still business partners, and we all know Mom was not above using unscrupulous means to her advantage. I know that is a horrible thing to say about one's mother, but it is the truth."

"Perhaps, but didn't your mother order that DNA test after Renton was killed?" Danielle asked.

With a frown, Melony considered the time line. "That's true.

Renton was already dead when Mother decided to have her DNA done."

"Plus, none of those results leading to your mom showed up on Brianna's account until I clicked the box to share information on your mom's account."

"Perhaps it is just a coincidence," Melony murmured.

"I guess this makes you and Danielle sort of cousins," Adam said.

FORTY

Absently circling the rim of her wineglass with the tip of her right index finger, Danielle listened to the lively conversation surrounding her. To her right sat Lily, and next to her, Ian. Chris sat to Danielle's left. Directly across the table was Melony, sitting between the chief and Adam.

The table they had been seated at wasn't directly next to the window, but it was close enough to enjoy the sunset now taking place over the Pacific Ocean. There wasn't an empty table in the house, which didn't surprise Danielle, as it was a Friday night in the height of the summer season, and Pearl Cove was the most popular seafood restaurant in Frederickport.

Melony was telling an amusing anecdote about her recent move to Oregon, while Danielle's mind wandered, recalling the comments Walt had made about Melony's feelings toward Adam. Her gaze shifted from Adam to MacDonald, back to Melony. An impartial viewer might have a difficult time determining which of the men was Melony's date. *Maybe neither one is,* Danielle told herself. What was clear, evident in the body language, Melony felt comfortable with both men.

Just as she was about to pick up her wineglass to take a sip, Danielle felt a light pat on her left knee. She glanced over to Chris, who had just removed his hand from said knee, and was greeted with a quick smile and wink.

Returning the smile, Danielle picked up her wine. In that moment she realized her relationship with Chris was as clearly undefined as Melony's and Adam's. Glancing to her right, she noticed Ian lean to Lily and whisper something in her ear. Lily laughed and then turned to Ian and gave him a quick kiss on the lips. *There is no confusion what their relationship is*, Danielle thought. Setting her wineglass back on the table, she gazed unseeing into the merlot that filled half the glass.

"Well, Danielle, are you?" Adam asked several minutes later.

Danielle looked up abruptly from her glass to Adam. "Umm… am I what?"

Adam laughed. "You weren't even listening, were you?" Brief laughter rose from the other friends at the table.

"Oh, hush, you guys," Lily admonished, using her left hand to reassuringly pat Danielle's back. "Dani's had a rough week. She's entitled to zone out if she wants."

Danielle blushed. "Thanks, Lily. Sorry, Adam, I guess I did zone out. What was your question?"

"We were talking about the open house," Lily explained.

"Adam wanted to know if you were going to wear the Missing Thorndike this year," Melony added. "I for one would love to see it. I've heard about it all my life, but I've never seen it before. Well, at least not in person."

"To be honest, I haven't really given it much thought."

"Dani hasn't given the open house any thought," Lily added.

"Hey, I promised this weekend I'll get my act together."

In a conspiratorial voice, Lily said, "I'm hoping the open house will give us some leads on who's behind the Mystery of Marlow House website." Quickly glancing around at her dinner companions, she asked, "Could it be someone sitting at this table?"

"What are you talking about?" Adam asked.

Lily told them about the anonymous blog they'd found online spotlighting Marlow House.

"Are you sure that's not one of your brilliant marketing schemes?" Adam lifted his wineglass to take a drink.

Danielle laughed. "Hardly. If it was, I would have used a much better picture of myself."

"So what about the necklace?" Ian asked. "Will you wear it again this year? It did bring in the crowds and, since this year is a fundraiser, would be for a good cause."

Danielle glanced over to the chief. "You think it would be a problem?"

"I'm sure we can work something out." The chief picked up his glass of water and before taking a sip added under his breath, "We know it won't be a problem inside the house."

Melony looked to Edward. "Why's that?"

Silently Chris, Danielle, and Lily thought, *Because of Walt.*

DANIELLE STOOD with Chris on the beach. They could hear the waves breaking on the nearby shore. Behind them, down the beach to the right, the lights of Pearl Cove lit up the shoreline.

"So this is why you decided to take your car when we picked you up." In one hand Danielle held her purse and in the other her pair of shoes. She started to walk down the beach, away from the restaurant, Chris by her side.

"I thought a walk on the beach might be nice after dinner, and I didn't particularly want to go with Adam and Melony. As much as I like them, it seems we're always around other people."

Danielle strolled down the shore, her bare toes occasionally kicking at the sand. "We could have walked on the beach down at our houses after Adam dropped us off."

"No offense, I just thought it would be nice to take a walk away from *Marlow House.*"

Instead of making a reply, Danielle kept walking. A moment later she was brought to an abrupt stop when Chris reached out and grabbed her forearm, turning her to face him, the moonlight illuminating her features.

Eyes wide, Danielle did not attempt to move when Chris leaned closer and placed a kiss on her lips. The kiss deepened. A moment later, Chris pulled away, a confused frown on his face.

He studied her moonlit expression for a moment and then said, "I didn't get the feeling you were really into that."

Danielle quickly looked down, her hands still clutching her purse and shoes. "I'm sorry, Chris, I guess I just have a lot on my mind."

Chris started to say something but then paused. Instead, he removed his jacket and spread it on the sand. "Why don't you sit down. I think we need to talk."

With a nod, Danielle sat down, using Chris's jacket as a blanket. He sat on the sand next to her.

"Where are we going, Danielle?" They sat together under the night sky, each looking out to the sea.

"You know I really care about you, Chris." Her shoes and purse now sitting on the sand next to her, Danielle wrapped her arms around her bent legs and rested her chin atop her knees.

"Well, I'm crazy about you."

Danielle didn't comment.

"When I was younger, my mother used to talk about how Dad courted her. I always thought that such an old-fashioned expression and notion—*courting*. I imagine it's one Walt would use."

Danielle glanced to Chris and even in the moonlight could see he cringed after his own reference to Walt.

"Damn, even here Walt is between us," Chris muttered under his breath.

"Is he?" Danielle asked.

Chris shook his head. "I don't know. But in all fairness, I have to acknowledge other factors. My business trip, dealing with the deaths of Jolene, Steve, and Hillary, and just when I thought we could get away and enjoy ourselves, there was the hijacking."

"No, I don't suppose we can lay all that on Walt."

"Perhaps not, but that kiss a moment ago, I have to wonder how much he factors in."

Danielle sat up straighter, her chin no longer resting on her knees. "What are you talking about?"

"I suppose, in my own way, I thought I was courting you. But now, I just can't help but think of that movie *He's Just Not That Into You*, or in my case, *She's just Not Into You*."

Danielle let out a sigh and rested her chin back onto her knees. "I'm sorry, Chris. It's me, not you."

"Words that never made any unrequited lover feel better," he said dryly.

"I don't want to lose you," Danielle said, tears in her voice.

"Who said anything about losing me?"

Danielle looked at Chris. "It just seems that often happens when two people—well when they are at different places in a relationship."

"How do you feel about me, Danielle?" Chris asked in a whisper, his eyes searching. "I know you care about me, but do you think you and I could ever be closer than just good friends?"

"Honestly, I don't know what I feel."

They sat in silence for a few moments. Finally, Chris spoke. "Perhaps wherever I imagined we were headed wasn't necessarily stalled because of all that's happened in the last six months. Maybe we just aren't ready to get there yet—if we ever are."

"What are you saying?"

He turned to Danielle, their gazes locked. "I guess I'm saying, like you, I don't want to lose what we already have. I'm not ready to give that up."

Furrowing her brow, she asked, "So what does that mean?"

Chris smiled at Danielle. "Maybe for now we can be okay with how we've been going. And later, if it seems like the right time for you, maybe we can try that kiss again."

WALT STOOD at the attic window, looking out into the night. He was alone in Marlow House. Even Max had deserted him, having taken off through the pet door an hour earlier.

Across the street, the lights were on at Ian's house. The blinds were shut, but Walt knew Lily was over there. They had returned from dinner at Pearl Cove thirty minutes earlier. He wondered when Adam would be returning with Danielle. But it wasn't Adam's car that drove up to the house twenty minutes later, but Chris's.

From the shaded window Walt watched Danielle get out of Chris's car. He noticed that Chris didn't bother turning off his engine, nor did he get out of the car to open Danielle's door. Neither did he walk her to the house. Instead Danielle got from the vehicle, shut its door, and waved to Chris before turning and racing to the front door. Walt was relieved that at least Chris waited until Danielle was safely in the house before he drove off.

"In my day a gentleman walked his date to the front door," Walt told Danielle from where he stood on the second-floor landing, looking down the stairs.

Holding onto the handrail, Danielle looked up at Walt as she trudged up the stairs. "I told Chris it wasn't necessary."

"It's always necessary," Walt said when she reached the second floor.

"Good night, Walt. I'm really tired."

Walt paused in the middle of the hallway and watched Danielle, whose back was now to him as she walked to her closed bedroom door.

"Are you alright, Danielle?" Walt asked in a soft voice.

Danielle paused by her bedroom door, preparing to open it. She glanced over her shoulder at Walt. "Yeah, like I said, I'm just tired. Goodnight."

Without another word, Danielle opened her bedroom door, stepped into the room, and closed the door, leaving Walt standing alone in the hallway.

———

DANIELLE OPENED HER EYES. Overhead a black velvet blanket covered the night, bejeweled with random diamonds, each demanding attention, twinkling, some brighter than others, lighting the sky. Sprawled before her, countless city lights competed with the night sky and in its centerpiece an illuminated iconic tower.

"Are we in Paris?" Danielle asked in surprise. Looking to her right, she found Walt sitting next to her. Looking down, she noticed they sat on a patchwork quilt situated on a grassy hillside.

"How did you know?" Walt asked with a smile.

"That's the Eiffel Tower, isn't it?"

"Yes." Walt leaned back on one elbow, stretching out on the blanket. He looked up at Danielle as she eagerly drank in the land-scape. "I looked through those letters Marie had given you. One was written when I was in Paris. I would have loved to have taken you to Paris."

Danielle let out a sigh and lay down on the blanket. Rolling to her side, she faced Walt, mimicking his pose as she too propped one elbow on the blanket while her cheek rested against a balled fist. Their eyes met.

"I thought you might be mad," Walt said in a soft voice.

"Mad why?"

"You said you were tired. Perhaps I should have just let you sleep."

Danielle grinned. "I am sleeping."

"Did you have a nice evening?"

"Dinner was good." Danielle rolled over onto her back and looked up at the sky.

"I thought Adam drove you and Chris tonight?"

"When we got to Chris's house, Chris said he wanted to take his car, so I went to the restaurant with him." Danielle continued to look up into the sky.

"I see Lily and Ian got back from dinner much earlier than you and Chris."

"Chris and I took a walk on the beach after dinner."

"He seemed in a hurry to get home after he dropped you off."

Danielle turned to Walt. "What's this about?"

Walt stared at Danielle. "It really is none of my business, is it?"

"You didn't answer my question."

"I hate to admit it, but I think Chris is a good man," Walt said reluctantly.

"Umm…yeah…so do I. Again, what is this about, Walt?"

"I want you to be happy. I don't want to do anything to interfere with that."

"I'm not sure where this is coming from." Danielle sat back up and turned to face Walt, who was now also sitting. She studied him a moment as he looked out to the city lights. "Are you suggesting Chris should have walked me to the door—he should have kissed me goodnight?"

Walt visibly cringed. "Well, not if I could see it—the kiss, that is. But I do want you to be happy and with me here—I wonder some-times—if it keeps your and Chris's relationship from reaching its inevitable conclusion."

"You want me to have an *inevitable conclusion*—is that like code for an intimate relationship with Chris? That's what you want?"

Walt looked at Danielle and frowned. "Hell no. That's not what I *want*. This is what I want."

He didn't hesitate as he had on the *Eva Aphrodite*, when he had taken her face in his hands, teasing her lips with his warm breath. That time Danielle had claimed the kiss, but this time Walt did not allow common sense to cloud his judgment.

When the kiss ended, he, unlike Chris, would not doubt Danielle's commitment to their brief intimacy. He would, however, question his own judgement.

THE GHOST WHO LIED

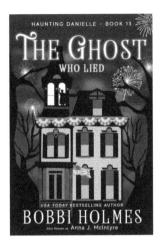

RETURN TO MARLOW HOUSE IN

THE GHOST WHO LIED

HAUNTING DANIELLE, BOOK 13

Reluctantly, Danielle agrees to celebrate the First Anniversary of Marlow House's Grand Opening. Her friends insist it is a way to move past the tragic events that occurred the past year. She even agrees to wear the Missing Thorndike for a second time.

But when one of the guests is murdered at the party—surrounded by more than a half dozen possible suspects—Danielle begins to wonder if there is something to the curse of the Missing Thorndike.

She understands that the ghost of a murder victim doesn't always know the identity of his or her killer. But this ghost knows, and she isn't telling. And she isn't leaving Marlow House.

NON-FICTION BY

BOBBI ANN JOHNSON HOLMES

HAVASU PALMS, A HOSTILE TAKEOVER
WHERE THE ROAD ENDS, RECIPES & REMEMBRANCES
MOTHERHOOD, A BOOK OF POETRY
THE STORY OF THE CHRISTMAS VILLAGE

BOOKS BY ANNA J. MCINTYRE

COULSON FAMILY SAGA

COULSON'S WIFE

COULSON'S CRUCIBLE

COULSON'S LESSONS

COULSON'S SECRET

COULSON'S RECKONING

UNLOCKED HEARTS

SUNDERED HEARTS

AFTER SUNDOWN

WHILE SNOWBOUND

SUGAR RUSH

CPSIA information can be obtained
at www.ICGtesting.com
Printed in the USA
LVHW091635130621
690121LV00008B/1608